"I want to thank you, Lucas, for all the help you've been to me and my son."

Virginia's voice was low and urgent. "It was a huge thing for me to come back to Glory. I only hope I've made the right decision."

"Hey, Virginia." Lucas held her gaze and felt something start to hum and burn inside his chest. She had this effect on him; she'd always had this effect on him.

"You've been terrific. And…and I really appreciate it. Especially since things aren't always the way I'd like them to be with Mother and Father."

Lucas had noticed that she always referred to her parents rather formally. It seemed odd, since everyone in town knew how much Doc and Doris Lake had doted on their only daughter.

Lucas wanted to reach out and touch her. Suddenly he did. He leaned forward and placed both his hands on her shoulders. "Listen, Virginia, I'm happy to be a good friend to you. But that's not all I want to be. When we're at work, I'm a hundred percent professional. But when we're not…I intend to court you. Seriously."

There was a moment of strained silence. Then "S-seriously?" Her voice was faint.

"Damn seriously."

"Oh, Lucas…then *kiss*

Dear Reader,

There's a wrong side to every town.

Sometimes it's the east end, if the prevailing wind is from the west. Sometimes it's across the tracks, where the cinders and smoke once flew and the freight whistles meant sleepless nights for the nearby residents. Sometimes it's on the far bank of the river or creek, with a graveled path leading toward it, away from the brighter lights.

Rarely it was a hilltop. Generally that's where "Society" lived, with a good view of those less fortunate folk below.

Lucas Yellowfly is poor, half-Native American and from the wrong side of town. But he's got big plans for himself.

Maverick daughter of the local surgeon, Virginia Lake is definitely from the right side of town. But she returns in disgrace, a young son in tow and no husband in sight.

Now, twelve years after they both left Glory, they've got a second chance. This time, will love prevail, no matter what the neighbors think?

I hope you enjoy Lucas and Virginia's story. How could two wrongs come out so right?

Sincerely,

Judith Bowen

P.S. I'd love to hear from you! Write to me at P.O. Box 2333, Point Roberts, WA 98281-2333

Other "Men of Glory" titles by Judith Bowen:

THE DOCTOR'S DAUGHTER
Judith Bowen

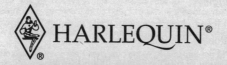

HARLEQUIN®

TORONTO • NEW YORK • LONDON
AMSTERDAM • PARIS • SYDNEY • HAMBURG
STOCKHOLM • ATHENS • TOKYO • MILAN • MADRID
PRAGUE • WARSAW • BUDAPEST • AUCKLAND

ISBN 0-373-70835-1

THE DOCTOR'S DAUGHTER

Copyright © 1999 by Judith Bowen.

This edition published by arrangement with Harlequin Books S.A.

Look us up on-line at: http://www.romance.net

Printed in U.S.A.

To my good friend, Kathy Garner

CHAPTER ONE

IT NEVER CEASED to amaze Lucas Yellowfly how, in this life, you couldn't discount coincidence. Sure, good luck was good management, but sometimes you had to wonder.

Look at today's mail, for instance. How likely was it he'd get an invitation to a baby christening, a letter from his sister, who never wrote when there was a phone in town, and a job application from a woman he'd once loved? Twelve long years since he'd seen her. No woman had ever measured up quite that way since.

Pete Horsfall, his law partner, mostly retired but still in the office a day or two a week, had tossed the application on Lucas's desk after lunch. Lucas had just picked up his personal mail at home and read the invitation to the christening of Joe and Honor Gallant's baby boy. His sister's letter he'd tucked in his pocket unopened after examining the postmark. Somewhere on Vancouver Island, in British Columbia. He wanted to think about it on his short walk back to the office.

So Theresa had ended up on the coast again. With her daughter, presumably. Lucas's sister had had her share of problems. He was always ready to help her, no questions asked, especially since Tammy's birth eight years ago. He just wanted a few minutes to think about what Theresa might be up to this time before he opened the envelope and found out.

And then, as soon as he sat down at his desk, there was that application for the legal assistant's position from Virginia Lake staring him in the face, on top of the handful of six or seven applications Horsfall had already opened and read. Lucas wondered if Virginia was on his partner's short list. If she wasn't, he pondered briefly how he'd get around the old man and get her hired.

Because that was what he intended. He didn't care what her qualifications were. He'd train her himself if he had to—he wanted to see Virginia again. He wanted her back in Glory.

When had he seen her last?

Graduation night. Her graduation. He'd come back to Glory with one thing on his mind—to show the town that had never had time for the Indian kid from the south side of the tracks just how wrong they were. He'd had a freshly inked bachelor of arts degree in one pocket and a letter accepting him to one of the country's top law schools in the other. He'd planned to ask the doctor's daughter to the dance—the one girl in town who'd been considered completely beyond his reach. All she could do was turn him down, right?

But she hadn't turned him down. She'd said yes, and Lucas wasn't sure his life had ever been the same again.

He'd had his eye on her all through high school,

although she was several years behind him. She'd been wild. Crazy and wild, and it seemed there wasn't anything she and that boyfriend of hers, Johnny Gagnon, wouldn't get up to. She was the bane of Doc Lake's life. His only daughter. His and that stiff society dame. As if there was any society in the town of Glory!

But Doris Lake did her best to pretend there was. Only, it was extremely difficult with a flame-haired daredevil of a daughter who drag-raced her daddy's Oldsmobile on the abandoned airfield five miles out of town and thumbed her nose at every convention in the book.

Maybe that was why she'd accepted his invitation to the senior prom. Because he was hands-off. A half-breed. A no-good with a drunk for a father and a brittle, worried, worn-out mother who somehow kept the family together by cleaning houses in the fancy district up on Buffalo Hill. Doc Lake's wasn't one of them. Lucas didn't think he could have borne the shame at eighteen, no matter how proud he was of his mother now, at thirty-five. The old man was dead finally, of a rotten liver and a broken heart, a salmon-eating Fraser River Sto:lo dead in prairie Blackfoot country, home of the buffalo-eaters. And a few years ago, Lucas had bought his mother a retirement apartment in south Calgary, which she shared with her older and only surviving sister. Family was a part of his life Lucas rarely talked about. The truth was, nobody asked.

Or maybe Virginia Lake had accepted his invitation because her boyfriend was in jail.

Johnny Gagnon had a string of petty charges against him by the time he quit school at sixteen. Joyriding, public mischief, shoplifting. He had a laughing, darkly handsome face and a devil-may-care attitude to match Virginia's. Even when he went to work as a grease monkey for the local mechanic, Walter Friesen, he hung around the high school, revving up his old Thunderbird in the parking lot, waiting for Virginia to finish class. When Virginia was out of town, Lucas would see him driving up and down Main Street with any number of other female companions. Or steaming up the car windows with some girl at the Starlight Drive-in.

The day of Virginia's graduation, Johnny was in jail for grand larceny. Car theft. He wasn't a young offender anymore and the *Glory Plain Dealer* didn't call it joyriding in their "This Week in Court" column. He got six months, was out in three, but by then Lucas had taken his girl to the senior prom and earned Gagnon's enduring enmity.

Not that Lucas Yellowfly gave a damn. Where was Johnny Gagnon now? Ha. Lucas hadn't thought of him in years. Probably in a maximum-security pen somewhere. Dorchester or Kingston. Well out of society's hair, anyway, he presumed. Lucas had grown up and dedicated his life to the law. He'd put the violence of his own youth behind him. The bar fights, the rodeo brawls, the lies dreamed up to protect his no-good father and tired mother from the town's scorn—all of it behind him. He believed in the law now. In the power of justice.

And his profession had been very, very good to

him. He had an excellent income, a knockout wardrobe, savings in the bank, a stockbroker on retainer, holidays in the south every January, a BMW—he'd achieved all the trappings of success. And, best of all, he'd come back to Glory to do it. He'd shoved his success in the town's face and they'd had to take it. Now he could accompany any single woman in Glory to any dinner party, anytime. He was in demand. Fathers brightened when they saw him arrive with their daughter on his arm. Where were the scowls of the old days?

Lucas enjoyed every minute of it. Revenge, they said, was sweet. Indeed, it was.

He frowned slightly as he examined the facts on Virginia's resumé. Thirty, diploma in office management and legal research, past experience... He ran his eye quickly down the list and frowned again. It seemed she'd had an awful lot of short-term jobs in a lot of different towns. He glanced at her cover letter.

Then his eye stopped. His heart stopped. She had a child. A boy, five years old.

Lucas pushed back his chair and put his feet up on the desk, hands behind his head. He stared out the window.

Single. With a child. Coming back to Glory. What had happened in Virginia Lake's life?

Lucas told himself he'd do everything right. He'd let Pete handle it; otherwise, she might remember that prom date and the night they'd spent together and maybe change her mind. When he saw her, in person, it would be different. There'd be no embar-

rassment on either side. She'd know he cared. The
way he always had. She'd know he'd never do anything to hurt her. She'd know she'd come to the
right place. If he could help her, he would.

Yes, he'd let Pete take care of things. Lucas
couldn't afford to blow it. He'd been waiting for
Virginia for a very long time.

CHAPTER TWO

Six years earlier

VIRGINIA PAUSED at the spring-loaded door to the Bragg Creek Grocery with an odd feeling that something was wrong.

What could be wrong?

It was a glorious morning, the trees were in full leaf and the wild roses were in bud. She'd just heard good news about a summer job at the Banff Springs Hotel and now she had a place to live, too, at the Prescotts' summer cabin just down the road. She didn't have to go home to Glory, didn't have to deal with her parents, after all. She could take care of herself.

Virginia frowned. Maybe the feeling had something to do with the shiny late-model Jeep that stood outside the store with its engine running. In winter, yes, people sometimes left their cars and pickups running, but on a beautiful May morning? She pushed open the door and stepped into the gloom of the old store.

"Well, well."

"Johnny!"

"Will you lookee who's here?"

Virginia was tongue-tied. She hadn't seen Johnny Gagnon since the summer her father had packed her off to Mount Allison University in Sackville, New Brunswick, four thousand miles away.

"Haven't seen you in a while, babe. Man, what a sight for sore eyes!"

She'd have recognized him anywhere. Handsome as ever, maybe even more so now that he was a man, fully grown. He wore a mustache, which suited him, and his hair was fashionably long. His teeth flashed white in his swarthy face when he grinned at her, and, as always, she found it hard not to grin back.

Johnny Bandito.

But what was he doing here?

Then she noticed his right hand stuffed awkwardly in his jacket pocket and, slung over his shoulder, a stained and worn canvas cash bag that was stenciled faintly with "Bragg Creek Grocery." He was sweating profusely and his dark eyes were all over her and all over the store at the same time. Where was Mr. Gibbon? Where were the other customers? The old guys who gathered every morning in the country store to shoot the breeze with the proprietor?

Virginia heard a muffled thump from behind the high wooden counter. That was when she noticed the wall phone was off the hook and the connection had been ripped out.

Her eyes shot to Johnny's. *"What are you doing here?"*

"C'mon, babe," he shot back, winking at her. "Lighten up, eh? Just a little grubstake, that's all."

He pulled his hand out of his pocket, leaving a bulky-looking object behind. *A gun. He had a gun in his pocket.*

He grabbed her arm. ''Come with me, sweetheart. I could use a good-looking hostage.'' He grinned again, but this time Virginia felt no inclination to smile back. Her insides were frozen. *He was robbing this store. She'd walked into the middle of a robbery.*

''Where's Mr. Gibbon?'' she demanded, wrenching her arm away from the man who'd been her first lover and, once, her closest friend.

''Aw, he's fine. Tied him up with a little of his own stock. Panty hose.'' Johnny nodded in the direction of the counter. ''Little trick I learned in the pen. You know I'd never hurt anybody, Ginny,'' he said irritably.

Virginia stepped closer, trying to peer behind the counter. ''My God!'' She turned to rush to the aid of the three people on the floor—one of whom was Mr. Gibbon—gagged and bound together by the feet. But Johnny grabbed her arm again.

This time it hurt. This time she knew he meant it. He was going to take her with him, just as he'd said.

''Look, they're fine. I tied 'em up so I could put a few miles between me and this dump before they called the cops. And I ripped out the wires just to give 'em a little more challenge, eh?'' He winked at her, then reached out and scooped up half-a-dozen beef jerky and pepperoni packages from the display on the counter. ''Come on, Ginny. Let's get out of here.''

He stuffed the jerky and pepperoni in the cash bag and gripped her arm. Virginia cursed herself for not doing something when he'd let her go. Why hadn't she run out of there screaming? She ought to be able to raise the alarm herself even now—run, get help at the nearest occupied cabin. Where was that at this time of year? Not many Calgary people spent more than weekends at their Bragg Creek cabins this early in the season.

It was too late. He had her arm in a viselike grip and he wasn't letting go. Maybe she should play along. Maybe she could talk him out of this, talk him into giving himself up. Convince him that this kind of stupid crime was no way to have a life.

Johnny doused the lights with his free hand, twisted the doorknob lock and flipped the plastic sign hanging on the window beside the door to Closed. The lock wasn't secure, but it would halt most people, though they might wonder why Mr. Gibbon hadn't opened up yet.

Then, holding her tightly, he turned and yelled back into the silent store, "Remember, old man. I got a gun and a hostage—just stay where you are and don't do nothin' and nobody'll get hurt!"

He slammed the door shut, then frog-marched her to the driver's side of the running Jeep. "Get in, Ginny, and don't try nothin' funny. We got a lot of catching up to do."

Virginia clambered across the driver's bucket seat and the gearshift into the passenger seat. By the time she was reaching for her seat belt—a matter of habit—Johnny had thrown the Jeep into gear and popped the clutch. He left the small parking lot in a spray of gravel and grinned at her as she jammed her seat belt lever home. "Just like the old days, eh? You and me? Bonnie and Clyde—"

"This is nuts, Johnny. You'll never get away with this."

His eyes narrowed. "Who says, babe?"

"Me. You can't do this." She made a wild gesture at him, at the vehicle, at the blur of trees lining the roadside. "Whose Jeep is this, anyway?"

"Friend of a friend, you might say. Just borrowed it." He winked at her again. She noticed then that there was no key in the ignition. He'd hot-wired it. That was why he'd left it running.

Johnny tossed her the cash bag with one hand as he pulled out to pass a gleaming stainless-steel dairy tanker. "Dig in there and throw me a chunk of that pepperoni, will you?"

Obediently Virginia rummaged in the bag. There wasn't much cash. Probably just Mr. Gibbon's float for the day. Or maybe his receipts over the weekend. She was disgusted. Imagine robbing a store for a couple hundred bucks or less. Then she caught herself—stealing was stealing, no matter what the amount. She'd just finished her second year of law school and she knew where this kind of thing led.

She'd have had more respect for her former lover if he'd planned and carried out something big. This nickel-and-dime stuff, this hot-wiring and stealing cars—all it did was add up to a ruined life and a string of jail terms. Not that robbing a bank and going to jail for twenty years in a federal penitentiary wouldn't ruin a person's life. But at least it took some brains. She tossed Johnny a bag of pepperoni strips, which he caught with his free hand.

"Thanks, babe. So—" he tore the bag open with his teeth "—what've you been up to since the last time I saw you? Four, five years ago now?"

"More than that." She paused. She didn't feel like filling Johnny in on her life over the past six years. This was no social picnic or school reunion. She was in the middle of a crime that was still taking place. He had called her his hostage. Armed robbery. She hadn't guessed wrong; he'd told Mr. Gibbon and the others that he had a gun. Car theft. Now kidnapping. Did he mean it? Or was he going to drop her off somewhere, maybe in the next town or on one of these back roads, and ask her not to go to the police?

She wasn't sure where they were headed, except that they were traveling west. The Rockies loomed, snowcapped and gleaming in the sunshine, in the near distance. Bragg Creek was in the wooded foothills twenty miles west of Calgary. To the southeast was the Stoney Reserve and, south of that, ranch country. Longview, Priddis, Black Diamond, Turner Valley, Millarville, Glory. If they stopped in one of those towns, she could jump out. Then what? She supposed she'd have to turn Johnny in and even testify against him when the time came. She didn't want to be involved. She wished she hadn't decided to walk to the store for a cellophane-wrapped Danish for breakfast this morning. She wished she'd settled for the dry cereal her first check of the Prescotts' cupboards had yielded.

What luck. And Mr. Gibbon's stock of bakery goods would likely have been a week old, anyway.

"Where are you taking me?" she asked finally.

Johnny swallowed the mouthful of pepperoni he'd been chewing and turned to her. "Place I know. Nice little cabin up here off the Powderface Trail. Give us a chance to visit. Nobody to disturb us, if you know what I mean." He laughed and bit off another chunk of the pepperoni.

Virginia relaxed slightly. He couldn't intend her any harm if he'd told her where they were going. He must plan to let her go soon, maybe after this "visit." Oddly, even with the gun she knew he had, she wasn't particularly worried. She wished he'd just let her go now. She had nothing to talk about with him. They had nothing in common anymore, probably hadn't since high school. She'd gone to her prom with that half-Indian guy she'd always secretly admired, Lucas Yellowfly. Johnny had been in jail. It had been the last in a string of disappointments with Johnny Gagnon, and in a way she was relieved when her father, furious that she'd dated Yellowfly, had packed her up and sent her to university in New Brunswick.

She'd stayed with her aunt Sadie and attended Mount Allison for four years, long enough to get her bachelor of arts, and then she'd applied for law school in Edmonton and Calgary. Edmonton had accepted her. She'd wanted to come back to Alberta. Maybe not to Glory with her parents, but she'd missed the mountains and the wide-open spaces. She'd missed home.

But she hadn't missed Johnny Gagnon, although she hadn't forgotten him, either. You never forgot the first man you'd been with. You never forgot someone who'd been a good friend, someone who'd grown up with you and who'd once shared all the secrets of your teenage heart.

"What've you been doing, Johnny?" she ventured. Might as well play the game. For now, at least.

"You mean besides robbing dumpy little highway grocery stores?" He grinned at her and ripped open a bag of peanuts that had been lying on the dash. "Oh, this and that." He stuffed a few peanuts in his mouth. "Got married."

"Really!" Virginia was genuinely pleased. "Anybody I know?"

"Nope. Babe from Clearwater. In B.C. On the Yellowhead." Johnny frowned, chewed a mouthful of peanuts and swallowed again. "Hey—you hungry?" He offered her the open bag. She shook her head.

"So, got any kids?"

"Nah. Marriage went belly-up a few years back. She couldn't handle the life-style, know what I mean?"

That didn't surprise her. What woman could?

"Worked a few jobs here and there, tried to stay straight. Sawmills, oil rigs, drove truck for a while. Harper's Transport out of Olds." He glanced at her. "Nothing that amounted to much. Spent a little time in the clink—I already mentioned that, huh?'' Virginia had the distinct impression he'd spent more than a little time in jail, and maybe that had been the part of the life-style his wife couldn't handle. ''What about you?''

''Oh, this and that. I was down East for a few years. I'm going to law school up in Edmonton now, second year—''

''No kidding! So you can put guys like me behind bars, eh?''

''I guess so.'' She smiled. It was hard to stay mad at Johnny. She remembered that about him. He could always make her laugh, even during the worst times. Firmly she reminded herself that this was different. This was serious. Mr. Gibbon had no doubt freed himself and called the Mounties. Any minute now they'd hear a police siren and they'd be pulled over and Johnny'd be arrested and that would be the end of it.

Suddenly Johnny slowed the Jeep and they lurched off the road, which had been gravel for the past several miles, onto a rutted lane that wasn't much more than a grassy track. The vehicle heaved and bounced, engine growling.

Virginia held tight to the armrest. She didn't like this. She didn't like it one bit. At least the road they'd been on was public; there'd been a chance of flagging down another car, if she'd had the opportunity. But what could she do out here in some shack in the bush? Somehow, though, she didn't think Johnny was a walker. Too lazy. The cabin he'd mentioned couldn't be too far and she figured it had to be on some sort of road.

She was wrong.

They came to a stop in the middle of a clearing with a faint turnaround. There were tiny spring flowers and grasses growing in the tracks, indicating it hadn't been used for a while.

"What are we stopping for?" she asked, on the off chance this wasn't what she thought it was— their destination.

"We're here, babe. This is old-fashioned cabin country. You take the cash bag and I'll grab that duffel in the back. I'm banking on my buddy keeping the joint stocked. Otherwise it's pepperoni and peanuts or, if the lady prefers, peanuts and pepperoni." He laughed, as though it was a tremendous joke.

Reluctantly Virginia took the canvas bag. She didn't know what else to do. She was stuck out here now. She had to put her faith in Johnny's good nature. Surely he'd drive her back to civilization, or at least to the road, once they'd talked.

She shivered, realizing no one knew where she was. No one even knew she was in Bragg Creek, except Mary Prescott, and Mary was in France right now. Virginia had planned to call her parents and tell them about her summer job and the place she'd found to stay, but she hadn't gotten around to it yet.

No one would miss her. Not until she didn't show up at the Banff Springs Hotel next Monday for her new job. It was a horrible feeling.

She walked beside Johnny through the clearing

and over a small grassy knoll, through sparse group-
ings of birch and poplar and mountain ash. A few
conifers, spruce and pine, were interspersed with the
deciduous trees. It was a lovely time of year. Somewhere in the distance she could hear the sound of
water flowing. Snowmelt? Elbow Falls was somewhere up here. Were they near it?

The cabin was surprisingly comfortable, despite
its remote location. It consisted of two rooms, a tiny
bedroom with a sagging double bed and a larger
main room combining small kitchen, dining nook
and living room. A large iron woodstove stood in
the center of the main room. Seasoned firewood was
split and piled to the eaves outside the weathered
wooden door. The walls were log and the roof was
rusted tin. The place had a certain charm.

"You've been here before?" she asked Johnny as
he threw the duffel bag onto the old-fashioned sofa
draped in a granny-square afghan on one side of the
living room. She wrinkled her nose at the musty
smell in the air. Mice, definitely.

"Couple times. Buddy of mine owns it. Fishing
cabin." Johnny yanked open a window a few
inches, then went to the cupboards. He whistled with
satisfaction. "Man, ain't we lucky? Everything a
guy could want," he said, holding up some soup
mixes and other dehydrated-food packages in one
hand and a large bottle of rye whiskey in the other.
"Good thing we had a mild winter or this woulda
froze—and that woulda been a darn shame."

Whiskey. Virginia had a sinking feeling in the pit
of her belly. Johnny had always been a boozer.

She'd forgotten that about him. In fact, it struck her that perhaps he'd already been drinking. The Jeep, she recalled, had smelled faintly of old booze, along with cigarette smoke and damp canvas. Maybe to get his nerve up for the robbery. Suddenly this no longer felt like a lark—not that it ever really had. She wanted to go home.

"When are you taking me back, Johnny?" she asked nonchalantly, trying a smile. She had the feeling it wouldn't be a good idea to get into an argument with him out here. Not until she knew exactly where she stood.

"Oh, hell, Ginny," he said sharply, unscrewing the cap on the whiskey and splashing several inches into a water glass. "What's your rush? It's party time. Hell, I haven't seen you in six years and now you can't spend a couple hours with an old buddy? What's the matter? The doctor's daughter too good for old Johnny Gagnon now?" He held up the glass in a mock toast and smiled, but his smile didn't quite match the look in his eyes. Virginia felt a tiny shiver run over her flesh.

"I guess you're right," she said lightly. "Well, I'll start a fire." Why not play Girl Guide? Maybe Johnny wasn't welcome in this cabin, and someone would come to investigate the smoke. It was as likely as not that the "buddy" who owned the place was like the buddy who'd lent him the Jeep—a figment of Johnny's wishful thinking.

Virginia found some old newspapers on a rickety table in the bedroom, yellowed and dated the previous fall. Did that mean the owner hadn't been back since?

She crumpled up a few sheets and poked them into the stove. Johnny slouched on the sagging sofa, whiskey in his hand, watching her every move. She opened the door to get some firewood.

"Don't go anywhere, eh, babe?" he called out. There was no mistaking the warning in his voice, and Virginia shivered again. She looked out the door into the deep, quiet afternoon woods. She had no idea where she was. What were the chances of her running out of here, away from Johnny? Not great. She'd play for a little more time; maybe he'd get drunk and fall asleep.

"I'm just getting some wood for the fire," she said. She stepped off the stoop and ambled casually toward a large stump that had obviously been used for splitting wood. Dry chips lay all about the ground. Virginia bent to pick up a handful—starter for the fire. As she did so, she glanced toward the cabin. Johnny was watching her through the small window. So much for making a run for it.

Why did he want her? Surely not as a real hostage. That was crazy, just something he'd made up on the spur of the moment. Virginia carried in the chips, along with a few sticks of the firewood. She'd go along with him and stay as determinedly cheerful as possible. Any chance she had to run, she'd take it.

The fire caught immediately, and soon a welcome warmth penetrated the cabin, warming the chill, dank air and even driving off the mousy smell she'd noticed when she'd first walked in.

"Soup and crackers?" she asked Johnny, checking out the cupboard contents herself. "I didn't have any breakfast or lunch."

"That's more like it, babe. Make yourself useful. Sure, put on some soup. Throw in some of that beef jerky." Johnny grinned and raised his half-empty glass to her. He'd already refilled it once. "Let's party!"

Virginia didn't reply to that. She filled a pot of water from the outdoor hand pump, letting the rusty water seep into the ground until it ran clear. A squirrel scolded her from a nearby jack pine. In other circumstances, this could be quite pleasant.

The soup was good and filling, especially simmered with a handful of the jerky. Something new, she thought, almost smiling—cream of jerky soup. The crackers were stale, but she felt better after she'd eaten. Johnny was drinking too much and mumbling to himself. She ignored him. All she could hope was that he'd pass out.

When she'd cleaned up the dishes and pot she'd used for the soup, Virginia pawed through a stack of magazines and newspapers she'd discovered in a corner of the bedroom. She found an old *Reader's Digest* magazine and curled up on the rickety armchair to read and pass the time. He was definitely incapable of driving anywhere now. Johnny had progressed from mumbling to singing to himself on the sofa, a third—or was it a fourth?—tumbler of whiskey in his hand.

Oddly, she didn't feel threatened. She knew her captor too well. He was the same old Johnny. Impulsive, headstrong, a joker… He was too badly organized to carry off anything complicated or serious. Virginia had no doubt he'd be back in jail within days. And not for the last time either.

A sudden groan and then snoring from the direction of the sofa alerted Virginia to the fact that she'd finally had some luck. He'd fallen asleep. Or passed out. Now she could sneak out and find her way back to the main road—there was still an hour or two of daylight—hitch a ride to town and put as many miles between herself and her captor as possible. If she could avoid it, she wouldn't go to the cops. Let them catch him themselves; it wasn't as though anyone had been hurt in the robbery, including her.

Virginia got to her feet and walked quietly to the door, one eye on the snoring Johnny Gagnon. He'd knocked over his glass when he'd fallen asleep and the pungent fumes of twelve-year-old whiskey filled the room.

The key! It was missing. Virginia clenched her jaw in surprise and shock. Damn him. He wasn't as disorganized as she'd assumed. There'd only been an old-fashioned latch on the outside when they'd arrived, but she'd noticed an ancient skeleton key stuck in the rusted lock from the inside when she'd gone out to get the firewood earlier. That skeleton key was gone. She glanced toward Johnny, her lips compressed in annoyance. No doubt the missing key was in his pocket.

Then she realized he hadn't taken the gun out of

his jacket pocket and his jacket was hanging over the back of the sofa. She tiptoed toward it. Shuddering, she touched the icy-cold steel of the gun. She withdrew it, then panicked. It was a lot heavier than she'd thought it would be. What was she going to do with it? She didn't know; she just didn't want a weapon like that available to a man as drunk as Johnny. She looked around the small cabin. There weren't many hiding places. In the end she put it in the crisper of the old icebox, which hadn't been used for months. Johnny wasn't the type to rummage around for vegetables, anyway.

After that she searched through the cupboard and found a couple of packages of noodles and mix, which she decided to make for an evening meal. The discovery that Johnny had locked her in was a shock. She was stuck until tomorrow now. It would be dark soon, and even if she got out, she didn't think she'd be able to find her way to the road at night. It wasn't as though the Powderface Trail got a lot of traffic even in the daytime.

Johnny woke up for supper, cheerful but still very drunk. He ate two huge platefuls of the concoction she'd made, complimenting her on her cooking. Then he dug the key out of his jeans pocket with a sly grin at her and swaggered onto the stoop outside, where she could hear him relieving himself. When he came in, she went out with the same object in mind, finding some privacy behind a bush to one side of the cabin. There was no outhouse that she could see, but there was probably one a few yards down a nearby trail. She wasn't about to hunt for it,

though. Johnny was waiting for her on the stoop
when she returned.

"Thought I'd let you sneak off on me, eh?" he
said with a snort of laughter. "Not a chance, babe."

"When are you taking me home?" she demanded. None of this struck her as being the
slightest bit humorous.

"Whoa, don't get your shorts in a knot, babe. I'll
drop you off tomorrow somewhere. Canmore, Calgary, wherever you wanna go. No sweat." He followed her back into the cabin and locked the door
again.

"Why are you locking up?" she asked. She didn't
like the idea of a locked door with a fire in the stove.
Or Johnny. He was drunk. What if he upset an oil
lamp or something?

"Keep out the bad guys," he joked, winking at
her. "You can't be too careful these days. There's
a lotta riffraff out there runnin' around." He gave
her a significant look and dropped the key back in
his pocket. Virginia went into the bedroom to return
the magazine and surreptitiously tried the small window there. It was either nailed or painted shut. There
was no way she could get out without breaking the
glass. Well, if she had to, she would. Maybe when
he passed out again.

Half an hour later it was too dark to read. Luckily
her captor had shown no interest in lighting the
lamps that were lined up on the kitchen counter.
Johnny fell asleep sprawled out on the sofa, with
only an inch or two left in the whiskey bottle. Vir-

ginia hoped that was the only booze the cupboards would yield.

She tried the bedroom window again. It wouldn't budge. Then she went back into the main room and tried the window he'd opened earlier. It was stuck, too. She looked for some kind of tool in the kitchen drawer, but didn't come up with anything more lethal than a dull knife, which she took into the bedroom. She began chipping at the paint that covered the window frame.

"Whatcha doin', babe?"

Damn. Virginia put down the knife and cleared her throat. "Nothing," she called back. She froze for a few moments, then heard snoring again.

She was trapped here. But did she really want to get out now and try to make her way through the dark forest? She could get seriously lost. For tonight, anyway, things seemed pretty hopeless.

She might as well go to bed. She picked up an afghan that lay on the end of the bed and carried it into the main room. Johnny was stretched out on the sofa. She unfolded the afghan and draped it lightly over his snoring form. With any luck he wouldn't wake up until morning.

Then, just in case, she jammed the kitchen knife between the door frame and the door itself of the bedroom as a temporary lock and studied the sagging double bed. When had the sheets last been changed? Did she want to know? For extra security, she lodged a rickety chair under the latch, then took off her jeans and sneakers, leaving her socks, shirt and underwear on, and climbed between the fairly clean-looking quilt and blanket that covered the bed. She could only hope that morning would come soon. And that Johnny would be sober enough to drive her to the nearest town.

It was so quiet. Except for the soughing of the wind in the trees and Johnny snoring in the living room, there wasn't a sound. And it was getting so dark. There wasn't even a moon.

Despite her certainty that, exhausted or not, she wouldn't sleep, she did, only to awaken suddenly in a horrible fright, the room pitch-dark, and with the stinking, whiskey-laden breath of her captor in her face. He obviously had broken into the room somehow and fallen across the bed. He was trying to kiss her.

"Johnny!" She wrenched her face away. "Stay away from me!"

"Whassamatter? Doc's daughter too good for me now? Eh?" He persisted, rubbing his whiskery face over hers. She wanted to gag when his damp mustache swept across her mouth.

"Get off me!"

"Shut up, you stuck-up bitch," he growled, grabbing her hair. "Kiss me. The way you used to." Real fear stabbed Virginia's heart. This wasn't the Johnny Gagnon she knew. She realized at the same time that he'd taken off his clothes. He was stark naked on top of her on the bed, only the tattered quilt between them.

He plunged his tongue into her mouth and she gagged. He swore and grabbed the quilt off her and tore at her panties. Virginia fought him, scratching his shoulders and pulling his hair. She was filled with complete panic and the strength of ten women.

Johnny swore in French several times and slapped her, then fumbled with himself, his other arm holding her down on the bed. She realized he was trying to rape her. She screamed. He laughed. "Go ahead. Nobody's gonna hear you, babe." She screamed again and twisted, desperately trying to free herself. "Come on, honey, settle down. You used to like this, remember?"

He thrust and thrust again. Nothing happened. Obviously he was too drunk to maintain an erection. Then he slumped suddenly, weighing her down so heavily she could barely breathe. *Omigod.*

He'd passed out again. On top of her. Stark naked on top of her. Virginia wanted to scream again, this time with hysterical laughter. But she was afraid she'd wake him. The impulse turned to painful whimpers as she heard his breathing slow, and the wet, sloppy, ragged sound of his snoring again. His breath overpowered her and made her retch. She tried to wriggle out from under him, with no success. She told herself to calm down, to save up her strength for one huge effort once he was deeply, fully unconscious.

Gradually, over the course of the next hour or so—she had no idea how long she lay there, terrified—she wriggled herself ever so slightly away from him. Inch by tiny inch she moved, so that less of his weight pressed her into the lumpy mattress springs.

But it was no use. There was no escape. Johnny

woke up. He raped her twice before morning. The second time, the birds were singing mightily in the trees outside and it was nearly the gray of first light. Battered and feeling sick beyond words, Virginia pushed the unprotesting Johnny off her and swung her legs over the side of the bed. She no longer cared if he tried to stop her. There was nothing more he could do to her, except kill her.

She stood, shaking, and looked down at the man she'd once loved with all her innocent teenage heart. She hated him now. She hadn't known hate could flood the heart as hotly and thickly as love.

She groped in the dark for her jeans. She couldn't find her panties. She felt around for her shoes. She realized she'd put her hand on another pair of jeans, Johnny's, in the darkness. She thrust her hand in his pocket. The *key*. Then she groped around until she found her shoes.

"Where you goin', babe?" Johnny groaned sleepily, and she froze. She couldn't believe it. He acted as though they'd just shared a night of consensual sex. As though this was just the morning after, one among many morning afters.

"I'm just going out to pee," she said, willing her voice to steadiness.

Johnny moaned something indistinguishable and buried his face in the mildewed pillow.

She slipped into her jeans, shuddering. She had a few dollars in her pocket, for the Danish she'd planned to buy the morning before. She hadn't brought a purse. Then she walked to the door of the cabin, opened it, closed it quietly behind her and turned the key in the lock from the outside. Squeezing her eyes shut, she threw the key as far into the long grass as she could.

She made her way to the Jeep and, in the rapidly lightening forest, managed to hot-wire the vehicle with shaky fingers. Some of Johnny Gagnon's early lessons had been well learned, she thought ironically. The engine roared as she put it in gear and retraced the path they'd taken the previous day. If Johnny pounded on the cabin door, she didn't hear it. She didn't hear anything. All her thoughts were on getting away and blocking the entire incident out of her mind.

That afternoon, after she'd showered and scrubbed herself until she was raw, she phoned the police. A constable picked her up at the Prescott cabin and she gave a statement at the area headquarters. She knew Johnny was as good as in jail. She didn't mention the rape, and when they asked her if she'd been hurt, she said no, she was fine. A month later, she was subpoenaed to testify against Johnny Gagnon in court and he was sentenced to nine years for armed robbery, grand larceny, assault and kidnapping, to be served in a federal penitentiary.

Three weeks after that, Virginia knew her dreams of a law degree were over. She needed to make a living, starting right now. She was pregnant; she was going to have Johnny Gagnon's child.

CHAPTER THREE

"Y-YOU MEAN I HAVE the job?" Virginia sat a little straighter in the hard oak chair facing Pete Horsfall's desk.

The old man spread his hands wide, an indulgent smile on his good-natured face. "I don't see why not. Everything's in order here—" he rearranged a few papers on his desk, then leaned back, still smiling "—and if I can't do a good turn for the doc's daughter, I'd like to know why not."

"I don't want the job because I'm Jethro Lake's daughter," Virginia said firmly. But she knew that wasn't the real reason Horsfall was hiring her. It was because she was qualified, maybe even overqualified, for the job.

"No, no—you're not getting the job because you're a Glory girl, my dear. Heavens, no! It's because you know the work and I'm convinced you'll do a fine job for us. Have you seen Lucas yet?"

"No." The thought of working with Lucas Yellowfly made her a little nervous. She hadn't seen him in years, not since that crazy night they'd spent together after her graduation. Talking, laughing, kissing, looking at the stars. Not that anything serious had happened—but it had made Jethro mad enough that he'd shipped her off to New Brunswick on practically the next train. "You said he wasn't in the office?"

"No. He's stepped out for the afternoon to go to a christening celebration. You remember Joe Gallant?" the older man queried from beneath grizzled brows. "Farms out toward Vulcan way."

She nodded. She had a faint recollection of the Gallant family. Joe and his sister had been a few years ahead of her in school.

"Well, Joe's finally married. Last year, to a real nice girl from Calgary. Honor Templeman. A lawyer! Oil- and gas-business law. Maybe Doc and your ma told you, eh?" When Virginia shook her head, he added, "Honor may do some title work for us a few days a week when her baby's a little older."

"I look forward to meeting her." Virginia smiled. "Well, I'd better go. I left Robert with Mom for the afternoon." She stood up and extended her hand. Pete Horsfall shook it warmly.

"I'm looking forward to meeting the little gaffer. P'rhaps Doc and I can take him fishing one of these days."

"Robert would like that," Virginia responded, smiling. She thought of her small, serious, bespectacled son. Fishing on the Horsethief River with a couple of old men would be a fine experience for him. That kind of thing was exactly why she'd made up her mind to come back to Glory. It was time to settle down, to stay in one place long enough for Robert to make friends. He'd start school in September, kindergarten, and it was time she quit running and made some long-term plans in her own life.

Maybe she'd stop having nightmares about Johnny Gagnon and whether he'd ever find her or find out about Robert. Johnny Gagnon was in jail, after all, where he belonged.

Virginia hesitated when she reached the sidewalk outside the law office. It was the middle of the week, and many Glory merchants clung to the old-fashioned custom of half days on Wednesday. The streets were quiet. Virginia breathed deeply. She swore she could smell the ripening fields of grain and alfalfa outside of town blowing along Main Street. She could smell the pungent blossoms of the town's caragana hedges, for sure. Caraganas, lilacs and peonies. Rhubarb and crabapple trees. The harshest northern winter didn't kill the stubborn roots of those prairie faithfuls.

She glanced at her watch. Robert had been with her mother for about two hours now. Doris could probably handle another hour or so with this grandchild she'd seen for only a few days a year. They'd visited her parents every Christmas since Robert was born. She heard a distant church bell and remembered what Horsfall had said about a christening. Why didn't she wander over to the church? Maybe she'd see Lucas. She'd feel a lot better getting that first meeting over with. Now that she had the job, the worst of her worries was behind her. Next would be finding a place to stay and getting settled. Her parents had offered—grudgingly, she thought—to let her and Robert stay with them in the big brick house at the top of Buffalo Hill. Her pride did not allow her to accept.

She'd stood on her own two feet for quite a few years now. She'd given up law school and completed an office-management course before Robert was born. She'd worked and supported them both ever since, and was determined to continue as she'd begun. She'd never asked for favors and wasn't about to start now.

People—including her parents—could take her and Robert as they found them or not at all. She had never pretended to be a widow or divorced, and no one had had the nerve, so far, to ask any questions. Perhaps in Glory someone would. Small towns were small towns. No one knew that better than she did.

Still, their hometown would be the last place Johnny would ever think to look for her. If, indeed, he *wanted* to look for her.

Virginia approached St. Augustine's, conscious that although several people on the street had noticed her, no one had tried to talk to her. She wasn't sure anyone would recognize her after all these years. She still had the red hair she'd been famous for, but she'd grown up. Slender now, not scrawny. Red hair neatly tucked up, not flying wild. Crisp skirt and jacket, not scruffy jeans and a T-shirt. Of such were most people's memories made, or so she believed.

The christening was over and the large crowd had moved next door to the church hall, where the women's league always served tea and cakes after funerals and weddings and, obviously, christenings.

Virginia stepped up to the door, smiling at several people she knew. She couldn't tell whether they remembered her, but they smiled back.

The hall was noisy with talk and laughter. The big multipaned windows on each side spilled bright sunlight into the room. Virginia saw the postmistress, Myrna Schultz, who was a town fixture, and said hello, then walked farther into the room, confident that within very short order the entire population would know about her, Robert and her new job.

Holding center stage were a much-older-than-she-remembered Joe Gallant with a slim, brown-haired woman who must be his wife, a teacup and saucer in her hand. Honor Gallant chatted animatedly with an older woman Virginia didn't recognize. Several ladies stooped over the baby, who was decked out in white lace and satin and gazing quietly up at the world from a fancy bassinet. A gray-haired man leaning heavily on a cane stood proudly beside the bassinet, a rather spectral-looking man in a bowler hat at his elbow, solicitously holding a tray with two cups and saucers and a small plate of cakes.

Virginia fought a sudden ache. How differently she'd welcomed Robert into the world. She'd taken a bus to Regina a week before her due date and stayed with a friend, whom she'd sworn to silence, so that her baby would be born in Saskatchewan and wouldn't even be traceable in Alberta records. Now she realized she'd probably gone somewhat overboard in her desperate fear that the man who'd raped her might find out about Robert and make life more difficult than it already was.

Suddenly she spotted Lucas Yellowfly and caught her breath. He was even handsomer than she'd remembered, and he'd been handsome as a teenager, when all the other boys had been just gangly and awkward. His shoulders were broad, the man fulfilling the rangy promise of the boy, and he looked terrific in a suit she'd have sworn was handmade, it fit him so beautifully. His hair was still black as coal, and he was tall—he'd been tall at eighteen.

He smiled as he bent slightly toward a dark-haired woman Virginia vaguely recognized. No, she couldn't put a name to the face. Lucas's smile was warm. Was this the lady in his life? Although she hadn't thought of that possibility, Virginia felt some relief. Of course Lucas Yellowfly would have a woman in his life, whether he was married or not. He was too attractive not to be in some kind of relationship.

That would make working with him a little easier. Not that she herself was particularly attracted to him, not anymore. What she'd felt for him all those years ago had been nothing more than a teenage crush. She'd been involved with Johnny Gagnon. Lucas had just been a lucky, last-minute date for her prom and a chance—again—to thumb her nose at the town.

Lucas saw her then, and Virginia knew that the seeds of the attraction that had once existed hadn't gone away. How awkward, when they'd be working together. His eyes caught hers and she felt almost as if he'd reached across the crowded room and touched her, put his warm, strong hands on her shoulders, run the side of his thumb along her cheekbone…kissed her softly. She took a swift breath. What foolishness!

She forced herself to smile and walked into the room. Lucas moved toward her, his eyes never leaving her face. The woman he'd been speaking with accompanied him. Virginia swallowed hard.

"Virginia!" He took her hand in both of his and smiled in return. His eyes were tender and gentle and welcoming. She felt a prickle of emotion, which she pushed back firmly. She took a deep breath. She finally felt secure, wanted, as though she'd made the right decision in coming back to Glory. That was a great part of Lucas Yellowfly's charm, as she remembered it. He gave the impression that the person he was speaking to was the only person in the world. It had a great effect on women.

"Hello, Lucas."

He kept hold of her hand and turned to the woman beside him. "Donna, this is Virginia Lake, the woman I've been telling you about. I believe she's coming to work for Pete and me in the firm. Is that correct, Virginia? Virginia, this is Donna Beaton, an old friend. She runs a gift shop in town."

Virginia, Virginia… It was as though he couldn't stop himself from saying her name.

An old friend. "How do you do, Donna?" Virginia said formally, and shook the other woman's hand. "Yes—" she glanced at Lucas "—I'll be

starting in the office the first week of school, I believe.''

"Welcome to Glory," Donna said. "I hope you'll
enjoy living here. Well, Lucas, I think I'll head back
to the store now." She smiled apologetically at Virginia. "I catch up on my bookkeeping on Wednes-
days."

"Virginia," Lucas repeated, gazing deeply into
her eyes. He took her arm, and nodded as the other
woman moved away with a small wave, then leaned
toward her. "Listen, do you want to get out of
here?"

"Sure," Virginia said, quickly looking around.
"Maybe I'd better say hello to the parents of the
baby first?"

"Do you know Joe and his wife?"

She shrugged. "Not really."

"Well, then, why don't we leave? You can meet
them another time."

Lucas adroitly maneuvered her out of the crowded
hall, smiling and saying a few words to people as
they left. Then they were back in the bright sunshine, standing on the painted wooden steps that led
up to the hall.

"You bring a car?"

"No," Virginia replied, very conscious of Lucas's hand still on her elbow. "I walked over from
your office. I left my son with Mother."

"I'm looking forward to meeting him," Lucas
said. "What's his name?"

"Robert."

"Starting grade one?"

"Kindergarten. He's just five."

The unspoken question hung between them: *Who is his father?* Virginia bit her lip.

"I walked, too," Lucas said easily as they reached the sidewalk. He let go of her elbow, for which she was grateful, and adjusted his stride to hers, hands in his pockets. "So, what are your plans, Virginia? I suppose you'll be staying with your folks for a while?"

"A few days. I'm going to look for a place to rent while I'm here—"

"While you're here?" he interrupted, one eyebrow raised.

"Sorry." She felt herself flush slightly. "That didn't sound right, did it? I'm planning to stay. When I find a place to rent, I'll go back to Stettler and pack up our stuff."

"Stettler. That's where you've been living?"

"Yes." She could be as clever at not giving out information as he could be at soliciting it. She wanted to smile.

"It can be tough renting in Glory. Most people own, and there's not much in the way of apartments in a small place like this."

"I'm hoping Mother and Dad will know of something."

By this time they were at the far side of the square. Virginia noticed a delicatessen-café—Molly McClung's—that hadn't been there when she'd lived in town. Lucas gestured toward it. "Coffee?"

She hesitated, but only for a second. Lucas was not only going to be her boss now, one of them, but he was well connected here. He was also her friend, or he had been, years and years ago. She needed a friend in Glory.

"They've got great carrot cake," he teased, one hand on the door, the other reaching for her elbow again.

"Sounds good."

The interior was dim and cool and bursting with good scents. Homemade soup, fresh-baked goods, spices, peppermint tea, fresh-squeezed orange juice....

They sat in a booth next to the window. A plump woman came from behind the counter to take their orders, then Lucas turned back to Virginia with a devilish grin. She waited, trying hard not to smile herself.

"You aren't going to believe this, Virginia Lake, but I think I've got just the answer for you."

She toyed with her spoon. "What do you mean?"

"An apartment. I'm moving out of my place and as far as I know, Mrs. Vandenbroek hasn't rented it yet."

"You're moving out?" She added cream to her coffee, which had just arrived, and stirred it.

"Yes. You remember my sister, Theresa?"

"No." Virginia shook her head and took a sip of the coffee. It was delicious. Her eyes met Lucas's over her cup.

"Well, she's a few years older than I am." Lucas pulled his coffee toward him. "Anyway, she's got an eight-year-old daughter, Tammy—she's in grade three this year. Theresa's shipping her out to live with me for a couple of months, so I've bought a house. It's bigger and closer to the school.''

"Bought a *house?*''

''It was high time. I'd been thinking about it for a while.''

Virginia frowned. "Why is she sending her daughter to you?''

Lucas sipped his coffee, then set down his mug. ''Theresa's in a patch of trouble. She's had problems with substance abuse in the past, liquor mostly, and she swears she's going clean this time. She's checked into a sweat lodge or some damn thing on Vancouver Island. Something she thinks is going to do the trick for her. Get in touch with her Indian spiritual side, all that stuff.''

''You don't sound like you believe her,'' Virginia said flatly, still frowning.

''Hey, I've heard a lot of big dry-out plans from Theresa over the years. She's been through detox, through different twelve-step programs, you name it. I'll keep an open mind on the sweat lodge.'' He shrugged. "Who knows? It could work for her this time.''

''What about Tammy's father?'' Virginia didn't know why she asked that question. The whole thing was none of her business.

Lucas paused and their eyes held for a second too long. ''He's not in the picture. Theresa's never told me anything about him.''

The statement seemed to hover there. The waitress brought their carrot cake just then, and Virginia was glad of the interruption and determined to change the subject.

"I'll have a look at the apartment. Thanks. Is it close to town?"

"Alder Street. Not far from the office."

Virginia thrust a fork into her cake. It was very good. She tried to ignore the statement about Tammy's father, but she couldn't. Lucas—everyone, the whole town—must be wondering about her son. *Who was Robert's father?* Well, she did know that, although sometimes she wished she didn't.

"The apartment's not big. Two bedrooms, one fairly small, which I used for a den, a kitchen, one bathroom, a small living room. It's on the top floor of Mrs. Vandenbroek's house. There's a separate entrance. She's okay. Decent landlady, not too nosy."

"Furnished?"

"Yeah. I had some of my own stuff, so she put a few things in the basement. She could rent it completely furnished, I'm sure."

Virginia didn't miss the curiosity in Lucas's dark gaze. He must wonder why she'd want a furnished place, like some oilfield worker moving in with a pair of jeans, two T-shirts and a case of beer for the fridge. The truth was, she hadn't accumulated much in the past few years. She'd moved too many times to want to burden herself with furniture. Apart from Robert's toys and their clothes, there wasn't much to bring down from Stettler. She could easily get it all in her car.

"Shall I tell Mrs. Vandenbroek to hold the place for you?"

Virginia met Lucas's gaze. "Yes. I...uh, I really appreciate this, Lucas. It makes things a bit easier." She barely recognized her own voice, low, hesitant, even slightly wobbly.

"Hey." Lucas covered her hand with his briefly and signaled for the check. "What are friends for?" he asked easily. "Do you want to go over and see it now?"

"No, I'd better get back to see how Robert's getting on with Mother. Thanks, Lucas."

Almost as though conscious that things were moving a little too fast—although in which direction Virginia couldn't have said—Lucas nodded. "I'm going back to the office for a couple of hours. Anything I can do for you?" He held the door open for her as they left the café.

"Not at all. You've been very helpful. Very kind."

He smiled. "I, uh, I guess I'll see you later."

Virginia nodded. "Thanks again."

"I'll call your folks and leave my landlady's number with them. You can see the place whenever. You don't have to wait until I move out."

"Okay." She watched him cross the street, then turned and began to walk slowly toward where she'd parked her car.

She was glad he'd left it at that. That he hadn't made her any offers she'd have had to refuse. *Friends.* They were thinking along the same lines, at least.

CHAPTER FOUR

LUCAS REALIZED he'd been counting the days until Virginia came to town. It was now precisely twenty-two days since he'd spotted her application and eight days since he'd seen her at the christening.

He peered into the fogged-up mirror and drew the razor carefully over his chin. It was Thursday, but he wasn't going into the office today. He was moving.

He'd better come clean with her right off the bat. No sense letting her go on thinking he'd forgotten everything that had happened twelve years ago. Maybe it meant nothing to her—just another date— but it had meant plenty to him. He'd never forgotten her, not in all that time. His thoughts of taking up where he left off when he'd looked over that application sure hadn't changed since last week.

She was beautiful now. Of course, she'd always been beautiful to him, even the first time he'd seen her when she was scrawny and maybe eleven or twelve. She'd been up a big sycamore, determined not to let any of the neighborhood boys into her tree house, and was pelting down anything she could lay her hands on—twigs, stuff from the treehouse, one of the other girls' sneakers. He'd just happened by with his buddy Adam Garrick. They were too old and too cool to get involved—must have been six-teen, at least—but he'd never forgotten it. Spit, vin-egar, sass. She'd been on fire with righteous indig-nation and he'd thought if she was a little older, he'd like to get to know her.

Well, she's a little older now. He whistled under his breath as he dabbed at the traces of shaving cream on his face and swiped the mist from the mir-ror with his towel.

He glanced out the small bathroom window, which he'd propped wide-open. Another gorgeous day. He was moving his stuff over to the new house this morning, and Virginia and her son were moving into this place on the weekend. Tammy was arriving on the weekend, too, on Sunday. He'd drive to Cal-gary and pick her up at the airport.

Lucas was still whistling as he finished dressing. Jeans, an old T-shirt, sneakers. Much as he enjoyed playing the lawyer-about-town, he liked getting into his old gear at home. He was looking forward to furnishing the new house on Second Avenue and settling in with his niece. He'd always gotten along well with Theresa's daughter, and this way afforded a chance to try out being a parent. Plus help his sister.

Not that he wasn't ready to make the big leap himself. Marriage. Kids. A mortgage. He already had the mortgage and now he had a woman in mind, as well. And she came complete with a kid already, which was just fine by him.

Robert. Kind of an odd little duff, with his glasses

and his serious face and big brown eyes. Somehow
Lucas had pictured a miniature version of Virginia,
only male, but Robert was dark, not fair. He'd met
the boy the day after he'd seen Virginia at the christening; the two had been downtown when he'd gone
to the hotel to meet a client for lunch. That was
Glory—business lunch was over a burger and a mug
of beer at the Glory Hotel, not a steak and a glass
of cabernet at the Palliser. Which was just fine with
him. Lucas's clients tended to be more of the break-
and-enter variety than the insurance-fraud type.
Which was fine, too.

He might have set up practice in Glory initially
to rub the town's nose in his success, but he had to
admit he'd grown fond of the place; now he couldn't
imagine leaving. That was why buying the old Murphy house hadn't hurt quite as much as he'd thought
it would. A house, after all, was a big commitment.

Two stories, white-painted, wide wooden veranda
with gingerbread trim, picket fence, lilac hedge, the
works. It was in an older neighborhood, close to the
center of town. Lucas liked everything about it, from
its hardwood floors and stone fireplace to the sunny
kitchen and the big yard out back with the raspberry
bushes and the Norway maples. Next on his list,
after he moved his stuff over this morning, was to
buy more furniture and get it delivered.

Maybe Virginia and her boy could help him pick
some out.

Lucas pulled the door shut behind him and clattered down the outdoor stairs.

Virginia and Robert were coming up the sidewalk.

"Hello!" she said, shading her eyes against the morning sunlight. "We just wanted to get a key from Mrs. Vandenbroek so I can show Robert the apartment. Are you leaving?"

"Just to grab some breakfast at the Chickadee." Lucas had most of his morning meals at the Chickadee Café, a low-end, no-nonsense place tucked in behind the Glory Hotel.

He peered in his landlady's kitchen window. Everything was spotless and shining and silent inside. "I believe she said something about going over to her sister's to pick peas this morning. Hey, come on up. I can show you the place."

"If it's not too much trouble."

Lucas regarded her for a few seconds. She looked gorgeous in khaki shorts and a plain, long-sleeved white shirt and sandals. Robert wore green shorts and an Edmonton Oilers T-shirt—in the middle of Calgary Flames country. He'd have to set the boy straight. "It's no trouble at all."

They followed him up the stairs.

The door opened into the kitchen. There was another door, a fire escape, off the main bedroom. Lucas stood back as Virginia and her son walked into the apartment.

"See, Robert? Here's where we'll be having our meals. Does the table stay?" She turned, her sea-blue eyes echoing the query.

"Table and chairs stay. Bed stays. Stuff in the

den goes. Sofa and chair stay. End tables and lamps go.''

"Coffee table?''

"It stays.''

Lucas leaned against the doorjamb, watching them. It felt weird to have Virginia in his apartment. It felt even weirder to think she'd be sleeping in what he'd thought of as his bed for well over a year. And she'd be sitting down at his table with her son.

"You mean this is mine? I get a room all to myself?'' Robert said, looking up at his mother in wonder.

She smiled quickly, glanced at Lucas, then back at her son. "Yes, Robert. All yours.'' She ruffled his hair in a gentle gesture and Lucas felt his heart go thump-thump.

"Do I get my own bed and *everything?*''

"Yes, honey. We'll have to buy you some furniture, won't we? For your very own room. A desk, maybe, and a—''

"And bunk beds?'' Robert grabbed his mother's hand. "Oh, boy! Bunk beds, so I can have a friend sleep over with me?''

Virginia paused, but just for a second. "Sure. Bunk beds.''

Lucas cleared his throat. "I'm, uh, I'll be doing some shopping myself when I get my stuff moved over. After lunch. Maybe you and Robert would like to come along.'' This was as good a time as any to jump in and show her that he had every intention of being a friend and more if she'd allow it.

"Here in town?''

"There's always Riddley's. Or we could go to Lethbridge or drive into Calgary. Make a day of it." Man, he was full of good ideas.

"Can we, Mom? Can we get bunk beds today? Yippee!"

Robert suddenly bolted into the bathroom and slammed the door. They heard his excited voice, slightly muffled. "I'm going to try out our new toilet!"

Lucas and Virginia smiled at each other. Lucas waited. He'd thrown out the invitation. The next move was Virginia's.

"Well, it's very kind of you to offer, Lucas. We've got our car, though—"

"I've got the pickup. Come with me. We'll take Robert over to the Grizzly Drive-in. You remember it?"

Virginia laughed. "Is that still around?"

"Yep. And Mrs. Perkins is still running it, too. Then we'll go shopping for bunk beds."

Virginia laughed again, then shrugged. "Okay. Sounds fine."

They heard the toilet flush, then the faucet, and Robert came out, wiping his damp hands on his shorts. "I like this place, Mom. It's cool."

"Good. Now let's get on our way. Mr. Yellowfly has lots of things to do this morning."

Lucas groaned. "Oh, please, Virginia. *Lucas.* Listen, Robert..."

The boy looked up at him, a tiny smile hovering on his too-serious face.

"Promise to call me Lucas, okay? Don't forget. Never Mr. Yellowfly—*never*."

"Okay...Lucas." The boy grinned up at his mother. "He said to, Mom!" he protested when she murmured something about manners. Lucas hadn't seen him smile like that yet. It suited the boy.

He stepped aside as they came back into the kitchen. "When do you want to go? Like I said, I was thinking of this afternoon. But if tomorrow's better for you..."

"This afternoon will be fine."

"I'll pick you up at your parents'?"

"Great."

"Let's make it before lunch so we can buy Robert a Grizzly burger. I should be finished moving this stuff by then." Lucas gestured to the stacks of boxes already neatly packed and piled on the kitchen floor. "Half-past eleven, say?"

Virginia smiled and nodded. As he left them on the sidewalk to make his way to the Chickadee Café for his usual two-over-easy and stack of hots, Lucas could hear Robert asking what a Grizzly burger was and Virginia trying to explain.

ROBERT'S EYES WERE HUGE when they drove up to the Grizzly Drive-in. The take-out diner, built in the shape of a bear's head, was a landmark in Glory, and Virginia had many memories of late-night swoops to the drive-in with Johnny or some of her friends for burgers and malts.

Lucas obligingly growled—a Glory tradition, albeit one usually practiced by children—and Mrs. Perkins growled back.

"Say, that you, Virginia?" she exclaimed, bending low from the counter inserted into the snarling bear's mouth to peer into Lucas's pickup. "Well, I'll be danged! Good to see you, dear. What'll ya have?"

It was said that Mrs. Perkins never forgot a face.

Lucas ordered a burger and fries for Robert, an order of onion rings for her and got himself a root-beer float. They parked on the side of the potholed parking lot and ate their meal with the windows of the pickup wide-open.

"What do you think, Robert?" Lucas asked, smiling at Virginia over her son's head.

"Cool!" He had his carton of french fries on his bare knees and was squeezing the hamburger a little harder than necessary so that mayo and ketchup dripped.

"Yuck!" Virginia wiped at her son's knees with a napkin.

"Here." Lucas handed her some packages of moist wipes from the food bag, which she used to finish cleaning up Robert. She hated to be too hard on the boy; it wasn't often that she'd seen him enjoy himself like this.

The onion rings were as good as she remembered. The hell with cholesterol, she decided, licking her fingers.

She sneaked a glance at Lucas as he sat, slouched back in his seat, one arm crooked out the window, the other holding his drink. He caught her glance and grinned. She smiled, suddenly brimming with good feeling. Simple. Uncomplicated. She'd found so few opportunities to relax in the past few years, certainly not with someone like Lucas, someone she'd known since she was practically a kid. She wondered who else from her school days was still living in Glory. Maybe she'd look up a few old friends soon.

Lucas seemed very relaxed, too. She was grateful for that. Obviously a lot of the stuff she'd thought about working with him was strictly in her own head. She'd have to make sure it stayed there.

They'd decided to drive to Lethbridge to check out Cooper's Department Store. Calgary would have been a better bet for selection, but a big-city mall was the last place Virginia felt like visiting on a sunny late-August afternoon.

They were driving down the highway that led to Lethbridge, deep in the St. Mary River valley, when Robert suddenly spoke up from his position on the bench seat between Lucas and her. He'd been quiet for the last five miles or so.

"Are you my dad?" He looked at Lucas wistfully. Virginia wanted the earth to open up and swallow her. She'd never heard anything like that from her son before.

"Me?" Lucas's startled eyes met hers over the boy's dark head. "Your *dad?*"

There was no mistaking the alarm in his voice. Virginia had to say something.

"Robert—"

"No, it's okay," Lucas said, and smiled at the

boy. Robert continued to gaze seriously at him. "No, I'm not your dad, pal. What made you think so?"

"You're a friend of my mom's. And you know her from a long time ago, so I just thought you might be my dad, that's all," Robert said evenly. He sighed and glanced up at her. She knew her face must be beet red.

"We'll talk about this later, honey," she said softly, about ready to die of embarrassment. *Oh, Robert, why did you have to bring this up now?* All she'd told her son about his father—and until now she'd seen little interest in the subject—was that he lived far, far away. Maybe Robert thought Glory qualified.

As though he knew intuitively that his question had unsettled the grown-ups, Robert went on, to Virginia's dismay, "It's just that I know I have a dad," he said solemnly, looking up at Lucas again. "*Everybody* has a dad, right?" Lucas nodded and smiled encouragingly at the boy. "It's just that I don't know who he *is.*"

Robert folded his hands in his lap and looked straight ahead. Virginia met Lucas's gaze again. He winked. "It's okay, you know," he said quietly. "I can handle tough questions. I'm a lawyer, remember?"

His remark, making light of Robert's query, made her feel a bit better. Next thing she knew, Lucas pointed out one of the hydraulic pumpers that dotted the landscape and was explaining to Robert how it brought oil out of the ground.

Later at the department store, while Robert tried out some of the BarcaLoungers, Virginia tried to explain. "Look, I'm really, really sorry—" she began.

"Hey!" Lucas put one hand on her shoulder in a casual gesture and squeezed gently. "It's no big deal. I can understand where the kid's coming from. He's just curious, that's all."

She looked into his dark eyes, waited a moment or two, then blurted out, "You wonder what the hell's going on, don't you?"

"Not really." Lucas shrugged. "It's none of my business, and to tell you the truth, who really cares? Except Robert, that is. It's your business."

"I'm not married. I've never been married. Robert was...well, he was an accident, I suppose you could say." She stared defiantly at Lucas, daring him to comment. He said nothing. "I'm a single mother. I've always been a single mother."

"I understand," he said. "You don't need to give me any explanations. These things happen." He shrugged again. "Let's go see the bunk beds, shall we?"

He steered her in the direction of the bedroom furniture, and Robert hopped off the BarcaLounger and followed them. "Oh boy! Bunk beds."

Virginia bought a maple model with drawers under the lower unit and headboards that had space for a row of books. Two mattresses and a child-size wooden ladder completed the purchase. Lucas sought her advice on some leather upholstered furniture, then ordered a sofa and chair in dark green, to be delivered on Saturday. She wasn't crazy about them and he said neither was he, but they'd do for his den. He also took Robert's advice and bought a white-lacquered single bed frame, mattress and matching dresser the boy thought suitable for a girl.

Lucas murmured to Virginia that it was a little fussier than he remembered his niece being, but ordered it, anyway. Virginia was warmed from the inside out that Lucas took Robert's opinion seriously. Robert had had very few men in his short life. Virginia had been so focused on work and on her son that she hadn't had time to develop relationships with men. Not that, after her horrific experience with Johnny Gagnon, she'd had any desire to.

The department-store employees loaded Robert's bunk-bed frame and mattresses into the back of Lucas's pickup. Their delivery van would bring the leather sofa and chair, as well as Tammy's new furniture on Saturday. Virginia settled on the passenger side for the return trip, wondering what questions her son would come up with on the way back.

Robert was quiet, paying attention to the landmarks Lucas pointed out, responding in his usual sober manner. Sometimes Virginia wasn't sure what to think about her small, serious son. She hoped this move to Glory meant he'd finally be able to make some real friends. He spent far too much time with his video games and watching television, in her opinion. Kindergarten would be a big change in his life. They'd moved so often that it had been hard for Robert to establish the kinds of relationships that meant birthday-party invitations and afternoon play sessions with friends. When she'd worked in Red Deer, she'd placed him in a licensed day care, but Robert had become so withdrawn and miserable that she'd taken him out and gone back to relying on baby-sitters, as she'd done when he was a baby.

That was something else she'd have to think about—after-school care. Her experience working with lawyers had shown her that the hours could be erratic. She'd have to find someone reliable to pick Robert up from school and stay with him until she got home from work. Maybe Lucas could give her some leads.

She bit her lower lip and glanced sideways. She'd already presumed on her former acquaintance with Lucas far too much. Besides, what would he know about child care or baby-sitters? His niece, Tammy, was arriving Sunday and he'd find out soon enough how much was involved in looking after children.

Lucas dropped her and Robert off at her parents' house at the top of the hill, insisting that he'd get a friend to help him unload the bunk beds at his old apartment. After that, he said, he'd have his hands full getting settled into his new place. He seemed about to add something else—had he been going to ask her to help?—but apparently thought better of it. She was amazed to realize she felt let down that he didn't ask. It would've been fun helping him arrange his furniture, and a way to pay him back a little for the outing they'd had today.

Robert wanted to play in the hammock that hung between two huge linden trees at the back of the Lake property, so Virginia went in through the kitchen door. She heard murmurs from the sitting room when she entered the house. Her mother must have company.

She'd paused to open the refrigerator door to inspect the contents for a cold drink when she heard the raised voice of her aunt Lily beyond the swinging doors of the kitchen.

"But, Doris, you *have* to insist she tell you who the boy's father is. I know Virginia's headstrong— she's always been a handful—and I realize what you and Jethro have had to put up with over the years, but don't you see? People are already asking. What am I supposed to tell them? That no one *knows?*"

She heard her mother's soft, fretful reply and suddenly Virginia lost her thirst. She shut the refrigerator door quietly and went up the back stairs to the room she and Robert were sharing.

Busybodies. All of them. Especially Aunt Lily. What if Robert had overheard that remark? Virginia felt her face flush. They made her so mad. What business was it of theirs? What was it about small towns that made everyone so darn nosy? It'd been like that when she was a girl here, and apparently nothing had changed.

Had she expected it *would* have changed?

No. Lucas had said, "Who really cares, except Robert?" Maybe Lucas believed that. But Glory was the same as it had always been. She was sure unmarried pregnant girls were still said to have gone to the city to take a hairdressing course, or gone to stay with a distant aunt to go to school.

Some things never changed. But she had. And the town of Glory would realize that soon enough.

CHAPTER FIVE

LUCAS STEPPED OVER a cardboard box and nodded to one of Gus McCready's employees, who was just clearing up the last of the paint, brushes, rollers and drop cloths, ready to leave after a week spent painting the place. Another employee had already carried ladders to the van.

The house looked terrific. Lucas took a deep breath, noting the pungent fumes of the last coat of cream semigloss that had been applied to the woodwork. The walls were a soft sage green throughout, with a deep mustard for his study on the main floor, a room that had once served as a bedroom for the Murphy family. The kitchen walls had been painted a soft butterscotch color with the kitchen cupboards, doors and framework all done in the same cream color as the woodwork in the rest of the house. The Portuguese tile countertop and black-and-white-checkered vinyl floor were new and shining.

Lucas had always been drawn to color. He wasn't sure if it was his native ancestry or just a personal preference, but color always made him feel good, and he wanted to feel good in this big Second Avenue house he'd bought. This was home now.

Lucas made his way up the broad staircase. He'd

had the hardwood floors refinished on both levels, and the deep walnut tones gleamed in the late-morning sunlight. Upstairs, the four bedrooms were all painted in an off-white, except for his, which was a restful but rich café au lait, again with the cream woodwork. A small Oriental carpet added a touch of luxury. He was glad he'd bought the bedroom furniture at an auction when he'd first moved to Glory and kept it in storage while he lived at Mrs. Vandenbroek's. Now, polished and sturdy, the old-Ontario armoire and dresser and chest of drawers fit into the room perfectly. The matching double bed was going into one of the bedrooms, which he planned to use as a guest room. Antique or not, Lucas had no intention of squeezing his six-foot-three frame into an old-fashioned double bed. A king-size model was coming this afternoon, along with the other furniture he'd ordered from Cooper's.

Lucas strode into the en suite bathroom, which one of McCready's crews had converted from a small bedroom or sewing room. Now the room was ready, complete with modern fixtures and ceramic tiles. Lucas felt something he'd never really felt before as he looked over his new home. Pride. Pride of ownership.

The house was too big for one person, no question. It had been the Murphy-family home for three generations. A lot of kids had grown up here, slid down the banisters, played in the attic, swung from the trees in the backyard.

Tammy would be here for a while, until Theresa was ready to take her back again. Who knew when that might be? Maybe he'd hire a housekeeper who could do the cooking and cleaning for him and his niece. And maybe one day he'd fill this house with his own children. It was a house that ached for family life. Lucas had enjoyed bachelorhood, but from time to time he felt that he should make a change. Get married. Settle down.

Somehow, Virginia Lake's coming home to Glory had put the idea right back in his head.

That reminded him—he glanced at his watch— he'd promised her he'd put Robert's bunk beds together after lunch. There wasn't much to do, just fasten a few screws and do some assembly work on the ladder and headboards. He was happy to offer and even happier when she accepted. Her father could have done it or she could easily have done it herself if she'd borrowed a few of her dad's tools, but he had the feeling Virginia didn't get on too well with her folks. She seemed awfully anxious to move into his old apartment and get settled in with her son.

Lucas could see a person not getting on all that well with Doc Lake. He had to be close to retirement age, in his midsixties, but was still head of surgery at the Glory Memorial Hospital. He was tall, lean and iron-haired, and was said to have an uncompromising personality. Definitely he had a certain unassailable position in this town, as a senior doctor often did, regardless of his temper. Lucas had to admit his memories weren't the best. Doc Lake had done all he could to blacken Lucas's name around Glory when word had spread that he and Virginia had spent the night together after her graduation. It didn't matter that his own daughter had told him nothing had happened or that Lucas had gone to his office and told him the same thing.

And even if something beyond a little moon-watching and stargazing and kissing *had* gone on, so what? It wasn't as though the doctor's daughter was the town virgin. Everyone knew how she'd carried on with Johnny Gagnon, and it wasn't as though Lucas was from a part of town any worse than the Gagnon clan's. Frankly it had irked the hell out of Lucas at the time, the doc's attitude, considering Lucas had been well on his way to making something of himself.

Maybe some things were too hard to change— like a person's skin color and the preconceived ideas of a small-town elite.

Well, those days were past, Lucas thought, whistling as he climbed into his pickup for the short ride over to Virginia's new apartment. Now the town fathers were more than happy to have him date their daughters. Lucas didn't harbor any grudges. He was too confident in his own abilities. But he had to admit he did enjoy their shocked expressions when he showed up in his BMW—ten years old but in perfect shape—with a big smile on his face and flowers for their womenfolk.

Virginia was at the apartment cleaning windows. She answered the door to his light knock—it seemed odd to be knocking at what still felt like his own door—dressed in shorts and a stained T-shirt, her hair tied back in a kerchief, her nose smudged with grime, her freckles vivid against her pale skin. She looked like a fairy-tale cleaning lady. Cinderella. He glanced down. Canvas sneakers. No glass slippers for this Cinderella—yet.

"Hey, didn't think I'd catch you here," he said, taking off his own sneakers at the kitchen door. He could smell fresh floor wax. "I'll have Robert's bed fixed in a jiffy."

"I thought I'd give the place a final going-over before we moved the rest of the stuff in," she said almost apologetically. "Robert's over at Mother's." She smiled, a delightful expression that made him want to bend forward and kiss the end of her nose. "He wanted to help, but I thought I'd rather do this myself. Take half the time. Besides, I think it's good that he's getting to know my parents better."

"I've got a couple tools with me," Lucas said, walking toward the bedroom where he'd unloaded the bunk beds, still encased in their packing plastic. "A screwdriver and wrench." He patted his back pockets. "If I need anything else, there's a toolbox down in the truck. Don't let me interrupt whatever you're doing."

"Okay," Virginia said a little uncertainly, still holding her cleaning cloth. "I'll make us some tea in a bit. Do you drink tea?"

"Sure." Lucas started stripping the heavy plastic from the furniture. Sometimes he had a hard time seeing the assertive, act-now-ask-later girl he'd known in this rather tentative woman. Yet there was something appealing about her vulnerability, something that upped the ante on the protective, tender feelings he already had toward her. And he was certain he glimpsed the determination that lay under that quiet manner. Somehow he didn't think Virginia Lake gave any more quarter now than she had then.

Assembling the bunk beds, he watched her from the corner of his eye. She had a serious look on her face as she attacked every glass surface with her cloth. She polished the windows in the living room, then went to work on the kitchen window, a little out of his line of sight. Which was just as well. It was a hot August day, but watching Virginia Lake in her cutoffs and skimpy T-shirt made the day a little hotter.

They worked quietly for a while and Lucas was just tightening the last screw on the headboard when Virginia came into the room with a tray containing two mugs and some store-bought cookies.

"You take milk or sugar?" she asked.

"Just plain." He tossed down his wrench and she offered him a mug.

"Thanks. Listen, why don't you help me lift this bed on top of the other one before we have our tea and then we'll have more room *and* an idea of what this is going to look like," Lucas said. He took the tray from her and set it down behind the door, where it was out of the way.

"Great." Virginia seemed pleased. She grabbed the footboard while he went around to the headboard.

"Now," Lucas began, "you just steady that end

while I lift. I'll help you with your end when I get this post onto the other one.''

In two or three minutes the job was done, and Virginia's face broke into a delighted grin. She looked about sixteen.

''Wait until Robert sees this,'' she said. ''He's going to be thrilled! I think it should go against this wall, don't you?'' She indicated the north wall. ''I don't want him falling out the window.''

''Good spot for it,'' Lucas agreed. ''We'll move it after our tea.'' He picked up the tray and sank onto the floor beside the bed, legs crossed. They still had the mattresses to unpack and hoist onto the frame. As Virginia knelt on the floor opposite him, Lucas handed her a mug. ''Robert's never had his own room before?''

Virginia frowned. She took a sip of the hot drink. ''I hadn't really thought it was important to him, but everywhere we've lived, we've either shared a room or sometimes he's had a sitter who stayed with us. When he was a baby we had a live-in sitter for a while.''

''Sounds like he's looking forward to having friends over, that kind of stuff,'' Lucas said casually. He took a swallow of his own tea. Virginia's past life was of enormous interest to him, but he didn't want to push her. He didn't want to appear to be fishing for information. And none of it mattered, anyway. Not really. Curiosity aside, the only thing that mattered was that she was here in Glory.

''Cookie?'' Virginia extended the plate to him and he took one.

"Thanks."

For a few minutes they sat in silence, but it was a companionable silence. Lucas wondered what she was thinking about—beyond where to position the furniture and what kind of curtains to hang, if she intended to replace the rather grim vinyl blinds Mrs. Vandenbroek had installed. His own mind wandered a little, to a difficult property case he was working on, and to whether or not he'd written Tammy's flight number in his day book—

"I want to thank you so very, very much, Lucas, for all the help you've been to me and my son since we arrived here." Virginia's voice interrupting his thoughts was low and urgent. She held her empty mug in one hand, and her eyes were troubled. "It was a huge thing for me to come back to Glory—I guess you know that. I only hope I've made the right decision. I'm determined to stay, no matter what happens—"

"Hey, Virginia." Lucas held her gaze and felt something start to hum and burn inside his chest. She had this effect on him; she'd always had this effect on him.

"What could happen?" he asked quietly. Maybe it was time he told her he had no intention of being just a friend.

"I mean it. You've been terrific. And...and I really appreciate it. It's meant a lot to us, especially since things aren't always the way I'd like them to be with Mother and Father." She paused and bit her lower lip.

Lucas had noticed that she always referred to her

parents rather formally. It seemed odd, since everyone in town had always known how much Doc and
Doris Lake had doted on their only child.

Lucas wanted to reach out and touch her. Suddenly he did. He leaned forward and placed both his
hands on her shoulders and began to massage. She
looked surprised momentarily, then relaxed into the
pressure of his hands, as though her shoulders or her
neck were tense and tight. Lucas continued to massage softly. "Listen, Virginia, I'm happy to be a
good friend to you. But that's not all I want to be."

Their eyes, only ten or twelve inches apart, held.
"Do you realize that?" he asked. "It's way too
early to kiss you, but that's what I'd like to do."
His voice sounded hoarse even to his own ears.
"I've been crazy about you ever since we were kids
and I only had the one chance to show it. Your
graduation. And we both know what happened
then."

He grimaced, expecting an answering smile, but
she stared at him steadily, her eyes huge.

"You're working for Pete Horsfall," he went on
quietly, "not me. I mean, you're working with me,
not for me. Do you understand? I'm giving you due
notice of the way I feel about you. I owe you that.
When we're at work, I'm a hundred percent professional. You can count on that. But when we're not
at work—" he studied her eyes, noticed that her lips
trembled ever so slightly "—I intend to court you.
Seriously. Very, very seriously."

He stopped massaging her shoulders and drew her
a little closer. "Consider yourself warned, Virginia

Lake. Unless you tell me that it's right out of the question for you. That there's no chance at all for me. For us.''

There was a moment or two of strained silence. Then, ''S-seriously?'' Her voice was very faint.

''Damn seriously.''

''Oh, Lucas…then *kiss me. Please.*''

He didn't need a second invitation. He pulled her into his arms. Her trembling stopped and she met his kiss with her own, warm and soft and tentative. He shivered. It was way, way too early for this. *What the hell was he doing?* She was vulnerable, she was new in town, and she was hurting in some way he couldn't begin to imagine.

Still, he'd made his intentions clear. Which was what he'd planned all along. Virginia moaned and he brought her even closer.

Well. He'd asked. And it didn't look as though the doctor's daughter was completely against the idea.

TAMMY'S FLIGHT WAS on time. His niece was the third one to appear in the arrivals area, accompanied by a smiling flight attendant. Tammy Yellowfly wasn't the sort of person to be bothered by late flights or schedule mix-ups or a mother in a sweat-lodge detox program. Tammy took everything in her stride. Beautifully. His niece was a survivor.

Lucas grinned when he saw her. Dressed in a cotton skirt and matching hooded jacket, she was carrying an Air Canada flight bag. She pushed her wire-rim sunglasses up on her nose and looked around.

"Tammy!" He wanted to swing her up in his arms and plant a big kiss on her chubby cheek, but some deep instinct told him she was no longer the baby he'd known. She was eight going on eighteen.

"Uncle Lucas!" At least she still sounded eight. That was a relief. Maybe the savvy was all for the flight attendant's benefit.

He bent and hugged her. "Got much stuff, honey?"

"One suitcase with clothes and one with my teddy bears. Mommy said you'd buy me anything else if I needed it," she said serenely, glancing toward the luggage carousel.

Smiling, Lucas shook his head. Trust Theresa. She knew him pretty well. Lucas didn't resent his sister's assumptions one bit. She was right: he'd be more than glad to provide for his niece. For as long as she was with him and any time afterward, too. It was the Indian way. You had, you shared. And, compared to Theresa, with her peripatetic existence of the past few years, Lucas definitely *had*.

"How's your mom?" he asked his niece as he joined her in the car after tossing the bags into the trunk of the BMW.

"Oh, pretty good, I guess," Tammy replied evenly. "She's getting in touch with her Indian side, you know. She's really serious this time, she says."

Poor Tammy. A little more informed than an eight-year-old ought to be, Lucas thought. But on the other hand, it hadn't seemed to affect the child adversely. She was as sweet and straightforward and self-possessed as she'd always been. Theresa might have gone wrong here and there in her own life, but she'd done a fine job raising her daughter.

He thought of Robert. Another kid with a single mom. Another kid who had no idea who his father was, according to what he'd blurted out in the truck. Theresa had never told him much about the circumstances behind Tammy's birth, either; all Lucas knew was that she'd gotten pregnant when she was doing a private job as a practical nurse in the Queen Charlotte Islands, many miles north of Vancouver. Who Tammy's father was, Lucas had no idea. Nor, until Virginia and Robert had come into his life, had he even thought about it much.

"You hungry?"

"Not really. We had lunch on the plane." Tammy folded her hands in her lap—a gesture that reminded Lucas oddly of Robert—and gazed out the window. He suspected she was just being polite.

"What'd you have? A Big Mac?"

She grinned at him. A gap-toothed grin that turned her into a beauty. She had the straight black hair, the high cheekbones, and the dusky color that gave away her heritage. Added to that was a glow of good health. "No burgers, Uncle Lucas."

"Oh, all right." Lucas grinned, too. "You're a growing girl. First McDonald's we see, we'll stop."

They arrived in Glory two hours later, after a leisurely lunch. Tammy was delighted with her room, complete with the new furniture Robert had picked out for her. Lucas had bought sheets and comforters and pillows at Riddley's, the local family-run department store, and had organized her room as best he could. There were still no curtains on the window, but he figured Tammy could choose them herself.

"Like it?"

"It's cool!" She threw her arms around his neck and kissed him loudly. "I love it! Thanks, Uncle Lucas. I'm going to love living here with you."

He left her singing some alternative music tune and happily unpacking her meager collection of clothes. Her teddy bears, all fourteen of them, she'd already positioned around her bed and pillow.

Lucas put on the coffeepot in the kitchen, humming to himself. He pulled out a couple of TV dinners to microwave for supper. Was this family life? Well, it was a start at least.

CHAPTER SIX

HORSFALL, HORSFALL and Yellowfly, Attorneys at Law, was a busy small-town practice. They took whatever came over the transom. Which meant plenty of mortgages, property disputes, break-and-enters, divorces, drunk driving, custody battles—and the occasional murder.

So far, Lucas had never defended a murder client. He'd done his share of divorces, civil suits, a ton of mortgages and wills and more break-and-enters than he could count.

Right now he was involved in a fairly complex property matter for Deverell Sparks, a local developer, which he hoped Virginia could assist him with. Sparks was trying to assemble some land for a golf course, and Lucas was having a hard time establishing legal ownership documentation on one of the properties.

Mrs. Rutgers, who'd been with Horsfall for longer than even Pete could remember, had finally retired. She'd started with the firm when Pete's father, the original Horsfall, was still alive. In one way, Lucas wasn't sorry to see her go—her interfering manner got on his nerves, although he'd always considered himself a pretty easygoing guy. In another way, he

missed her desperately. Along with her front-end reception duties, Mrs. Rutgers had been a pit bull for
research. She had no special training, had learned
the job as she went, taking on more and more research tasks to the delight of Pete, a lawyer who
enjoyed the town bonhomie and the people part of
the job far more than hitting the lawbooks. That, too,
was part of a successful small-town law career. You
had to get along with folks.

But everyone they'd replaced Mrs. Rutgers with
in the year or more since she'd left had been unsat-
isfactory in one respect or another. Either their research skills didn't measure up to the demands of
the two-lawyer practice, or they didn't work out
when it came to answering the phone and dealing
with the public. Finally Lucas and his senior partner
had decided to advertise in the provincial law ga-
zette and hire a proper, full-time legal assistant—the
job for which Virginia had applied. They had a nice,
bright young woman handling reception and typing
duties now, which worked out very well. Nancy often had time on her hands, and she put it to use
reading police procedural thrillers and true-crime
tabloids. From these she gleaned unusual legal no-
tions that she freely shared with Lucas and his partner. But Nancy's advice was easily ignored. They
only hoped she wasn't offering her oddly acquired
legal expertise to clients over the phone. So far
they'd had no complaints. Sometimes Lucas wished
she'd stick to *People* and *Cosmopolitan* for her reading material, but as long as she was there to deal

with off-the-street clients, to answer the phone and type documents, he and Pete were satisfied.

Virginia Lake came well qualified for the job of researcher. She'd had two years of law school herself, as well as an office-management course and plenty of experience doing research for law firms in small towns throughout Alberta. Every letter of reference spoke in glowing terms of her abilities and expressed disappointment that she'd left them after such a short time.

Lucas wondered about that. If she was so well liked, why had she abandoned so many jobs? It was one of the mysteries of Virginia's past—that and Robert's sudden appearance not long after she'd left law school. Maybe she'd had an affair that had gone wrong with someone at the university, another student or a professor, and she'd changed her plans as a result of it. Who knew? Lucas only hoped she'd meant it when she told him she intended to stay in Glory. He didn't want to lose her now that he'd found her again, and his feelings had nothing to do with the firm's need for an assistant.

He recalled that unexpected kiss in her apartment. She'd shocked him with her sudden demand. Then, after a kiss that reminded him of everything he'd ever felt for her, she'd sprung back and covered her face with her hands.

"I'm so sorry, Lucas."

"Don't be sorry, Virginia," he'd replied, stunned. "You know I'd never hurt you."

"You don't know!" she'd cried. "You don't *know* what can happen!"

He'd agreed, mystified, then drawn her into his arms and let her sob. After a few minutes, she'd pulled herself together and, face red, apologized again, offering him no explanation beyond the obvious one that she was overwrought, that there'd been too many changes in her life lately and she had a lot on her mind.

Who didn't? Lucas thought. That reminded him. He'd promised Theresa he'd call when Tammy arrived. He'd tried last night just after they'd gotten home, and there'd been no answer. Now he'd give her a call from the office.

"Theresa? How ya doin', sis?" Lucas always enjoyed his conversations with his sister. He was generally in touch with her at least once a month. He knew she called their mother in Calgary more often than that.

"Everything's cool with Tammy?"

"Absolutely. She loves her new room. She's already got plans for me to take her shopping before school starts. She's down at the library right now signing up for a card."

His sister laughed. "Sounds like my girl!"

"How about you? What's with this Indian spiritual stuff?"

"I know you think it's crazy, Lucas," she replied, "but I've made my mind up this time. I'm off the booze for good, and I'm turning my life around. The sweat lodge has worked for other people and it just might work for me. It's time, isn't it? For Tammy's sake."

"I believe you, sis." Lucas wasn't sure it would

work. Theresa had tried AA before, but the sweat lodge was new. Whatever she decided, though, he'd support her. One of these times something had to click. "Good luck with it, hey? And keep in touch. Tammy'd like a letter now and then. I'll get her to write. And I'll make sure she eats her vegetables and gets plenty of sleep. I'll look after her just fine, so you don't need to worry about that. I talked to Ma the other day and I'm going to take Tammy up there for a weekend soon."

"Thanks, bro. You know I appreciate it," Theresa said softly, and hung up.

Lucas stood and walked to the long windows that overlooked Main Street. Tammy had decided she needed a library card first thing, so he'd helped her fill out the forms, then left her browsing for books before heading into the office to check his messages and mail. He was taking time off in the last week before school began, but still needed to come in for a few hours here and there. Luckily Tammy was no baby who required looking after every minute of the day, but he'd still have to hunt up a reliable sitter. She was too young to be left by herself for long, even though the house was only about a ten-minute walk away.

He returned to his desk and pressed the call button to the reception area. "Nance? See if you can round up a list of sitters for me to check out. Some older teenagers. And preferably with references."

Might as well add that. He didn't want any party animals in *his* house.

He wondered how Virginia was doing with Robert. He was dying to see her again but wasn't going to push it. He didn't want to come across as a pest. Maybe he'd call and ask them to lunch with him and his niece later this week. Tammy and Robert might as well get to know each other before they started school. They'd be attending Sam Steele Elementary, a short walk from both his house and Virginia's apartment. Nothing in Glory was much farther than fifteen minutes in any direction.

Robert would be in kindergarten and Tammy in grade three. She'd be nine in January. It had seemed such a short while ago that Theresa had brought her to Alberta, a squalling pink bundle to show off to him and their mother. Husband or no husband, Theresa had been pleased as punch with her new baby.

Lucas shook his head. Man, soon he'd be saying stuff like *How time flies* and *It seems like only yesterday.*...

VIRGINIA CAREFULLY BALANCED the lemon layer cake she carried in one hand as she and Robert approached the big white house on Second Avenue.

Robert had been asking her to take him there ever since he'd heard that Lucas's niece had arrived. He wanted to see how she liked the new bed he'd picked out. Virginia hoped Tammy would be a friend for her son, even though she was older and a girl and things like that mattered to children.

She and Robert had moved completely into their own apartment now, and Robert was thrilled with his new room. Especially the top bunk, where he'd installed himself. He could see across the street through the window and had already played endless spy games by himself.

Maybe she should have called first. It was eleven o'clock. But if Lucas wasn't home, it wasn't much of a walk back to their place, and she knew the cake would get eaten regardless.

But he was home. Lucas answered on the first ring of the doorbell, tall and handsome in an old football jersey and jeans.

"Who is it, Uncle Lucas?" she could hear from somewhere behind him.

Lucas grinned. "Come on in." Then he shouted over his shoulder, "Visitors, Tammy. Couple of new neighbors."

A girl with long black hair clattered down the stairs behind him. "Wow. New neighbors."

Before Virginia could figure out what was happening, Lucas had introduced the two children and they'd vanished into the interior of the house. He had taken the cake from her and she was following him into the bright sunlit kitchen.

"Thanks for the cake," Lucas said, setting it down on the counter. "Looks terrific. You make it yourself?"

Virginia nodded.

"I'm impressed. I'm not much of a cook. Say," he suggested, "You want some coffee to go with this? Or a cold drink? And you'll stay for lunch—"

"Oh, no, we couldn't—"

"Absolutely. Tammy and I've been planning to ask you and Robert over before school started and we've been shy about it."

Virginia laughed. "You, shy? I doubt it."

"No kidding. I thought you'd want a few days to get settled in without me bugging you. After the other day—" to her rattled nerves, his pause was significant "—I thought I might be getting in the way a little." He laughed disarmingly. "You know, even with the best of intentions."

His reference to their last meeting, the day he'd put together Robert's bed and she'd kissed him and then wept all over his shirt, had her reddening.

"Iced tea? Coffee? Juice?" Lucas turned smoothly to the refrigerator. "Let's grab a glass of something and sit out back. I want to show you the yard."

They settled on lawn chairs under the big maple trees. Virginia felt relieved that the reference to their last meeting was well and adroitly behind them. She thought Lucas must be an awfully good negotiator, which couldn't hurt, considering his profession. He certainly was a diplomat.

Business. They could talk business.

"Are you working on anything particularly interesting these days? I don't suppose Glory is exactly a hotbed of sticky legal problems and serious crime," she began, taking a sip of her lemonade.

"You'd be surprised." Lucas frowned. "Right now, I'm trying to put together some land titles for a client and I'm having a hell of a time digging up the relevant documents." He grinned at her. "That's your first job next week. Track down some stuff at the courthouse."

"Sounds interesting." It did. Virginia had been

amazed to discover how much she enjoyed poring through dusty property documents and liens and mortgages in law libraries and government offices. She'd always thought her interest in law had been in the visible, courtroom part of the profession; she'd discovered she liked the background nuts-and-bolts research just as much.

"Who's your client?"

"On the land? Oh, some guy who wants to acquire a chunk to put in a golf course. A developer," Lucas said dismissively, his eyes traveling quickly over his backyard. "Small-time stuff, really. Hey, come and see my raspberries."

He grabbed her hand, almost an unconscious gesture, it seemed, then walked with her to the bushes at one side of the yard. She could see dull red berries under the thin leaves, almost bursting in the warm sun. Lucas picked a few and turned to her.

"Open up."

Unthinking, she did just that and he put two fat raspberries in her mouth. The sweet juice ran into her throat and she couldn't take her eyes off him as he popped a couple of berries into his own mouth. She couldn't breathe. She wasn't sure he could, either.

Lucas swallowed. "Damn," he said softly, his eyes on hers. "This is going to be even tougher than I thought, Virginia."

She swallowed, then croaked, "Tough?"

"Keeping my hands off you. Business or otherwise."

"We, um, already talked about that." She swallowed again, stepped back and took a deep breath.

"You're right. We did." He turned toward the back of the house. Virginia followed his gaze. White curtains blew out of a bedroom window on the second floor. The whole scene was impossibly domestic. The two of them. The garden. The fresh-baked layer cake in the kitchen. The children in the house.

"Let's go see what the kids are up to, huh?" Lucas grinned, the amiable old Lucas she remembered, not the potential lover she'd glimpsed so often since she'd arrived in town. "Come on, race you to the back porch!"

And, giggling, she did.

THAT NIGHT VIRGINIA SAT before her mirror and stared into it long after she'd put down her brush. Robert was asleep, tired and happy from the day spent with his new friend. Virginia had thought she'd read for a while, but had decided on a bath and early bed. She, too, was tired.

And happy.

Lucas Yellowfly had a lot to do with that. He was so easy to be with, so relaxed. He was one-hundred percent male, no question, and the sexuality that positively simmered below the surface was nothing any woman could ignore.

Did she *want* to ignore it?

Virginia examined her face in the dim lighting. She had only one small bedside lamp on and the sun had set hours ago, although it wasn't completely dark outside, a benefit of the long northern summer.

She was moderately attractive, she guessed. No beauty, that was certain. The years had taken their toll. There were fine lines beside her eyes. Her mouth, always full-lipped and generous, had a new firmness, a maturity. It hadn't been kissed, except by Lucas, in a very long time.

She took a deep breath, then let it out slowly and allowed herself to remember why that was. Still, she'd responded to Lucas's kiss, not like that other time she'd tried to date. To have a normal life. With that lawyer from Lacombe. His kisses had thrown her into a panic. She hadn't liked kissing him at all, hadn't responded, except with revulsion. And why was that?

Johnny Gagnon.

He'd ruined her life. With other men, it seemed—at least some men—and with her son. She'd been on the run for so long. She'd been terrified of something happening to Robert. Of Johnny finding out about him. She'd had nightmares for years about that horrible day and night in the remote cabin out past Bragg Creek. She'd never even gone back to that part of the country, although Mary Prescott had offered her the cabin several times just to get away from it all, especially after Robert was born, and been hurt when she refused.

She'd had nightmares about Johnny showing up and snatching Robert. Taking him away from her forever and ever.

It was like a toothache that wouldn't go away. Johnny Gagnon was safely in jail, had been for years, but somehow she still couldn't quite accept the idea that he was out of her life and wouldn't be part of it again.

Why hadn't she told the police about the rape? Many times she'd awakened in a cold sweat, terrified, sick at heart about what she eventually saw as her complicity. She'd allowed him to escape the charge of rape, thinking at the time that it was a freak happenstance that he'd raped her. He'd been so drunk. Not that that was any excuse. Except, until recently, it too often was. *I didn't know what I was doing, Your Honor. I was too drunk.*

And she'd have had to suffer through questions about her own past relationship with Johnny, in a trial. She might have had to answer a lot of very hard questions. Not fair, certainly, but the entire legal system was based on the presumption of innocence until proved guilty. And, fundamentally, Virginia believed in that system. She'd known there was plenty of evidence to convict him on the armed robbery, including her own testimony, so she'd kept her mouth shut about the rape.

But what if she'd been wrong?

If he'd raped her, how could she have been so sure he wouldn't have raped someone else? She hadn't seen him in a long time when she'd happened upon him in that highway grocery. He could have changed a lot since high school. *She* had.

Virginia picked up her brush again and limply drew it through her hair, oblivious to the tears that ran down her face. She'd been through this so many, many times. It was no use. It was a question that would never be answered. All she could do was protect Robert. She could never tell her son who his real father was. She could never tell him he'd been born as the result of his mother being kidnapped and raped. She could tell no one. All she could tell her son was what she'd already told him—that his father was far away and couldn't be part of their lives.

She'd sworn to quit running, to come back to Glory and make a home for herself and Robert. She'd face whatever the future brought.

Even Johnny Gagnon, if he showed up in town?

Virginia bit her lower lip until it hurt. She couldn't say. Until she confronted that particular horror, how could she guess what she'd do? She hoped she'd never have to decide. She reminded herself that Glory was the last place he'd dream of looking for her—if, indeed, he had any thoughts of finding her again. And why would he, after their last encounter and after her testimony had helped send him to jail? He must hate her for that.

Lucas, she knew in her heart, would be the friend she so desperately needed. He said he wanted to be more, but she didn't know if she was capable of more. Not just with Lucas, but with any man.

Only time would tell.

Until then, she knew she could count on him. Everything about Lucas Yellowfly spelled strength and stability. Trust. Honor. Integrity. Dependability.

Earlier today they'd dined al fresco on the patio behind his house, munching on delicious things that came out of boxes from Molly McClung's Delicatessen. Lucas swore he was one of Molly's best customers. Virginia could understand why. The good scents she'd noticed that day she'd had coffee and cake there with Lucas were borne out in the excellent focaccia, couscous salad, hot Buffalo wings, potato salad and fruit punch, freshly squeezed and delicious with real strawberries and lemon slices floating and real cherries bumping along the bottom of the pitcher. Lucas had ducked out to pick up the food, leaving her and Tammy and Robert to set the outdoor table.

They'd had fun. Tammy was a delightful girl and Virginia was thrilled to see how well the two children had hit it off. Whatever social skills Robert seemed to have missed out on due to their frequent moves Lucas's niece seemed to have in spades. Her sunny, outgoing personality was an interesting balance for Robert's natural stoicism.

And, of course, they all had lemon cake and ice cream for dessert, melting mouthfuls between the laughter.

Virginia got up with a sigh and pulled back the quilt on her bed—the bed that had so recently belonged to Lucas, but she stifled that thought as she'd done each night since she'd moved in. Lucas *was* a special man.

He was a man who could make things work out right. All kinds of things…

CHAPTER SEVEN

THE TUESDAY AFTER LABOR DAY, dawned brilliant and blue. Virginia walked the three and a half blocks to Sam Steele Elementary with Robert, relieved to discover how short a distance it was. Ten minutes at most. Robert was quiet and held her hand all the way. He had on brand-new clothes, which she'd bought him the week before at Riddley's Department Store, an old-fashioned establishment that had been a fixture in Glory for longer than anyone could remember.

Robert brightened when they approached the school playground, alive with the shouts of children, mostly dressed just as he was, in brand-new back-to-school wear, including bright white running shoes. Spanking new backpacks were tumbled in heaps by the play equipment. She felt him tighten his grip on her hand, even though he gawked with interest at all the children. Virginia knew this was a big deal to Robert. It was to her, too.

Mrs. Brown was a plump grandmotherly person who looked as if she was exactly where she'd always wanted to be—in a kindergarten classroom. She greeted each child with a pat on the shoulder and a sweet welcoming smile, and Virginia practically felt Robert's sigh of relief. The class was relatively small, just eighteen pupils. The paint on the walls looked fresh, the big windows sparkling clean. Sam Steele was a two-story brick building, with tall, old-fashioned windows dating from the days when schools depended more on daylight than electric lights.

Virginia left Robert happily playing on a sand-and-water platform with two other boys. She told him she'd pick him up at noon. First day for kindergarten was a half day.

On the way out of the school, she passed Lucas and Tammy going in. Lucas was obviously dressed for the office, in a suit and tie. He looked devastatingly handsome, with his dark complexion and dark hair. He greeted her with a smile and an apology that he couldn't talk; they were running late. Tammy grinned and waved. She wore jeans and a white T-shirt, her glossy dark hair pulled back in a ponytail.

Virginia didn't see either of them when she returned for Robert at half-past eleven. Her heart leaped when her son appeared at the classroom door, his small face lit with excitement.

"This is Teddy and he's my new friend," he said, pointing to a sandy-haired boy who hung back shyly. "He wants to see my new bunk beds and play Spy with me. Can he come over?"

Virginia looked helplessly around, meeting the eyes of the woman who must be Teddy's mother. "I'm Virginia Lake," she said, extending her hand, which the other woman shook briefly.

"Marcia Herrara."

"I'd love to have Teddy come over, but we've promised his grandmother we'd have lunch with her today—"

"Awww!" Robert scowled, and she hushed him with a gesture.

"How about a little later?" Virginia continued. "Maybe Teddy could come over around two o'clock? We'll be home by then."

The other woman smiled and patted her son on his tousled head. "That's fine. You're upstairs at Mrs. Vandenbroek's?"

"Yes," Virginia said, surprised, knowing she shouldn't be. In small towns, news traveled. "I guess you know where that is?"

"Sure. We'll be over about two." Marcia beamed at the two boys. Perhaps, thought Virginia, she's as pleased that her son has found a new friend as I am. "See you then, Robert?"

The boys nodded and raced down the hall together. The two women followed more slowly.

"You're new, aren't you?"

"Yes. I'm starting work tomorrow at the law firm."

"Lake, hmm. Now, would you be any relation to the doctor here in town? Jethro Lake?"

Virginia hesitated a second or two then smiled. "Yes. He's my father."

"Really? Believe it or not, he delivered me. My husband, too. My husband's Paul Herrara. He works for the gas company."

"Dad probably delivered half the people in

Glory,'' Virginia said with another smile. Despite her own problems with her parents, she was proud of them. Her father was a well-respected man in town. He'd always had time for his patients, day or night.

''No kidding! Well, nice to meet you. See you this afternoon.'' Marcia collected her son and Virginia started down the walk with Robert. She didn't have to say a word; Robert chattered the whole way home.

It was a different story when they got to her parents' place. Virginia had been annoyed at her mother's insistence on hosting a family luncheon today to celebrate Robert's first day of school. It was such a silly, old-fashioned ritual, in Virginia's eyes. She remembered too many similar occasions when she was a young girl, before she'd discovered she could rebel.

Lacy dresses, fancy-cut sandwiches frosted with cream cheese, juice and lemonade, sweet milky tea when she got a little older, the mothers perching in upholstered chairs with their china cups and matching cake plates...

Robert was noticeably quieter at his grandparents' house. Virginia was glad they'd moved into their own place so soon after coming to Glory. *Thanks to Lucas.* They'd moved so often, and Virginia was determined that this time she'd make a real home for herself and her son.

Shortly after Virginia and Robert arrived, her father drove up to the house. She knew that most of his time was spent on administrative duties rather than the actual practice of medicine these days, but she was still surprised to see him break away from the hospital to come home for Robert's lunch.

"Couldn't miss the young man's first day at school, could I?" her father boomed jovially. It was always disconcerting to hear such a big voice from such a thin man. Her father had iron-gray hair now that he was in his late sixties and prided himself on his fitness, his lean frame carrying not an ounce of excess flesh. She'd adored him as a child. He'd taken her fishing and swimming at the lake and taught her the names of many of the birds that frequented the fields and woods around Glory. It was only when she'd reached her teen years and discovered she had a mind of her own that things had begun to go wrong between them. Events had culminated in his outrage at her grad date with Lucas Yellowfly and he'd shipped her off to New Brunswick. That had been the end of her relationship with the man she'd called her daddy, as far as Virginia was concerned. She'd had to grow up fast. She'd been fully aware that it wasn't so much "for her own good" that he'd sent her away, but that he'd once and for all removed the source of embarrassment she'd become as the Lakes' maverick daughter. They'd washed their hands of the problem, hoping Aunt Sadie would make a lady out of her.

It hadn't happened. What would her father say if he knew Lucas Yellowfly had expressed his intentions of becoming more than a friend now that she was back in town? Maybe it wouldn't matter anymore. Maybe now that Lucas was a pillar of Glory society himself, the fact that he'd once been considered the bad boy from the wrong side of the tracks was conveniently forgotten. The half-Indian kid, son of a drunk and a cleaning woman. Hardly fit company for the doctor's daughter.

Sometimes Virginia wondered when she'd become so cynical.

Her mother ushered them into the breakfast room, where the round mahogany table had been set for a fancy lunch. Sun streamed in the windows and there were fresh flowers and a white tablecloth, as well as Doris Lake's fine china. Virginia sighed. Hot dogs on the picnic table outside would have been so much more fun for a five-year-old.

Her mother was fifteen years younger than her father. They'd married when Doris Burns was just twenty, a red-haired beauty from High River. Virginia's father, never married and already chief of surgery at Glory Memorial Hospital, had been quite a catch. The years had not been particularly kind to Doris, as was so often the case with pale redheads. Virginia wondered if she'd look as faded and washed-out at her mother's age. Doris Lake had recently abandoned touching up her once-titian tresses, and the streaks of gray in her stiff shoulder-length bob did not improve matters.

Still, she was a kind person, Virginia told herself, with many fine qualities. She was a marvelous hostess for her father; she'd been a loving, if nervous, mother. That she'd never found a place for herself outside her father's long professional and social shadow was hardly her fault. She'd been content to be the doctor's wife. Many women of her generation were in the same position.

"Sit down, darlings," she said to Virginia and Robert, and they took their seats at the table. Virginia motioned to her son to unfold his linen napkin and spread it on his lap. They didn't dine formally very often.

"Can I help you, Mother?" Virginia called as her mother disappeared into the kitchen.

"Not at all, dear. I've got everything under control," she said, beaming as she returned with a tray of Royal Worcester soup plates, which she placed before each of them before taking her own seat with a smile.

"What's this, Mom?" Robert whispered.

Virginia dipped her soup spoon into the creamy, chilled concoction.

"Vichyssoise, Robert," she said quietly, smiling to encourage her son as he made a face. "Cold potato soup. Isn't that nice?"

"I thought it would be a sensible choice on such a hot day," her mother said, dipping her own spoon into her bowl. "And we've got some lovely crab salad with Russian dressing and raspberry shortcake to follow. And ice cream!"

Virginia wanted to forget the rest of the luncheon as she drove home with Robert an hour later. They'd begged off croquet on the lawn, which, Doris told her, her father had had especially mowed that morning for the game. Thank heavens Teddy Herrara was coming to play at two o'clock. They had a good excuse to leave.

Midway through the soup, her father had turned to her son and boomed, "Well, young man, what did you learn in school today?"

"Nothing."

"Nothing?"

"Nothing, sir."

"Come now, you must have learned something!" Dr. Lake said, surveying her and her mother with an indulgent smile. Virginia knew her father preferred to be addressed as "sir," another old-fashioned habit that she found simply annoying in today's world where so many children called adults by their first names. Robert rarely remembered. "Who have you got for a teacher this year?"

"Mrs. Brown," Robert replied quietly, taking a man-size spoonful of his vichyssoise and not making a face. Virginia was proud of him.

"Mrs. Brown, eh? I took a nasty appendix out of her husband a while back. Must be twenty years now. So what did Mrs. Brown do with the class today?" her father persisted.

"She asked us our names and if we knew how to spell them and I did," Robert said.

"That's a good thing to know. Very good," her father said. "You bet! What else, young man?"

"She asked us if we had any brothers or sisters and what their names were. And she asked us if we had any pets and what their names were and I said I didn't have a pet but my mom said we could maybe get a gerbil or something and if we did, I was going to name it Sam," Robert volunteered.

"Sam, eh?" her father replied.

Virginia heard her mother's faint contribution to the conversation. "Gerbils. Aren't they some kind of rodent?"

"Uh-huh. And she asked what our mom and dad's names were and I said my mom was Virginia Phyllis Lake and I had a dad but I didn't know his name 'cause he doesn't live with us."

The atmosphere froze. Virginia could picture icicles hanging over the crab salad, about to puncture her lungs and heart. Her parents both stared at her, rigid with shock, then hastily dropped their gazes to the snapdragons and daisies in the center of the table.

"It's true, isn't it, Mom? I do have a dad, right?" Robert looked earnestly up at her. Somehow she'd hoped this day would be a long time in coming. Somehow she'd hoped it wasn't a question he'd ask for many years yet. After all, single moms were no rarity in any of the towns where they'd lived. Robert had had friends before who didn't live with their dads. *But they all knew who their dads were.* Until they'd come to Glory, Robert had never asked so insistently about his father, or lack of one.

"Yes, Robert. Of course you have a dad, just like every other little boy." She gave her son a we'll-talk-about-this-later look. "Now, finish up your soup, honey, and hand Nana your plate."

Robert didn't mention the subject when they got home, just ten minutes before Teddy arrived. The two boys raced to Robert's bedroom to play Spy, and Virginia sank thankfully onto her couch, clutching a cup of hot tea.

A reprieve. But it was time she faced facts. Robert wanted to know who his father was. And he wanted to know soon.

VIRGINIA FELT a little disappointed that Lucas didn't appear for her first day of work. Pete Horsfall was there, and Nancy. Pete explained that Lucas had had to travel to Calgary to consult with another lawyer about something the two of them were working on.

Nancy ushered her into the office and told her where to put her coffee mug and her coat when she brought one. Pete showed her to the little cubicle they'd cleared out for her, a small space that had once been a storage area. Thank heavens it had a tiny window, Virginia thought, regarding the desk, chair and filing cabinet with dismay. The small collection of furniture filled the room. Lucas's office was on one side, Pete's on the other. Pete rather sheepishly confessed that he wasn't in the office all that often. One or two days a week, he said, but he "dropped in regularly. Most regularly."

The firm's law library was located on one wall of Lucas's office, which was the largest on the premises. That meant she'd be working there a lot, she realized. She'd also need a computer. Pete told her they'd been meaning to expand for some time, and now that they'd hired her, they'd start drawing up some plans. Perhaps this fall.

Virginia hoped so. She was amazed to discover that they didn't have Internet access, which she'd used for some of her research with other law firms. They had one computer, an old model, which Nancy used for word processing. Perhaps Lucas had a laptop, although there was no evidence of one.

Virginia knew that a lot of lawyers were skeptical of new technology, particularly regarding client privacy. Still, there were software programs specifically developed for the legal profession, and she could see that one of her first tasks would be to drag Horsfall, Horsfall and Yellowfly, kicking and screaming if need be, into the current century, never mind the next.

"By the way," she asked Nancy when the two of them went to lunch, turning the sign to Closed on the office door as if they tended some old-fashioned grocery or pharmacy, "who is the second Horsfall?"

"Oh, that's old Mr. Horsfall. He's dead. And Mr. Horsfall Jr.—that's Pete—has a nephew he keeps hoping will come into the firm, so they've never bothered to change the sign." Nancy tackled her Reuben sandwich with gusto, then added, "At least, that's what Lucas told me. That's Mr. Yellowfly. I guess you know him, right?"

Virginia nodded, her attention wandering. How was Robert enjoying his first lunch at school? They'd purchased a Barney lunch box and he'd given her a list of the things he wanted her to buy for him to eat, none particularly nutritious, but she could gradually change that. She couldn't believe that her little boy was growing up. School now, then girls and a driver's license. And one day, he'd leave her. Move out of her life.

She wrenched her attention back to Nancy and her

own salad. She picked up her fork, returning to Nancy's remark. "Mm. Lucas and I went to the same school, although he was several years ahead of me."

"Ohhh," Nancy moaned, with a tender expression on her freckled face. "He's such a *hunk,* isn't he? I never thought a lawyer could be so good-looking and to think I get to work for him! All my friends are so jealous. Makes up for old Horseface, that's for sure— Oops!" She covered her mouth and giggled. Virginia smiled. Nancy was going to be an asset to the office atmosphere, she could see that.

At quarter past three, Lucas walked in, handsome in a pale blue shirt, rough linen jacket and tan trousers. Virginia knew exactly what Nancy meant by "hunk."

"Come on," he said, crossing to her desk and grabbing her hand. "Work's over. Let's go pick up the kids from school."

"I—I've got a couple more things I was going to do before I left," she said weakly at first, unable to resist Lucas's broad smile. "Well, okay. Let me call Mrs. Vandenbroek and let her know I'll be picking up Robert." She made the brief call, then stood, trying to ignore his open admiration. She was wearing office garb—a pale green cotton shirtwaist and low pumps today. She realized he'd only seen her in jeans and shorts, except for the day of her interview. She knew she could look good if she put some effort into it.

"You leaving for the day, Mr. Yellowfly?"

Nancy called. Pete hadn't returned after lunch. "I'll tell your callers you're not in?"

"You do that, Nance," Lucas said.

Nancy giggled. "Okay," she chirped, and opened the tabloid weekly she'd stopped at the drugstore to buy on their short walk back to the office. Virginia had only caught a glimpse of the lurid headlines, something about a twenty-two-pound baby being born to a twelve-year-old.

Lucas's car was parked at the curb out front. He held the door for her and she got into the passenger seat. His car was clean and comfortable, leather-lined and very masculine, with only a few newspapers on the backseat and his briefcase tucked behind the driver's seat. No fast-food wrappers, single socks or toys on the floor. A BMW. An older model. Well, Glory's bad boy was definitely on the right side of town now.

Lucas released the emergency brake and they glided away from the curb. "How's Robert liking school?"

"Fine. He seems very happy, actually. He's got a new friend."

"Oh?"

"Teddy Herrara. You know the family?"

"I know Paul. We've golfed a few times."

"Golf?" she teased. "I thought you let Pete do all the firm's golfing."

"Oh, I get in a few games. The odd charity tournament. Try as I might to do all the things a proper lawyer's supposed to do, I just can't handle golf."

He chuckled. "Rather be riding a green-broke colt out at Adam Garrick's any day."

Adam Garrick. Virginia searched her memory. She couldn't put a face to the name. He must have been one of Lucas's ranching buddies from out of town.

They reached the school and Lucas found a parking spot on the side street. Parents who accompanied their children to and from school usually walked.

"Listen." Lucas made no immediate move to get out. He turned to her and she paused, one hand on the door handle.

"Yes?"

"I lined up a baby-sitter for tonight. For Robert and Tammy."

She raised her eyebrows. "*And?*"

"Yeah. I want to take you out, Virginia. Nothing fancy. Just a burger and shake out at Pop Jenkins's place—" a diner out on the highway toward Nanton "—maybe drive around a little. We'll be home by nine."

"Robert goes to bed at eight-thirty."

"We'll be home by eight-fifteen, then. What do you say?"

"Who's the sitter?" Why didn't she just refuse? After all, tomorrow there was school and work, and Lucas, frankly, had already presumed quite a lot by making these arrangements.

"Natasha Jarvis. She's sixteen. Works at the library in her spare time. Got a few friends who can pinch-hit for her when necessary. Joe Gallant's niece, Phoebe Longquist, for one. Hey!" He touched her shoulder lightly and smiled. "You can use my secret list of baby-sitters anytime. Company perk. I got Nancy to check 'em all out."

He was joking, but his eyes were deadly earnest. The man-about-town was actually worried she'd turn him down.

"All right."

She smiled and his eyes blazed hot and intense for a split second. Then he reached for his door handle. "It's settled then. I'll pick you up at five."

Five would be early, she thought, getting out. She'd promised Robert she'd take him to the small pet department at the back of Riddley's after school to pick out a gerbil and cage. She wasn't wild about the idea; she wasn't sure how she felt about having a rodent in the house. But Robert was looking forward to it so much she didn't have the heart to refuse. And a gerbil, safe in a cage, was better than a cat, which she used to be allergic to when she was a girl, or a dog, which would have to live in their cramped apartment and be walked several times a day.

At Robert's age, a small caged animal was better than no pet at all, she supposed. No matter how hard it was for her to imagine anything with beady eyes and whiskers and a long skinny tail as a pet.

CHAPTER EIGHT

POP JENKINS'S PLACE was a roadside diner situated in an old remodeled train caboose, five miles from town on the way to Nanton. It was patronized mainly by locals from the rural area and from both towns, as it wasn't on the road to anywhere else. A few tourists probably stopped in from time to time, intrigued by the caboose.

Virginia didn't recall until they'd parked in the gravel lot that she and Lucas had come to Pop's diner the night of her graduation, after they'd left the dance to drive aimlessly around Glory and the back roads, talking. They'd passed the caboose and noticed the lights were still on. Pop kept irregular hours and the local cops figured he was a bootlegger, although he'd never been arrested.

He made great burgers. Or his wife did, a tired-looking woman who was generally on the prem-ises—if not behind the counter, then sitting in a booth, smoking and reading a paperback novel.

Virginia and Lucas had raced across the parking lot in a light rain that night. She remembered grab-bing her long skirt, shrieking at the puddles she'd had to jump. Halfway across the lot, Lucas had scooped her up in his arms and, grinning, ducked into Pop's. What a sight they must have been, Lucas in his tux, tie stuffed into his pocket and collar studs open; her, giggling and bedraggled in a filmy silk formal. She'd never forgotten that. It had seemed so impossibly romantic at the time. Her eighteen-year-old heart had been charmed. Lucas was older; he'd been to college, was a man compared with the boys around town. He was tall and handsome and he wanted to take her to the grad dance. She'd said yes, thrilled that he'd noticed her enough to ask.

Johnny had been in jail that month. Not for the first time, either. And he'd never been the slightest bit romantic, although they'd slept together several times. He treated her like one of the guys, which usually suited her. She'd enjoyed their escapades, even if some of them bordered on the criminal. She loved thumbing her nose at the conventions her parents revered, and Johnny was full of ideas in that department. From driving down Main Street stark naked after a dip in the Horsethief to the time they'd hidden a pailful of garter snakes in the mayor's garage. Immature, maybe, but worth a lot of laughs later with their friends.

Now Virginia saw some of her activities with Johnny as cruel. Or at least thoughtless. The mayor's wife must have been horrified when she'd opened the garage door. At sixteen or seventeen, Virginia hadn't given much thought to that side of things.

Consequences were something she'd learned about quite a bit later in her life.

Tonight she was relieved to see that they weren't the only customers. It was just past six o'clock, and two pickups and a car with out-of-province plates were already in the parking lot. Lucas parked and turned to her, one hand on the door handle. "Remember this?"

He came around the car to let her out. That was twice in one day. When had a man last opened a car door for her? Probably Lucas twelve years ago.

He tucked her hand casually under his elbow and walked beside her. In his dark glasses, jeans and T-shirt, he looked more like a college quarterback than a successful small-town lawyer. She'd opted for casual, too. Jeans and sweater and sandals. She didn't want Lucas to get the idea that this was a *real* date. Instead, they looked like they'd known each other for years. And they had, in a way.

Friends.

Lucas took off his sunglasses and hooked them in his shirt pocket as he held the door for her. Not much had changed. The aqua Formica countertop still struck a jarring note in the painted tongue-and-groove interior of the caboose. Booths had been built along one side, and the kitchen was at one end, behind the counter. It was just a fast-fry joint, with great milk shakes and malts. Two booths were occupied, one by a couple of cowboys and the other by a man and woman. A man in a cowboy hat was hunched over a plate of fries and a T-bone steak at the counter. He glanced at them in the fly-spotted mirror and nodded at Lucas, who put his hand briefly on the man's shoulder as they passed and said, "How you doing, Noah?"

The man grunted a monosyllabic response, then

returned his attention to his meal. Virginia and Lucas slid into one of the vacant booths.

"What'll you have?" Lucas pulled the paper menu closer and scanned it quickly. "Not much new. I don't think I've been back since we were here last."

Virginia smiled. She didn't need to study the menu. "I'll have a chocolate malt and a turkey club on brown, extra mayo. If they've still got them."

Lucas popped a loonie into the small jukebox that was part of each table. "You pick."

Virginia eyed the choices. Plenty of yesteryear country-and-western with a sprinkling of new country and some Shania Twain. She punched in her selections. Ian Tyson's "Summer Wages" filled the diner and she caught the cowboy's eye in the mirror. He seemed to approve.

After all, this was Tyson country. The singer and composer had a ranch not far from here, at Longview, where he raised cutting horses and ran a few cattle.

Lucas leaned against the vinyl seat and rested one arm along the back. He smiled at her. "What do you think? Good place to take a date?"

"I'm not a date, Lucas, not really," she said slowly, tracing the swirly pattern in the tabletop. "We both know that."

She met his eyes briefly, then continued. "I appreciate your asking me out this evening, and arranging for the sitter and everything, but I'm not in the dating mode these days. I'm more of a loner than I used to be. Things have changed for me. A lot.

I've carved out a pretty simple life for Robert and me. I like it that way.''

"Why's that?"

"Why's what?" She looked at him.

"Why no men in your life? You're an attractive woman. Smart, savvy. A good mother. It doesn't figure."

What he really meant was, what about Robert's father? *Was he the one who hurt you so badly you don't want to date any other man?* Of course, that wasn't it, either, but how could she tell Lucas?

Virginia was seized with a powerful desire to tell him everything. The kidnapping six years ago, the terrible fears she'd had that Johnny would learn about Robert and come after him, the way she'd been on the run ever since, determined that her son's father would never find them.

But she'd never told anyone. Not even the friend she'd stayed with in Regina before Robert was born. No one knew she'd been raped. She'd never breathed a word.

Virginia tried to laugh off the question. "You know what it's like—busy, busy all the time." She shrugged. "Guess I've never found a man I cared enough about, that's all I can say."

"I've never forgotten you, Virginia." Lucas's voice was low and intense. He took her hands in both of his across the table. Virginia prayed that the woman behind the counter would come and take their orders. "Not since I first saw you when you were about eleven, up a tree, firing stuff down on some boys who'd been bothering you. I'll bet you don't even remember."

She shook her head.

"I've dreamed about you ever since that night we spent together. I've always felt guilty that your father sent you away after that. Responsible, somehow. I went to see him, did he ever tell you?"

She shook her head again, unable to speak.

"I went to see him at the hospital. I told him nothing had happened between us that shouldn't have happened. He was pretty mad." Lucas gave her a crooked smile. "At you and at me. I guess he figured I had no business taking out his daughter in the first place."

"I know." Virginia stared at their intertwined hands. "He's such a snob. He was then and he still is. My mother's the same. Or if she isn't, she never says anything to disagree with my father. I hated them both back then, Lucas." She gazed into his eyes. He looked so kind, so understanding. It was so hard not to tell him everything.

"What a rebel!" he teased. He let go of her hands and grinned. "Don't all kids hate their parents at that age? Hey, I could see his point. Beautiful daughter, only child. I'm sure he had higher hopes for you than getting mixed up with some bad old Indian boy—"

"Don't say that!" Virginia's vehemence surprised her. "They were just stuck-up. Snobs. Do you think Johnny came from some upper-class family? No way! He just wasn't part Indian, that's all."

Lucas eyed her curiously. "Whatever happened to him? Johnny?"

"He's in jail, last I heard," Virginia said breathlessly, looking around for the waitress. "Where I hope he stays."

Lucas frowned. She prayed she hadn't said too much. Just then, thank heaven, the waitress decided to honor them with her presence. She came up, wiping her hands on her gingham apron. "What'll you have, folks? There's none of the Wednesday special left, meat loaf, and only one kind of pie. Pop makes apple this time of year, that's it."

They ordered their meals. When the music wound down, Lucas plugged in another two loonies and this time *he* chose. Some sweet, slow songs, including a rendition of "Unchained Melody." Virginia couldn't meet his eyes. She felt herself color. The band had been playing that song the first time Lucas had kissed her. At her grad dance. A kiss that had gone on and on and on. They'd left shortly after.

They'd necked in his borrowed pickup, then they'd driven around, just talking. They'd parked for a while at the local lovers' lane, a dead-end road at one of the buffalo jumps outside town. If Lucas had permitted it, she would've made love with him right there on the bench seat of the pickup, or under the stars on the wet grass. He'd held her tight, talked some sense into her, told her they weren't ready for that yet. She hadn't seen him again until she'd come back to town a few weeks ago.

They were both a lot older now. Did he really still feel the same way? He insisted he did; Virginia had a hard time believing it. He was just being kind. He'd saved her from herself twelve years ago, but no one could save her now. She had changed. He'd changed, too. He must have known a lot of women since then. What had happened twelve years ago was only a silly high-school date with a lot of heavy necking. And now? Now he maybe felt a little sorry for her, that was all. Nobody felt the same way about someone twelve years later.

"What about you, Lucas?" she asked, taking a big pull on the straw in her malt. *Enough about her.* "Tell me a little about what's happened since I last saw you."

Lucas gave her a surprised look. "Okay. Starting when? I spent my last fifty bucks on that tux rental for your grad dance and borrowed my buddy Adam's pickup to take you out. I couldn't afford a car. I'd made up my mind I was putting my faith in the justice system. I'd been accepted into law school. No more fighting, no more rodeos, no more drinking too much on payday. Every cent I made was going to tuition and books. I planned to continue shamelessly milking the system for everything I could get. First Nations money, that sort of thing."

He grinned. "Well, heck. It was just lying around all over the place, waiting for some ambitious Indian to come along. So I picked up some of it and got an arts degree. I'm part Indian. I've always figured it was up to me to make something of myself. So I did what I had to do to make it happen." Despite Lucas's background, and she knew it had been rough, he seemed to bear no ill will toward anything. No grudges.

"Then, after your daddy packed you off, I got a job on the rigs, made a whack of money and went back to school the following year. Law school. Vancouver. My sister was out there and I kind of wanted to get in touch with her again. That was a little after Tammy was born. Theresa had been working up north in the Queen Charlottes until then. Private nurse. Anyway... You still interested in all this?"

"Sure I am."

"Okay. So I got my law degree, articled with a big firm out there, did some stuff in Edmonton, got my Alberta papers and came back to Glory to rub the town's nose in my good fortune. Including your dad's."

Virginia smiled. Lucas looked extraordinarily pleased with himself. "And did you? Rub their noses in it?"

"You bet." He took a final bite of his burger, chewed, then swallowed. "Now the ladies in town can't wait to invite me to this and to that. But you know—" he raised one eyebrow and leaned toward her confidentially "—I won't go out with just anyone. I'm picky."

Virginia laughed and noticed the cowboy at the counter glance at them in the mirror again. "Your mom and dad still around?"

"Dad died shortly after Tammy was born. He'd never felt right living here in buffalo country. I'm not entirely sure why he ever left B.C. He never fit in anywhere, married to a white woman. Seems it's okay for white guys to marry Indian women, but not the other way around. He was a Fraser River Indian, from near Chilliwack. Sto:los. Guess that makes me half salmon-eater, huh?'' Lucas grinned again. ''Ma's in Calgary in a seniors' condo with her sister, Alma. She's fine. A little arthritic, that's all. I'll take you up to see her one of these days. You and Robert.''

Lucas seemed to assume she was part of his life now. He'd obviously looked after his mother, he'd taken in his sister's daughter, and now he was taking Robert and her under his wing.

''There must have been a few women in your life since then.''

''A few.'' He didn't seem inclined to elaborate and she wasn't going to ask. Surprisingly, though, she found herself wondering. Who were they? Was the woman she'd met at the christening one of them?

He had her home by eight-fifteen, as he'd promised. Robert had spent the evening at his house, with Tammy and the baby-sitter, a tall, quiet, dark-haired girl. They'd ordered pizza for supper and played video games. Robert had obviously had fun. He came running into the foyer to greet them and threw his arms around her neck. She'd hugged him close, reveling in the feel of her son's scrawny little body. Oh, Robert! What would she ever have done without him?

When she'd put him to bed, she sat down to think about the evening. After they'd left the diner, Lucas had driven home by an indirect route, very likely along some of the same back roads they'd taken twelve years ago. She couldn't remember. He'd made no attempt to kiss her or do anything beyond showing her around, talking, and pointing out the various sights. Some antelope in the distance. A copse of aspens that had already changed to brilliant gold. A view of the Horsethief Valley from a high point on a gravel road that led to Pekisko Creek. He obviously loved the area and knew it well. She suspected he'd come back to Glory for reasons other than to flaunt his success.

She'd felt better after their meal and the leisurely drive. It was as though she'd been dreading the "more than friends" Lucas had said he wanted. She felt as though she'd been holding her breath since she got to town, not sure what her role would be. Now, after visiting some of those same places she'd gone with him twelve years ago, she'd been able to breathe again. Able to remember. She could put the past in the context of *now,* as a woman of thirty, with a child. A successful, working, single mother. Not the doctor's daughter. Not the eighteen-year-old rebel.

It was time to look up other old friends. It was time to find her own place in Glory.

LUCAS HAD TO ADMIT he was shocked to see Virginia and Robert sitting in the Stardust Theatre on Saturday afternoon with Bruce Twist, an insurance salesman from Fidelity Farm and Home, the office across the street from Horsfall, Horsfall and Yellowfly.

What in hell was she doing going out with a jerk

like that? Well, maybe not a jerk, he revised, thrusting his hand into the popcorn barrel he was sharing with Tammy. Bruce Twist was okay. He was about his own age, midthirties, sandy-haired, thinning on top, glasses—about as meek and nice a man as anyone was likely to meet in Glory. Nice? Since when had Virginia Lake gone for *nice?*

At least Robert was sitting between them. Lucas decided he wasn't all that interested in what was on the screen, some kiddie adventure flick Tammy had wanted to see. He had plenty of time to keep his eye on those two.

Then he felt like a high-school kid, spying on his girlfriend. That wasn't his style. And Virginia wasn't his girlfriend. She'd never given him one lick of encouragement, no matter how frankly he'd stated his position. That kiss in her apartment was an aberration.

Maybe he'd made a mistake with her—coming on too strong right away. He'd figured honesty was best. He'd wanted to stake out his position early. *And scare off the competition?*

Well, maybe, he admitted grudgingly. But what about her? If she'd really meant what she'd said about being a loner and not interested in having a man in her life, then what was she doing sitting there with Bruce Twist?

Lucas forced his attention back to the screen. At least Tammy was having a good time so far in Glory. Her teacher had already said she thought Tammy was very bright for her age and had recommended an after-school enrichment class. He'd

discussed it with his niece and been mildly amused
but not surprised that she'd turned down the opportunity. She'd said she wanted to take swimming lessons and dance lessons this year and maybe play
girls' hockey, and that would mean she wouldn't
have time for extra schoolwork.

What a kid. No wonder Theresa had had her
hands full. He was glad his niece and Virginia's son
had hit it off. They were sharing an after-school sitter now, the Jarvis girl, who walked both children
home. Some days they stayed at Lucas's house, and
some days Virginia made other arrangements for
Robert with other sitters, notably his ex-landlady,
Annie Vandenbroek. He hadn't known Mrs. Vandenbroek was partial to children, but Virginia had
told him that she set Robert to shelling peas and
cutting pictures out of her Dutch magazines, and
kept him stuffed with *zaandtarten* and *kanootjes* and
sousas and similar good Dutch baking. Sometimes
Robert went to his grandmother's after school,
where, she'd reported with a grimace, he watched
Disney videos and played croquet by himself and
learned to do a good job of polishing his grandfather's wing tips.

Lucas took a deep breath and offered the popcorn
to Tammy. Maybe it was time to back off. Maybe
it was time to recognize that just because Virginia
Lake had come home to Glory, it didn't mean she
wanted him to bulldoze into her life and take over.
Fine. He'd back off for a while. Then he'd revise
his plans.

Maybe honesty wasn't the best approach. Maybe

she'd prefer some real old-fashioned courting. He sneaked a glance at the trio eight rows ahead. All three seemed engrossed in the movie. No footsies going on there.

He smiled to himself in the dark cinema and stretched out his long legs under the seat in front of him.

Roses, dancing, special dinners out at fancy places, Sunday drives, sweet talk—he could do that. He felt better about the whole thing already.

FIRST THINGS FIRST. He'd have a talk with Doc Lake.

The following Tuesday was the hospital-board meeting, and Lucas was on the board. As chief of surgery and acting administrator—until the board could find a replacement—Jethro Lake would be there, too.

Lucas found an opportunity during the coffee break to approach Virginia's father. Doc Lake was always cordial to him these days, had been ever since he'd moved back to Glory. Twelve years was a long time ago.

"You drive over this evening, sir?" Lucas inquired amiably. He knew very well that Dr. Lake generally walked to the meetings. He was very proud of his fitness level for his age, which had to be close to seventy.

Jethro Lake snorted indignantly. "No. Walked over as usual."

"I'd like to drive you home, if I may," Lucas

said. "I've got something I want to talk to you about."

"Fine, fine. I'll see you after the meeting."

In his car, Lucas didn't waste any time broaching the subject. "I'll bet you're glad Virginia's back. Pete's probably mentioned what an asset she is to the firm."

"Eh? Yes, yes." The doctor cleared his throat. "No question. Doris is pleased as punch. I am, too."

"And that little Robert. He's some kid, isn't he?"

"You bet," the older man muttered. But even in the dim interior of the car Lucas could see that he was frowning heavily.

"Taken him fishing yet?" Lucas knew that his partner and Doc Lake were avid fly fishermen who spent many weekends in the summer, armed with insect repellent and hip waders, staked out in some river or other, waiting for rainbow trout to bite. Or holed up in Pete's garage workshop tying flies.

"No, but Pete suggested it to me the other day. We're going to take him soon. Need to talk it over with Virginia. See if the little fellow can swim or not. You've got to do these things right, you know." Virginia's father suddenly peered at him. They were approaching the drive that led up to Buffalo Hill. "Say, Yellowfly, what's your point here? I regret what happened back at Virginia's graduation, you know that. I acted rashly at the time, but maybe you can understand a father's concerns about his daughter, young girl of eighteen and all…"

"I'm glad you asked, sir," Lucas said. He glanced at his passenger. "The truth is, I like Virginia a lot. I always have. And now that she's back in town, I expect to take her out from time to time."

"*Date* her, you mean?" The doctor sounded incredulous, seemed unfamiliar with such a notion.

"That's right. I'd definitely like to establish a relationship with her. A romantic relationship. Maybe more."

"But...what about the boy?"

"Robert? What about him?" Lucas cast his passenger a narrowed look. What was the doc getting at?

"Well, she's made no beans about it, has she? No one knows who the boy's father is," the doctor blustered on. "It's a crying shame, that's what it is. Scandalous. It's broken her mother's heart."

Lucas wondered why the old man couldn't admit she'd broken his heart, too. And why, after all this time, did something like that matter? Didn't Robert count? Wasn't it enough that the boy was his live, flesh-and-blood grandchild? His *only* grandchild?

"With all due respect, sir, I can't say that means much to me." Lucas slowed the car. They were close to the Lake residence now. "I imagine you're familiar with my own family circumstances?" he added dryly. "My niece is here with me now, and my sister's never told any of us who her father is."

"Er, yes," the doctor mumbled, obviously ready to leap out the instant Lucas stopped the car. "I believe Doris's sister did mention something about that."

"So you have no objection?"

"Objection?"

"To me courting your daughter." That was straightforward enough.

The doctor seemed uncomfortable. "Look here, Yellowfly. I know you've had your problems in the past—"

"That's true. Brawling, no money, a drunk for a father…" Lucas couldn't resist interrupting with a drawled recital of the facts.

"Never mind that! No sir! A fellow can't help who his people are. You've made something of yourself, young man. That's what counts."

"So you have no objection," Lucas persisted.

"None at all. None at all. Besides, she's a grown woman. She makes her own choices. Her mother and I have nothing to do with it anymore." He got out of the car then, and Lucas could have sworn the old man's expression was one of relief.

Doc Lake would be more than happy to marry off his only daughter. If not to him, then to any other man who'd have her. The sooner, the better. Lucas realized it was beyond the old doctor's frame of belief to think that any man would want his daughter, a woman of a certain age, complete with bastard son. *Soiled goods.*

It was an extraordinarily outdated concept.

Lucas drove slowly back down the hill, careful not to disturb the snoozing burghers of Glory. He had a bad taste in his mouth, and it wasn't from the squares that had been served with the coffee.

Virginia was a woman of principle. She deserved better from her own folks. A whole lot better.

CHAPTER NINE

NEXT MORNING Lucas ordered a fall bouquet from Mindy's, a specialty florist in south Calgary. Mindy's guaranteed next-day delivery and promised satisfaction. He'd never been disappointed yet. The florist specialized in unusual flowers and arrangements and, in the past, Lucas had only felt the expense justified if he was romancing a very special lady. There'd been a few over the years. Usually he shopped locally.

Virginia was a special lady.

He said nothing, but when she came to work Friday, the day after the delivery, he could tell by the sparkle in her eyes and the smile on her face that she was pleased. She carried a mug of coffee into his office midmorning and closed the door behind her.

"The flowers are gorgeous, Lucas," she said in a low voice. She raised the coffee to her mouth, and Lucas watched her.

"You like them?"

"They're stunning."

"What did they send?" Lucas crossed his arms and leaned back in his chair. He was curious. He rarely specified the flowers he wanted, preferring just to pay the bill and be as surprised by the arrangement as the lady he was romancing.

"Michaelmas daisies," she said with a slow smile. "One of my favorites. Blue, pink and purple. How did you know?"

Hey, was he going to take credit for the mind-reader florist at Mindy's? "I didn't," he confessed finally, grinning. "But I do now."

"And half-a-dozen glads, dark red and pink."

"Oh?"

"And some little bundles of wheat stuck in here and there, very Alberta, and some Japanese maple branches and leaves and, I don't know, some sort of sticks or something. Maybe willow. And a few unusual chrysanthemums, shaggy-looking things. It's gorgeous."

"No baby's breath?" he asked, raising one eyebrow.

"No baby's breath," she said, smiling again. She finished her coffee, then walked around to his chair behind the desk.

"And?" He looked up at her. She was wearing a pink angora cardigan and blouse, and pearls and a dark gray skirt. The pink with her hair was…beautiful. Simply beautiful.

"And you are a very, very sweet man. Thank you." She bent and kissed him on the nose. He resisted the powerful urge to pull her onto his lap and kiss her properly. Not yet, he told himself. *Wait.*

"Sweet isn't exactly what I had in mind," he said dryly, with a belated warning to himself—*Not so fast.*

"Oh?" Luckily she didn't take him up on his challenge. "Now, what would be the occasion for such a gorgeous bouquet of flowers?"

"How about 'Welcome to Glory.'"

"Very nice," she said, nodding. "Thank you."

"Or how about 'Beware, sweet lady, Lucas Yellowfly, man-about-town, is about to romance you and seduce you the way a woman deserves to be romanced and seduced'?"

Virginia giggled. Lucas hadn't heard her giggle since she was a teenager. She'd come back to town too serious and too sober by half. It was a wonderful sound to hear.

"So," he said, "would you say this'd be a good time to ask you out for dinner?"

She considered him with mock seriousness, but he saw the telltale trembling of her lips, which he knew was a smile struggling to emerge. "Yes," she said finally, her eyes softening and the smile emerging. "I'd say it was a very good time."

"Tonight?"

Her brow furrowed slightly. "I've got plans for tonight. Sorry."

Damn. Probably the farm-insurance twerp. Bruce Twist. Lucas could be cool. And sophisticated. And flexible. "Sunday, then?"

"Sunday? Well, okay. If I can get a baby-sitter."

"We'll get a baby-sitter. Guaranteed."

She stepped back and moved toward the door. "I thought you might be able to line something up."

With another smile, she left his office.

Bull's-eye.

Sunday. What could they do in Glory on a Sunday? There wasn't much open, except the hotels, and they didn't exactly specialize in fine dining. It wasn't what he had in mind, anyway.

Oh, well, Calgary was less than an hour away. Give them a chance to talk, too, on the drive there and back. Or maybe he'd cook, show her what he could do when he put his mind to it. On the other hand, maybe it was too early for that.

Lucas whistled softly and felt in his pocket for his list. *Let's see...flowers. Dinner out. Then chocolates.* Dinner again, and maybe some dancing. Then maybe perfume. He had a question mark beside that one—women were so fussy about perfume. This one, that one, whatever. He preferred none at all. Still, you couldn't go wrong with Chanel. Then, after the perfume, a little snuggling on his new sofa? Some soft music? Maybe even... Well, he could hope.

Finally, jewelry. Preferably a ring.

The flowers had gone over very well. Lucas crossed off the first entry on his list, then got out the Calgary Yellow Pages and ran his finger down the *C*s. *Chocolate,* there it was. Belgian. Swiss. Dutch. He smiled and pulled the telephone toward him.

Every woman—and every kid—loved chocolate. Now, what could the experts come up with in *that* department?

NATASHA'S FRIEND Phoebe Longquist was available to baby-sit Sunday, but she told Lucas she'd have

to be home by ten because she had a big physics
test the next day.

No problem. Their reservation at La Lumière in
Calgary's trendy Eau Claire area was relatively
early—half-past six. He was picking up Virginia and
Robert at five and dropping the boy off at his house
to spend the evening with Phoebe and Tammy. Lucas planned to be back by half-past nine. That was
early for a date, but the whole thing was tough
enough to juggle with a sitter and two kids and
school the next day, not to mention work.

When they got to La Lumière, he couldn't find a
place to park. The streets were jammed. Odd, he
thought as he handed the car over for valet parking
near the restaurant. Must be some sports event going
on in town, maybe an exhibition hockey game.

It was a fine evening. Virginia was wearing a
navy coat, a light wool or something over a soft,
sage-green dress, and matching beret. She looked
absolutely gorgeous. Lucas was having a hard time
restraining his instincts, which were to move fast.
Very fast. Never mind this romancing. He wanted
her. He wanted her like no other woman he'd ever
met. He was ready for marriage, he was ready to
settle down—he just had to convince the woman at
his side.

At the restaurant, the maître d' met them at the
door with a worried expression. "Monsieur, we
have a disaster for you. We have a party of twenty
from the premier's office in town for some meeting
and we have no room, but can we say no? No." He
spread his hands eloquently, shaking his head. "Can

you come back later, say, eight o'clock? We will have tables then and a special for you, champagne, compliments of Gaston. So sorry—''

Lucas graciously accepted defeat. The date at the classy French restaurant was out. He reassured the maître d' that he wasn't put out in the slightest and that they would come another time. The mademoiselle had to be home early tonight, so they wouldn't be able to take his offer of an eight-o'clock table.

Virginia grasped his arm as they left the restaurant and giggled. It was starting to be a habit with her. One he liked. She leaned against him and he smiled down at her. ''What now?'' she asked, smiling back.

''All dressed up and nowhere to go, eh?'' he said, holding her arm securely against his side. ''Got any suggestions?''

''We could go to a hotel.''

''For dinner?'' He winked wickedly; he couldn't resist.

''Of course!''

''We could've done that in Glory.''

''Sure, the Glory Hotel, I suppose.''

He didn't think she'd ever been in the Glory Hotel. ''How about the Palliser?''

''No.''

''Why not? They've got decent food.''

''It's the kind of place my parents would go.''

''Okay. How about Nestor's?'' He named another exclusive Calgary dining spot.

''Too stuffy.''

''Your call.''

"Let's just walk around for a while and if we see something, we'll go in. Serendipity."

He bent quickly and kissed her nose. "Good idea. I like serendipity."

That was how they ended up at a noisy Lebanese restaurant half an hour later, jostled into a corner among a crowd of older men arguing loudly, politics obviously, at a table near the bar. University students in jeans and sweatshirts lounged here and there. An intense-looking young man with half-a-dozen dishes in front of him sat at a table in the window. And two cats sprawled on top of the bar fridge, clearly in violation of the city's restaurant bylaws.

They insisted the waiter choose their meal for them, and after a moment of extravagant surprise, the waiter—who turned out to be the owner—was happy to oblige. His wife and aunt, he told them proudly, were in the kitchen, and his daughter was on the cash register. Virginia wondered aloud where his son was—if he had one. In medical school, he replied proudly. She and Lucas both congratulated the owner, who was clearly pleased by their interest.

They ate terrific finger foods—*mezze*—followed by a delicate chicken-and-yogurt soup, eggplant and tomato salad, and a main course of *escabeche* for two, a cold dish of fried, pickled fish, as well as a hot dish of lamb meatballs with a highly flavored rice pilaf, all followed by a date-and-banana dessert and plenty of lashings of sweet Turkish coffee.

At eight o'clock, they spilled back onto the street,

sated with delicious Middle Eastern food and warmed by the totally unexpected experience.

"I loved that!" Virginia said, smiling up at him. He turned to her and adjusted the collar of her coat against the chill wind. The street was dark, with only the streetlights' eerie glow, and their car had to be seven or eight blocks away, near La Lumière.

Lucas smiled. "I did, too. Put your gloves on, honey. It's cold."

She did, and then on impulse he pulled her into his arms and covered her mouth with his. Her lips were soft and warm and tasted of coffee and cinnamon and vanilla. She met his kiss eagerly and for a few moments they stood entwined on Tenth Street, completely in their own world, while passersby stepped around them and one cyclist gave a wolf whistle as he pedaled past.

Lucas took his time, holding her tightly, kissing her thoroughly, reminding himself that it wasn't often he had the chance. He wanted her to remember this evening, and him, as he was going to remember her. Remember her! He was going to marry her.

Finally he relaxed his grip and she smiled up at him, looking a little dazed—which, he thought, was exactly as it should be.

"Thank you for the lovely evening, Lucas," she whispered. "You're a very nice man."

Very nice. Still wasn't where he wanted to be. But it would do, for now.

They were back in Glory by half-past nine. He took her and the sleepy Robert to their apartment while the sitter stayed with Tammy. Luckily Phoebe had her own car and could drive herself home once he'd returned. Virginia had worked out the logistics for him; he wasn't used to having to arrange his life so Tammy wouldn't be left alone for too long.

Then, before he went into his home office to do a little last-minute work, he got out his list. *Dinner*. He crossed it off carefully. He'd call the chocolate company in the morning and tell them to deliver on Wednesday.

THINGS DIDN'T GO SO WELL that week. It wasn't the chocolate store's fault—the delivery was on time and well-received. The store had suggested seven chocolate, cream-filled antique cars, one for each day of the week, for the boy, and two pounds of their special "romantic occasion" chocolates for the lady—a mix of truffles and heart-shaped creams and white chocolate daisies and roses and delicately sculptured shells. Lucas had agreed with this suggestion.

Virginia told him she was delighted, grateful, overwhelmed. Lucas stopped by her apartment that evening, out with Tammy for their regular walk, and Virginia threw her arms around him, kissed him and insisted they stay for coffee and to share some of the chocolate.

Tammy was only too happy to oblige, and chose a milk-chocolate Edsel from Robert's collection. The two children sat on the kitchen floor, pretending to drive their candy cars, stopping to lick their fingers regularly. They finally sat cross-legged beside each other and nibbled at the cars until they were gone. Then they ran off to play with Robert's new gerbil.

"Lucas?" Virginia poured him a second cup of coffee and pushed the chocolate box toward him. He declined, as he had at her first invitation. He wasn't particularly fond of chocolate.

"Hmm?" He stirred sugar and cream into his cup. He liked what she'd done with the kitchen. New curtains and wallpaper with an ivy design really perked the place up. He'd never thought of doing anything to it while he lived there. It was a rental; whatever the landlady wanted was fine with him.

"Flowers last week," she began slowly. "Then chocolate this week."

"Yes?"

"Do I detect a pattern here?"

"What kind of pattern?"

"You know, flowers, chocolate, maybe some perfume coming up..."

Lucas gave her a look of mock dismay. "Hey, that's guy stuff. You're not supposed to figure it out. But didn't I tell you I intended the full, classic courtship? One hundred percent? No holds barred?"

"Lucas." She made a slight frown. "You know what I told you. I—I'm just not ready for this sort of thing. I like you a lot, don't get me wrong, but—" her troubled gaze sought his "—it's just Robert and me for now. It has to be that way."

"What about old Bruce?"

"Bruce Twist?"

"Yeah. You're seeing him, aren't you?"

"Well, yes." She laughed, sounding genuinely amazed. "But he's just a friend. There's nothing romantic going on there."

"Uh-huh. Wonder if old Bruce thinks there's nothing romantic going on."

"Oh, Lucas! You're crazy." She got up and took her cup to the counter. "You think every guy's after me, just because you're…well, interested."

Lucas got up, too, and went to where she stood, hands behind her back, at the counter. He put one finger on her chin and lifted it until she met his eyes. "I'm more than interested, honey. You know that. I'm in love with you. I've been in love with you since the first time I saw you up that tree. I was fool enough to tell you that right off the bat when you came back to Glory and I can see maybe it scared you a bit. Now I've changed my tactics."

"I see that." She gave him a crooked little smile.

"But that doesn't mean I've changed my mind. Just going about it differently. I was going to make sure you felt the same way about me before I brought it up again, but now that you mention it—"

"You…you really mean it, don't you?" she asked breathlessly. She sounded surprised. Now why would she sound surprised? Didn't she believe what he'd told her?

"You bet I do. I've never been more serious about anything in my life. The only thing that's going to make me back off is if you tell me right now, straight out, that you're not the slightest bit interested, that me doing this—" he lightly touched her mouth with his, just a second or two "—doesn't make your toes curl. The way mine do," he finished softly. "So, are you going to say it?"

She hesitated. He felt his heart stop beating. Then she said, "No, Lucas, I'm not going to say that. I'm...going to keep my options open."

"You do that." He dropped another quick kiss on her lips. His heart started beating again, in quick time. "You just keep those options open, honey."

Virginia laughed and busied herself with clearing the table. "You're a very persuasive man, Lucas. You know that, don't you?"

"I guess I can be," he admitted. "It's how I make my living."

Persuasive. Still not what he wanted from her— but they were getting somewhere.

She couldn't go out with him that weekend, as she'd already made plans for Friday evening with her parents and for Saturday evening with some old friends from high school. Lucas was only slightly relieved to learn they were female friends. He felt as if the weeks were slipping by and he wasn't making the progress he should be. It was dinner-and-dance time, to be followed promptly by perfume. He had an elegantly wrapped bottle of Chanel No. 19 in the glove compartment of his car, all ready for the right occasion.

The fact that she'd gone out with Bruce at least once more, and that the jerk had had flowers delivered to the office, a dozen roses, didn't make him feel any better. He wasn't worried—not really. *I mean, roses?* he asked himself. *Doesn't the guy have any imagination?* But it didn't make him feel great to know she really was keeping her options open, as she'd said. For all he knew she was seeing *other* men, too.

ON SATURDAY Tammy had a friend sleeping over. The pair had finally gone to sleep and Lucas had turned in, too, when his phone rang.

"Yes?" He glanced at the clock. It was 2:00 a.m.

"Lucas!" Virginia's horrified whisper pierced his brain and had him sitting up.

"What?"

"Sam's out." Sam? Was that a new guy? What was he—a jailbird?

"What are you talking about?"

"He's out! He's somewhere in the house. I can't find him. Oh, Lucas, I'm—"

"Wait a minute, honey. Who the hell's Sam?" If this was some guy in her house, he was definitely going to go over there and kick the bastard out. Maybe there was a robbery in progress. Somebody she knew. This Sam maybe. He was trying to put it together. His brain felt soggy. "Have you called the cops?"

"Cops? For a gerbil?"

Sam. Robert's rodent. It had escaped. And Virginia was having fits about it in the middle of the night.

Lucas leaped up and hastily scribbled a note for Tammy, saying he was at Virginia's and he'd be right back. He checked that there was nothing on the stove, turned on a night-light for Tammy and

Andrea, and double-checked that all the doors and windows were locked.

Then he jumped in his car. *Man, when trouble looms—who's she gonna call?*

Me.

Maybe things *were* working out. Maybe they were working out much, much better than he'd expected.

CHAPTER TEN

HOW HARD COULD IT BE to catch a gerbil?

Virginia must have been listening for him because she opened the door before he'd even knocked. She held one finger to her lips, as though she was afraid they might wake Robert.

"Is Tammy okay for a few minutes? I'm so sorry, I forgot about her," she whispered.

"She's fine. She's got a friend staying over. Now where's this rat?"

"Not a rat. A gerbil."

"I know, I know." Lucas grinned. "Gerbil. Anything to get me out of bed and into your apartment in the middle of the night, eh?"

"Shh! Over here." Virginia tiptoed toward the living room and, stupidly, Lucas found himself tiptoing behind her, like a couple of clowns in a Peter Sellers movie.

She knelt down gingerly by the coffee table and gestured. "He's really fast, so— Oops!" She covered her mouth and he thought she was going to fall over. He'd seen a streak of something dark whip out from one corner of the sofa and under a nearby table with a low shelf.

"Easy now." He gripped her shoulder. She was

wearing a fuzzy pink bathrobe, rather tatty around the lapels. It was endearing somehow, so normal. So domestic. Her hair was a mess, most of it tied back loosely with a small silk scarf. She looked adorable.

"Oh, thank heavens you're here, Lucas. I've been chasing this damn thing for the last hour." She was thoroughly disheveled, obviously at her wit's end. *And she'd turned to him.*

"How'd you find out he was loose?" Lucas whispered from his squatting position beside her.

She shuddered. "Yuck. I heard some rustling in the closet. Then, before I knew it, he was on my bed and running across the blanket. Little creep." She shuddered again. "I don't know why I let Robert get him. I hate rodents. Tammy warned him about this, too. She said they were nocturnal. Robert gets mad when I call him a rat. He thinks he's so cute sleeping all day. Then he's driving me nuts on that squeaky wheel of his all night. But I don't see how I can get rid of him now. Robert would have a fit. But I'm definitely going to make sure he can't get out again, even if I have to nail him in there. Do they live long, do you know?" She stopped suddenly and looked up at him anxiously. "Am I babbling?"

"You're babbling, honey." Lucas grinned. "Now just go into the kitchen and stand on a chair or something, and I'll catch this little doofus."

Easier said than done. After ten minutes of the gerbil scooting from one end of the sofa to the other at the exact instant Lucas lunged for him, and Virginia standing on a kitchen chair, beet-red, giggling enough to nearly fall off and yet trying to stifle her giggles so as not to wake her son, he was ready to change tactics.

"Have you got a broom, or something with a long handle?"

She went to the kitchen closet and came back with a broom. "Don't hurt him," she warned.

"Virginia," he replied, exasperated, "I can't get *close* enough to hurt him—"

Virginia handed over the broom.

"—yet."

"Oh!"

"Never mind. Now, I'm going to stick this under there, and when he scoots out, you grab him—"

"I'll do the poking. *You* grab him," she said firmly, grabbing the broom. She began poking awkwardly under the sofa. "I can't see anything, can you?"

Lucas got down on his hands and knees and peered. "He's there all right. Keep poking." The little beast was standing on its hind legs and thumbing its pointy little nose at them both. "I swear he's sticking his tongue out at us, Virginia—"

"There!" She gave a mighty swipe.

"Okay…" Lucas lunged and missed. Then he swore. The rodent dashed back to his starting place. "Poke him again!"

This went on for at least another ten minutes. Then Virginia turned the broom around and tried to sweep him out with the brush end. The gerbil did not cooperate. He hopped, he skipped, he did double backward somersaults.

"I can't believe how fast that little fella is," Lucas said, sitting back, breathing hard. "And we're supposed to be at the top of the food chain? Not sure I get it." Damn, at this rate, he'd still be here in the morning. Not his idea of spending the night with Virginia, that was for sure. "Wish I had a snake."

"Oh, don't say that. What if Robert heard you?"

"Well, what about a cat? We could get Mrs. Vandenbroek's cat."

"Lucas!"

Virginia thought for a moment. "What if he gets into the heat register or into the wall somehow?" She shuddered once again. "I know. Let's try putting a bucket or something at one end. They like to go into little sheltered places. Maybe he'll think it's his house or something."

"It's worth trying." At this point, anything was worth trying.

Either the gerbil was tired of their antics or he really did think it was a nice little house. A minute or two after Virginia wedged the plastic pail at one end of the sofa and started calling softly, "Here, Sam. Come here, little gerbil," the darn thing waltzed into the bucket in response to a poke from Lucas. "Tip it up!" Lucas said urgently. "He's in!"

Virginia instantly righted the bucket and there was the little beast, hopping in rage inside, but unable to make it up the slick sides.

"Where you going?" Lucas felt abandoned. Virginia had immediately started making cooing noises and was heading for the kitchen with the pail.

"I'm giving him a little treat for being such a good boy and going into the bucket the way he did."

"Good boy, all right," Lucas muttered, getting to his feet. He deposited the broom in the closet and watched as Virginia tried to entice the gerbil with a piece of lettuce and an almond. Sam the delinquent gerbil wasn't having any of it.

"He's obviously ticked off that you caught him," Lucas remarked dryly. "Where's his cage?"

"In Robert's room."

"Then I suggest leaving him in the bucket until morning."

"He might eat his way through it," Virginia said, looking worried again. "It's only plastic."

It must have been horrible waking up to find a ratlike creature skittering across your blanket. A woman really needed a man in her bed to deal with stuff like that. Mind you, this was no time to mention it. "I suppose he might."

"What should I do?"

"Put him in the bathtub overnight and put a window screen on top with some books on it to hold it down."

"You think that would work?"

"I was just kidding. But yes, I think it would work. He could play roller derby on the side of the tub to amuse himself."

Virginia tried to stifle her giggles again and carried the bucket to the small bathroom. Lucas went out onto the step and pried a window screen loose. It was October, time for storm windows, anyway. He carried the screen into the bathroom. It fit.

"Perfect!" Virginia said. The gerbil raced around the tub at top speed. He seemed to be having fun. Lucas noticed that she'd put the plug in—and wondered briefly if he would've been as conscientious. Still, Robert was going to get an awful surprise in the morning if he got up before his mother.

"I'd better go." Lucas checked his watch. "I've left Tammy for nearly half an hour now."

"Thank you so much. I don't know what I'd have done alone," she said softly. "I couldn't stand the thought of trying to go to sleep with that thing chasing around the apartment." Her eyes were starry and shining. It must have been the late hour. Or the lack of sleep. Or the chase. Or the scare of waking so suddenly with a rodent loose in her room. She looked so vulnerable and yet innocent and sweet. And luscious. Lucas couldn't resist. He bent down and kissed her softly.

"Good night," he said, kissing her gently again. "Call me any time you find a rat in your bed. Day or night."

She laughed. "I will. And thank you for—for coming to my rescue. I panicked when I couldn't catch him. I hope Tammy's okay."

"She's fine. Let's put it this way, honey," Lucas said with a broad grin. "I'm just glad you thought of me first."

What if she'd called Old Bruce?

THINGS WOULDN'T BE GOING Bruce Twist's way. Not if it was up to Lucas.

He wouldn't have done it if he'd thought Virginia

had any real interest in Bruce, but she didn't in his opinion and—again in his opinion—the man was getting to be a bit of a pain. Of course, even if she *had* a real interest…all was fair in love and war. And he was in love.

When Becky Fitzjames, the florist's delivery girl, knocked on the office door a few days later before regular office hours and handed Lucas a long white box for Virginia and a slip for him to sign, he signed.

The box just had to be from Twist, he'd already sent flowers once. But the card inside read: *To a lovely lady, Virginia. From Lenny.*

Lenny? Damn, wasn't that the new butcher at the IGA? So there were other guys after his woman already. Lucas got a blank card from his desk drawer and carefully printed, with his left hand: *To a lovely lady, Nancy. From Lenny.* And he set the box on the receptionist's desk. Nancy was currently between boyfriends, from what he could tell. He'd seen the way she eyed Bruce when he came into the office. So she didn't mind older men. Lenny looked mid-to-late thirties. Good job, regular hours… Nancy could do worse.

Twenty minutes later, when the receptionist arrived for work, there were squeals of excitement outside his office door.

Nancy burst in with an armful of yellow roses. "Lucas! Oh, I mean, Mr. Yellowfly—look what someone sent me!"

"They're lovely." He raised one eyebrow and cleared his throat. "Er, who from?"

"Oh, I don't know! It just says from Lenny—isn't that romantic? I wonder who that is." Nancy rushed out before Lucas could reply.

Then she popped her head back in, eyes alight. "Oh, I think I know who—that sexy new guy who works at the IGA. I think older men are *sooooo* sexy, don't you? Oh—" Face red, she suddenly disappeared. Perhaps she'd remembered that her boss could very well qualify as an older man, Lucas thought dryly.

Well, well. If Lenny the butcher wasn't—yet— romantically involved with one woman, he might find himself with another. Perhaps, after all, Lucas had done him a good turn.

Virginia was definitely out of the running, anyway.

With that pleasant thought, Lucas picked up the phone and started making his morning calls.

NEXT TIME Lucas took Virginia out, it was dinner and dancing at the Glory Country Club. Lucas liked to dance, unlike many men—according to confidences from previous dates—and they stayed out past midnight, a record so far with Virginia. Mrs. Vandenbroek baby-sat Robert.

He hadn't quite gotten up his nerve to offer the perfume. It was one thing for her to know how he felt about her, another to have her second-guessing his courtship strategies.

Then one Saturday toward the end of the month, he organized a picnic with Virginia and the two children down at the municipal park on the Horsethief

River. It was chilly, but they ate a pot of barbecued beans Virginia had prepared and then insulated in a picnic basket. They also had coleslaw and potato salad from the deli, and roasted hot dogs and sausages over a charcoal fire. Afterward, they took a leisurely drive over the back roads and wound up at the Dairy Queen in Pincher Creek for dessert.

The BMW wasn't quite up to it. The next day Lucas found marshmallow topping gummed to the upholstery in the backseat. Maybe the time would soon come when he'd have to trade in his bachelor car for a minivan. He'd thought the notion would hurt; surprisingly it didn't.

The first Sunday in October they drove out to the Blackfoot—known these days as Siksiksa—Reserve in the Porcupine Hills south of Glory and watched the dancing taking place at the annual fall powwow. Tammy was thrilled. Lucas was impressed with his niece. She was very proud of her Indian blood and didn't hide it from anyone at school or anywhere else. Lucas had never hidden his Indian background, either, for reasons other than Tammy's; his had had more to do with bravado or teenage fury. He was glad to see that times had changed.

Lucas was convinced he'd begun to win Virginia over. She welcomed his company—which she'd always done, but now it seemed there was something extra in her smile of welcome. Robert adored Tammy, and both children loved excursions outdoors. They were both loners who found each other good company, despite the difference in age.

One day down at the Horsethief, Robert found an

Indian flint arrowhead in the mud. He pried it out triumphantly and announced that now he had one, just like Teddy. Then Lucas overheard Virginia tell him that Grandpa had quite a collection he could show the boy.

"Do you think he will?" Robert had asked his mother wistfully. "Do you really think he will?" Lucas knew that Doc Lake had yet to take the boy fishing. If the old man didn't do it soon, Lucas would swallow his distaste for the sport and take the kid himself.

Of course, the year was getting late. In a month or so, the river would start freezing over, and fishing would have to wait until spring.

But all Robert knew was that his grandfather had promised and then let him down. Lucas hoped it would be different with the Indian artifacts.

One morning later that week, there was ice on the step outside and frost on the grass. It was unmistakably autumn, with winter soon to come. The raspberry canes lost their few remaining leaves and the pumpkin vines turned black. The previous tenants in the house on Second Avenue had been gardeners, and Lucas found a few onions and turnips in the grass behind the maples, and pumpkins planted along the fence. Tammy and Robert rescued a couple of the best ones to save for Halloween.

Virginia and Robert had been back in Glory for nearly two months now. Lucas didn't think Virginia was seeing much of Bruce Twist anymore. Lenny had been dating Nancy, he'd heard. He was pretty sure he was the only man in Virginia's life.

By Christmas, he told himself. By Christmas, he'd definitely propose. He'd already purchased a diamond engagement ring. A solitaire from a custom jeweler in Calgary. All he needed was to find the right occasion to ask her to marry him. Virginia had said she wasn't ready for a man in her life, but he thought maybe she was changing her mind. She seemed happier and more relaxed now—as though whatever cloud she'd been under when she came back to town had blown away.

By Christmas, he promised himself, he'd have a real wife and a real family. He was prepared to wait. He'd already waited for Virginia for twelve long years. What was a few more months?

CHAPTER ELEVEN

"WHERE'S VIRGINIA?"

Lucas flipped idly through the Friday-afternoon mail that Nancy had picked up on her lunch hour. He'd come back from the morning court session, after a long lunch with Deverell Sparks, dying to tell Virginia what the developer had found out. Apparently the current owner of one of the parcels he was trying to acquire for the golf course wasn't the owner at all—it was Indian land belonging to Danny Weaselfat and it had never been sold. At least, the proper documents had never been executed thirty-seven years ago, the time of the supposed transaction.

"She didn't come back," Nancy mumbled, finishing up the giant chocolate-chip cookie she'd bought at Molly McClung's.

Lucas dropped the wad of mail onto the receptionist's desk. "What do you mean, didn't come back? She sick or something?"

"She didn't feel all that well after lunch."

"She told you this?" Lucas felt vague alarm. Virginia had seemed her usual quietly cheerful self this morning when he'd seen her before he'd headed for the courthouse.

"She called in. About half-past one." Nancy screwed up the wax envelope the cookie had come in and neatly tossed it into her wastebasket. She fished in her purse, drawing out a lipstick, and began examining herself critically in her compact mirror.

Lucas walked back to his office, frowning. That wasn't like Virginia. She wasn't the sickly type, unless she'd eaten something bad at lunch. Maybe it was Robert. Maybe the school had phoned and she hadn't wanted to tell Nancy that her son needed her.

But that wasn't like Virginia, either. She was very honest, or at least he'd always had that impression. And surely she trusted him and Nancy. And Pete. It wasn't as though she'd get fired for taking an afternoon off.

Lucas stood with his hands in his pockets, facing the long window in his office. He narrowed his eyes against the bright sunshine. Damn it. He didn't like the feel of this. He decided to go over to her place and see what was wrong.

Once he'd made up his mind, he acted immediately. He locked his office door behind him—he didn't want to take a chance that his papers on the Sparks property would be seen by anyone until he'd sorted everything out—then headed for the outer door.

"You leaving, Mr. Yellowfly?" Nancy looked perturbed.

"Just for an hour or so." This shouldn't take too long. "I'll be back around three."

As Lucas walked to Virginia's apartment, he noted that a lot of the big maples and poplars had already lost their leaves. The weather, for mid-October, was unseasonably fine. He'd been thinking about taking Robert and Tammy on a little overnight camping trip. Last one of the season. Maybe this was the weekend for it.

Virginia's car was parked in her driveway. Oddly the headlights were on. The car wasn't locked, either. Lucas reached through the open driver's window and turned the lights off. He took the steps two at a time and knocked on the kitchen door.

He heard nothing inside and knocked a little harder. "Virginia, it's me. Lucas!"

After what seemed an interminable amount of time, the door opened a crack and Virginia's tear-streaked face appeared. Her eyes were wide with fright.

"What's wrong?" Lucas went inside and pulled her into his arms. She held back a second or two, then collapsed on his chest. He shook her gently. "Is it Robert? For God's sake, tell me!"

"Robert's fine," she said. Then she stepped back. "Oh, for heaven's sake—look at me!" She wiped at the tears on her cheeks and tried to smile. "I'm so sorry. I'm a mess."

She was wearing what she'd worn at the office that morning, a gray tweed skirt and white blouse. Her hair was down, though, tangled and wild. He wanted to pull her back into his arms, kiss her until…

Then he spotted the cardboard boxes on the floor. Household items had been hurriedly thrown into several. There were glasses and dishes of every sort taken out of the cupboards and stacked in a hodge-podge on the kitchen counter.

"What the hell's going on?" he demanded, looking from the countertops to her again. "What's wrong?"

"Oh, Lucas," she began tremulously, "everything's wrong. I—I've got to leave. As soon as Robert comes home from school, I've got to tell him—"

"Tell him what?" Lucas moved toward Virginia and grabbed her upper arms. A chill horror struck him—could she be talking about leaving *town?*

"We've got to go, Lucas. Find somewhere else to live. I can't explain it all. It's too much...." She ran her fingers through her hair in a frantic gesture, obviously not for the first time. "Oh, I wish I could tell you...."

He reached forward and picked her up in his arms. She smiled through the tears and bit her bottom lip. He stepped over and around the boxes in the kitchen and carried her into the living room, where he sat down on the sofa, with her in his lap. He freed one hand to scoop up the phone on the end table and punched in the office number.

"Nancy? I won't be coming back this afternoon," he said, then interrupted Nancy's questions. "Yes, I know, I know. Tell her I'll see her first thing Monday. All right. Yes—" he glanced at Virginia "—everything's all right. Fine." He hung up the phone.

"You had an appointment."

"Old Mrs. Reeves. She changes her will every third week. First one daughter gets all the family teacups, then the other one gets them. She can wait until Monday. Now," he said firmly, "tell me everything."

She took a deep breath and made an effort. "Okay. I saw Cecilia today, at the grocery store—"

"Hold on. You mean Cecilia Gagnon?"

"Yes." She gulped. "Johnny's aunt."

Lucas frowned. "So?" He had a bad feeling. He always had a bad feeling when Johnny's name came up.

"She…she said he's getting out of jail. She thought I'd be pleased to know. She said they weren't sure, but they thought he could be out by the end of November. Maybe earlier. Christmas for sure. She said he'd probably be living with her and Phil for a while. Until he got his feet under him, she said." Virginia half sobbed, half laughed, then went on bitterly. "As though he'd *ever* get his feet under him!"

Lucas thought hard. Johnny Gagnon was in jail, as Virginia had told him earlier. And obviously he was getting out on parole. But why should that concern Virginia? Send her packing? Where did all this bitterness come from? Their relationship was long over and she hadn't shown any interest in Gagnon, none whatsoever, since her return to Glory. Surely Cecilia's news was no cause for tears. Guys went to jail—and then they got out. This wasn't anything out of the ordinary.

Packing boxes. A suspicion, ever so faint, slid into his mind.

"I don't get it. What's all this about Johnny Gagnon? Who cares?"

Virginia squeezed her eyes shut, forcing fat tears to run down her cheeks. Her jaw trembled.

"I think you'd better tell me everything, honey," he said gently. "Right from the beginning."

After what seemed like a very long time, Virginia opened her eyes. She gazed straight ahead. "Johnny is Robert's father, Lucas."

Lucas was thunderstruck. He never would have guessed. Johnny Gagnon was Robert's *father?* How in hell—

"Robert doesn't know. No one knows," she whispered, pausing to blow her nose on a tissue she'd tucked in her sleeve. "I've never told anyone. I've never told Mother or Father or anybody. You're the first. I...I just can't keep it to myself anymore. I'm so tired of running, Lucas—" her teary eyes pleaded with his "—so tired. I thought I was finished with running. It's been six years, nearly seven. I never dreamed, *never,* that he'd come back here. I thought this was the one place I'd be safe from him."

Safe from him.

"What do you mean, Virginia," Lucas said slowly, "'safe from him'? How can he harm you? What are you so afraid of? If he's Robert's father—"

"He raped me, Lucas."

"That son of a bitch!"

"He raped me after he'd robbed a grocery store. He had a gun. I happened to walk in on the robbery.

Just bad luck, that's all. He made me go with him to some cabin west of Bragg Creek. In the mountains. He…'' She shuddered and he held her tighter. ''He got drunk and raped me.'' Her voice trembled. He heard the anger, still as loud as the fear after all this time. ''I managed to get away the next day, and then a month later I testified against him in court. He went to jail for armed robbery and kidnapping. And stealing a vehicle. He got nine years.''

Lucas stared at her, hardly able to believe what she was telling him. He'd never heard about any of this. It had happened long before he'd come back to Glory himself. ''Not rape?''

''No,'' she said, so quietly he could barely hear her. ''I never told anyone about th-that part. And then…then I found out I was pregnant and had to quit school.'' She shrugged. ''I had to get a job. I couldn't ask my parents for help, not after they sent me away and everything.''

And that was partly his fault. For taking her out knowing full well her parents didn't approve.

Lucas's mind was spinning. He was furious. He wanted to find that Gagnon bastard and rip him apart. He felt all the fury and rush of blood he used to feel in a good bar brawl or a bunkhouse fight or a scary rodeo event. The heat that had given him the courage to hurt people. He hated the feeling. But he'd put all that behind him years ago.

He forced himself to think clearly. ''What does Johnny know about Robert?''

''Nothing.'' Virginia's sea-blue eyes searched his. ''No one does. I'm so afraid, Lucas, that he'll put two and two together if he knows I've got Robert, and he'll try to take my son away from me. It wouldn't take a genius to do the math, would it?'' She burst into tears again and Lucas rocked her in his arms.

No one was going to hurt this woman. Or her son. Certainly not some piece of garbage like Johnny Gagnon. But she wasn't thinking clearly about this, not at all. ''Look, what kind of chance would he have, Virginia? None. You must know that. Are you talking custody? Hell, you're Robert's mother. You've looked after him all these years. You've supported him, you've raised him. Nobody could take him from you.''

''No!'' Virginia sat up straight on his lap. Her eyes flashed fire. ''No, that's not true! He could make my life miserable. He could make Robert's life miserable. He could tie me up in legal crap for years. You know what it's like, Lucas. Or he could just grab him one day, steal him away. I'm not going to take that chance! I don't want Robert to know about him—ever!''

Lucas bent forward and kissed her on the brow. Her skin was hot and damp.

''Would you want to know?'' she went on angrily. ''Would you want to find out your father was a criminal? A man who'd spent half his life in jail? That you'd been born because of a *rape?*''

''He's still his father—'' Lucas began.

Virginia scrambled off his lap in a burst of energy. He reached out to grab her again and she turned, furious. ''He *raped* me, Lucas. Don't you get it? We're not talking about an ordinary criminal here. Some…some purse snatcher!''

Lucas pulled her back onto his lap, and her resistance, strong at first, suddenly collapsed. She put her arms around his neck and wept loudly.

He kept his mouth shut. She was right. How the hell could he know how she really felt? He pushed back her hair, smoothed it away from her face. She closed her eyes again. ''Look, Virginia. Listen to me. The fact is, you can't keep running every time this guy shows up. Or every time you think he's going to show up. What kind of life is that?''

She shook her head mutely.

''And what kind of life is it for Robert? You're staying here, honey. We can face this together, you and me. I'll help you. Your son's not a baby anymore. This is your home now. Robert's got his grandparents here, he's got Tammy, he's got his little buddy Teddy Herrara.'' He paused. ''He's got me.''

Virginia opened her eyes. Wild and distraught as she was, he knew he'd never seen a more beautiful woman. And he never would. Damn, if only he'd been able to break through that reserve she'd put up ever since she'd come back here—

''And h-he's got his bunk beds?'' She tried a smile.

''Hell, yes. He's got his bunk beds. Nobody's taking those away from him, I guarantee.'' Lucas smiled, too. ''Not even you.''

That was when he covered Virginia's soft lips with his. She was stock-still at first, rigid, then her mouth moved under his and she kissed him back, moaning softly. He held her tight, relishing her closeness, the warmth and softness of her on his lap, her sinewy strength as she clung to him. He loved kissing her, he always had.

"Oh, Lucas," she whispered.

He wanted her. No one else. There was no way on God's green earth he was letting her get away from him now that he'd found her again. Johnny Gagnon or no Johnny Gagnon. "You're staying here, honey," he said as firmly as he could, feathering her face with kisses.

Virginia leaned against him and sighed.

"I'm serious. You're staying here with me. We can deal with this character. Send him on his way if he causes trouble."

She was silent for a long moment. Then she raised her head and looked at him. "I know you're right, Lucas. I know you are. I...I panicked. I didn't know what else to do. I've dreaded this for so long, and when Cecilia came up to me in the store and told me—" she bit her lip and shook her head "—I just fell apart. Everything I'd planned—the job, my promises to you and Pete—everything just flew out the window."

He held her close and nuzzled her hair with his chin. This was where he wanted to be, *how* he wanted to be, holding this woman in his arms. Kissing her. Taking care of her and her son. Loving her. In his big, new house on Second Avenue.

"Virginia, you know the way I feel about you," he began, his voice rough. "I've been crazy about you for a long, long time. That's no secret. I've never tried to hide it. I couldn't possibly hide it." He gazed into her eyes and smiled. "Marry me. Stay here with me and I'll protect you and Robert. I'll promise to love, honor and cherish you. I already do. I know you don't feel the same way about me…yet." He ran his fingers through her soft curly hair. "You will one day, I hope. I'll take steps to adopt Robert right away. Legally. There's nothing Johnny Gagnon can do to hurt you or Robert. I *promise*."

She looked at him and said nothing. She seemed to be considering his words. He took a slow deep breath. Could he really be lucky enough?

"Then—" he ran his fingers through her hair again "—if it doesn't work out, if you find you don't really feel about me the way I do about you, well…" He shrugged. "I'll still adopt Robert and be his father, whether we're together or not. I'll protect him to the best of my ability. He'll be my legal son. What do you think?"

"Little Robert Yellowfly?"

"Yeah." He grinned. "That's got a nice ring to it."

"And Virginia Yellowfly?"

He laughed. "You don't have to go that far. You can keep your name. It's up to you."

Virginia stared at him for a long time. Then she leaned up and kissed him softly on the lips. She smiled through her tears. Her eyes shone. "I think you're a very good man, Lucas Yellowfly. Much better than I deserve."

"Does that mean yes?" he asked, hardly daring to frame the question.

"Yes. I'll marry you. I care about you. Do I love you? Sometimes I think I do. But I...I don't know what love is anymore, Lucas. I wish I did." She shrugged slightly, her eyes clouded. "I'm sorry."

"That's okay, Virginia. I look forward to showing you what it is. In every possible way."

She smiled, then added quietly, "I'd be proud to be Virginia Yellowfly. I like the sound of it. I've been carrying another man's name—my father's—long enough."

"Babe!" Lucas held her against him so she couldn't see his face for a few seconds. He blinked back the emotion that overwhelmed him. He'd wanted this for so long. He'd wanted Virginia since the first moment he'd seen her.

"I don't think we should have a big wedding, though, do you, Lucas? Shall we just go to the courthouse and get it over with?"

"You're damn right we should have a big wedding. The biggest. I intend to get married only once, and I plan to do it properly. The biggest and the best—and the quickest. How long to pull off a decent wedding?"

"Two weeks, maybe three," she murmured, her eyes soft. She was smiling again. "Maybe a month. I don't know, I've never been through this before. I'll have to check with Mother."

"And she'll have to check with her sister, Lily."

Virginia giggled. "Yes."

HE REALLY DID NEED a different vehicle if he was going to be a family man. He needed something besides a luxury sedan like the Beemer or a truck. Lucas glanced at Virginia in the passenger seat of his pickup and the two children strapped into the seat belt in the middle. It wasn't legal or safe, really, but the best he could do. At least they weren't on a government road, and there was no traffic at all.

They were on their way to find a campsite along one of Adam Garrick's range roads. Sure, it was October and cold at night, but the kids had insisted when he'd broached the idea of camping. He knew a good spot up by one of the creeks that led into the Horsethief. Virginia and Lucas had unpacked the few boxes she'd filled in her frenzy, and by the time Robert arrived, accompanied by Tammy and Natasha, there was no evidence that only a couple of hours before, Virginia had been planning to leave town.

They'd decided to keep their decision to get married to themselves for a few days. Just to get used to it. And to have a chance to talk to Robert about it first.

Now that he was about to become an instant father, Lucas suddenly felt unsure of himself around Virginia's son.

As soon as he'd pulled up to the clearing on the banks of the stream, the two excited children piled out and started running around, flopping down in the long dry grass and laughing. Lucas unloaded the truck and carried everything to a flat area he thought was a good place to pitch the tent. Virginia walked around aimlessly, generally getting in the way.

"You ever camped before?" he finally asked.

"Of course I have. Daddy used to take me out with him all the time. Not that we stayed overnight all that often. We'd usually just be fishing or canoeing." Virginia gazed around the isolated spot. "This is a lovely place. You must have been here before."

Lucas tried to see it through a newcomer's eyes. "Yeah. Me and my buddies used to come up here as kids. Teenagers. Do a little drinking, a little fishing, a little yarning. Me and Adam and Cal Blake and his brother, Jeremiah. Sometimes Jesse Winslow came along. Once in a while, his brother, Noah." He smiled. That seemed like a long, long time ago—and it was.

"Hey, Lucas! Can I help put up the tent?" Robert ran toward him, eyes bright, cheeks flushed. He had grass in his hair and looked the picture of health for a five-year-old. It was hard to believe this was the same wan, pale boy who'd arrived with Virginia in mid-August.

"Sure can, buddy." Lucas spread out the tent. It was just a small one. Virginia and the kids could sleep in it; he'd take his Montana bedroll under the stars. "Pull that corner out—that's it. Now, take those tent pegs out of the zipper bag and lay one beside each peg loop."

He glanced at Virginia. Robert crouched by the tent, lower lip tight between his teeth, counting the pegs. Virginia was giving him, Lucas, a very tender look over her son's head. Her expression surprised Lucas. Maybe there *was* a chance for the two of them. A real chance. It wasn't as though this marriage business was unexpected. Not to him, at least. It was just that Johnny Gagnon's coming along had hurried things up a little, that was all. Lucas had made up his mind years ago that he'd marry Virginia Lake if he ever got the opportunity.

The fact was, maybe he owed the Gagnon bunch a debt of gratitude—Johnny for planning to come back to town, and Cecilia for being so quick with the news.

That night, as the campfire blazed under the stars, Virginia and Lucas sat close together. Lucas had his arm around Virginia's shoulders. His gesture didn't go unnoticed by the children. Robert whispered loudly to Tammy that his mom and Lucas were holding hands and Tammy shushed him and dug him in the ribs with her elbow.

"Did you bring any marshmallows, Uncle Lucas?" Tammy suddenly said, getting to her feet. She pulled her Swiss Army knife out of her jeans pocket. Any chance the kid had to cut or sharpen something, she took it.

"I did. They're in that cardboard box just inside the tent. I suppose you're going to cut a few sticks to roast them with."

"Can I?"

"Sure. But be careful, honey." He turned to Virginia. "I never realized when I sent her that knife and a fold-up fishing rod for her last birthday that I'd ever have to supervise her with it."

"Serves you right," Virginia said cheerfully.

The children disappeared down the bank of the stream where the willows grew. Lucas pulled Virginia toward him, cupping the back of her head in his hand. She turned easily, meeting his mouth with hers. He kissed her lightly, then a little more deeply, finally breaking off the kiss with a groan. "This isn't a good idea, is it?"

"Mmm. Not really, I guess. Not with the kids around."

She seemed relaxed and comfortable, leaning against him. He had something on his mind. They hadn't talked about their upcoming marriage since this afternoon, when he'd asked her to marry him.

"Virginia," he began, "there's one thing I want to make crystal clear before we get married."

"What's that, Lucas?" she asked softly, looking up at him in the falling dusk.

"This is what I've always wanted, you know. To marry you, Virginia. I love you. I told you that already."

Her eyes clouded slightly. "Go on."

"What I want you to know is that I want a real marriage." He stared deeply into her eyes and saw the shadow of fear there, quickly gone. "I'm not marrying you just to keep you safe from Johnny Gagnon, although it might seem like it now. I'm marrying you because I love you. You know that. I want a wife in my bed, Virginia, not just under my roof."

"I know," she said. "I...I'll try." The fear was back. He kissed her swiftly. He couldn't bear the look in her eyes. If Johnny Gagnon had done this to her, he'd kill the bastard, he didn't care what the law said. There was the law, and then there was justice. They didn't always mesh, no matter what he'd been taught.

"We'll take it slow and easy, honey," he murmured against her ear. "We'll take all the time you need. But I want you as my real wife, Virginia. I love you more than I ever dreamed I'd love anyone. I want this marriage to work. More than anything."

"I know, Lucas," she whispered. "I know."

CHAPTER TWELVE

VIRGINIA HAD NEVER THOUGHT she'd be a bride. Certainly not the white-lace-and-roses type of bride you saw in magazines and movies.

She was doing this for Lucas, she told herself. And for her mother.

Doris Lake had been shocked for a total of three seconds when she and Lucas had gone to her parents' house and announced their desire for a speedy marriage. She'd rushed forward and flung her arms first around Virginia, then Lucas. Afterward she'd clasped her hands together, her face mottled with excitement.

"Oh! I'm going to call Lily immediately. We've got to get on this right away. There's so much to do." And she'd rushed off. Virginia overheard snatches of the excited conversation from the next room—"the country club" and "off-the-rack, I suppose" and "champagne cocktails" and "Oh, no, Lily, I don't think so—not this time, *surely*"—and smiled to herself. At least someone besides her and Lucas and Robert was pleased about their marriage plans. Leave it to her nosy aunt Lily to ask why they were in such a big hurry.

Her father was pleased, too. Virginia might even

have said he looked relieved, but perhaps that wasn't fair. He shook Lucas's hand warmly and offered brandy all around. It was early evening and they'd hired a baby-sitter for Robert and Tammy. Virginia didn't think telling her parents would take more than thirty minutes, but it was an hour before they left the big brick house on Buffalo Hill.

Lucas said nothing as he drove through the winding streets toward the center of town.

"Second thoughts?" she teased, knowing very well that he didn't have any. Nor did she, although sometimes she had to pinch herself to realize that this was reality, not some virginal maiden's dream. Well, hardly a maiden's dream, not with a five-year-old son in tow at the wedding.

"Never!" Lucas laughed. "Just thinking how pleased the old boy was tonight, when a few years ago he'd have run me out of town with a shotgun if I'd even dared suggest I had my eye on you."

"Yes." Virginia looked out the window at the rapidly thickening darkness. "Times change, don't they?" she murmured. What hypocrites. Oh, well, at least she and Lucas knew where they stood. And Lucas was enjoying his triumph, which had nothing to do with her personally. It was his vindication against the good burghers of Glory that he was enjoying.

They owed him.

"You think Robert really likes the idea?" Lucas seemed a little hesitant. "Sounds to me, from what you've said, he's still stuck on finding his real dad."

Virginia shook her head. "No way. He's crazy

about you. Sure, he's asked a lot of questions lately, but I think he'll be content with us being a family now. You and me and him.'' Suddenly worried, she stared at Lucas in the light from the dashboard. ''Don't you?''

''Maybe.'' He turned to her and grabbed her hand and kissed it, then held it over the gearbox between them. ''I hope so. I'm looking forward to having your son for my son.''

DORIS AND HER SISTER insisted that Virginia had to have attendants for a proper wedding, so she had Marcia Herrara and Nancy. They'd become good friends in the few months Virginia had been in town. Lucas had rancher Adam Garrick and their mutual buddy, Jeremiah Blake, stand up for him.

It all seemed so silly, Virginia thought, but she kept her opinions to herself. Her wedding was the highlight of her mother's life at present. But she put her foot down at wearing a long, white bridal gown, and she and her aunt and mother purchased a gorgeous cream-colored crepe wool suit on a trip to Calgary. It cost a fortune, all the same, and with a few adjustments, fit her perfectly. Practical as always, Virginia figured she could wear it later.

Lucas was resplendent in a new Hugo Boss suit. The groomsmen had dark suits, and the bride's attendants wore wildly expensive and elegant cocktail dresses from a Calgary designer shop, in differing shades of coral and salmon, courtesy of Dr. Lake. Her father had insisted that he wished to spare no expense when it came to his daughter's wedding, regardless of the short notice, and Doris Lake had taken him at his word.

The church was full of flowers, and Virginia carried white and pale, apricot-colored roses, which went nicely with the shade of her hair. Lucas had asked her to wear it down, and she did, curly and unrestrained and irrepressible, well past her shoulders. It reminded her of her wild teenage years, and she was sure it would remind the entire town of those days, too.

The look on Lucas's face when she walked down the aisle on the arm of her father, who'd insisted on an old-fashioned morning tuxedo, made the whole wedding fuss worthwhile. Pride, tenderness, love— she didn't deserve it. Not any of it.

Virginia lowered her eyes to cover her unease. Was it right to draw Lucas into her troubles with Johnny? Somehow a straightforward marriage of convenience would have seemed more honest. But she was sure that the many, many townsfolk gathered to watch the Indian kid from the wrong side of town marry the doctor's daughter—the church was straining at the rafters, every pew filled—thought her downcast gaze was simply the bashfulness of a new bride.

Robert stood with the groomsmen, and Tammy stood, in a full-skirted floral dress, with Nancy and Marcia. When Lucas turned to Adam for the ring, his best man winked and smiled, and Robert stepped forward proudly and handed him the wedding ring.

It wasn't part of the script, but Virginia didn't think even her mother, who wept tiny, elegant, wedding tears in the front pew beside her father, would mind. Lucas's mother, Joan Yellowfly, a tall, angular woman with neat silvery hair, and her sister, Alma, sat quietly near the front on the groom's side of the church.

Lucas slipped the ring onto her finger. Then he kissed her, and it wasn't a perfunctory public or ceremonial kiss, but a kiss tender and passionate at the same time, sweet and bursting with all the promises they'd just made. They turned to face the congregation as the organist struck the first chords of "The Wedding March," and Virginia smiled up at her handsome husband and took his arm.

The deed was done. She was Virginia Yellowfly now and she didn't have any regrets. She was very close to loving her husband already, and she was sure that by Christmas, in the tenderness and intimacy and safety of marriage, she'd love him wholly and completely. She'd be *in love,* whatever that meant. For Robert's sake, she had to make this work. And for Lucas's sake. And perhaps even for her own.

Whether Johnny Gagnon came back to town or not.

After a luncheon at the Glory Hills Country Club, where 130 invited guests listened to music that dated more from her parents' day than hers and dined on smoked trout and filet mignon and hearts of palm— her mother's choice of menu—they managed to leave about midafternoon for their very abbreviated honeymoon.

Virginia's parents had insisted on keeping

Tammy and Robert with them for a few days, but Virginia was loath to leave Robert very long with his too-proper grandparents. And she had no idea how they'd take to the outspoken Tammy Yellowfly. Probably not well. So she agreed to go away with Lucas for only four days.

The wedding was on a Friday morning near the beginning of November. She expected to be back at work on Wednesday. Lucas was frustrated at her insistence on such a short honeymoon, but if anything, she felt more nervous than ever leaving Robert in town with Johnny's parole presumably just around the corner. She hadn't seen Cecilia Gagnon since the day they'd met in the grocery store, but that didn't mean things couldn't change. His parole could be moved up. When—*if*—Johnny Gagnon came back to Glory, Virginia wanted to be there.

Lucas booked a honeymoon suite at the Banff Springs Hotel for four nights, at a price too horrendous for her to contemplate. After all the years of pinching pennies and making do as a single mother with rent to pay and food to buy, she shuddered at the cost of the famous luxury resort in the Canadian Rockies.

And she shuddered for another reason. The Banff Springs Hotel was where she'd been working when she'd discovered she was pregnant.

She thought she could put that difficult time out of her mind—so much had happened since—and for a while she did. The drive to Banff was beautiful, with all the poplars and willows in full autumn color. The mountains, snowcapped and majestic, never changed.

They dined in the hotel's most elegant dining room, the Rob Roy Room. The finest china and silver, the snowiest linen and purest candlelight, the most romantic soft music from a harpist—but Virginia couldn't settle her jitters. Lucas finally noticed.

"Something wrong, Virginia? I mean, really wrong?" He looked tender and concerned.

"No. Just a little nervous, I guess." She laughed and sampled the minuscule portion of a bitter lime sherbet, the palate cleanser, that had come between their first and second courses. "Wedding nerves."

Lucas studied her for a few moments and she could imagine what was going through his head. *Nerves about what? Being married? To me?* But he simply reached across the table and squeezed her hand lightly. "We'll dance. Later."

The waiter poured some wine, a delicious Ontario white, and Virginia became aware of the gentle babble of voices of other diners, of quiet laughter, of the harmonious sound of conversations. She felt nervous all over again. It was better to get everything into the open.

"I worked here once, you know," she blurted, "as a summer student."

"Did you? So did I," Lucas said, smiling. "Well, in the area, anyway. I guess it must've been about fifteen years ago, before I went to college. What did you do here?"

"I worked on the desk. Answered the phone, that sort of thing."

"I was a wrangler's helper on a nearby ranch that rented horses to the hotel." Lucas laughed, as though remembering. "Out in the barn. Lousy pay and long hours. Another reason I wanted to come back here as a guest." He looked around the dining room briefly, then leaned toward her. "I helped shove the rich tourists into their saddles and made sure they stayed on the trail. Mind you, those horses would've had heart failure if anyone tried to lead them *off* the trail. So when were you here?"

It could have been a conversation between strangers.

"Six years ago. The summer after my second year in law school."

She could see Lucas counting up the years, making the deductions. "Before Robert was born," he said flatly.

"Yes. It was just before I started my job here that I...uh, that Johnny kidnapped me and, well, you know the rest." She glanced nervously around, but no one appeared to have overheard her. The tables in this dining room were all a discreet distance apart.

"I wish you'd told me," Lucas said in a low tone. "This place must have bad memories for you. We could have gone somewhere else. Calgary or the Kananaskis Lodge or anywhere." He frowned. "Damn it, Virginia, why didn't you say something?"

"I'm fine. I didn't even think of it, really, until now," she lied. "Never mind. It's ages ago, anyway."

Their meals arrived and nothing more was said.

But Virginia could see that Lucas wasn't pleased. It had ruined what should have been a wonderful evening for him, for them both.

How much influence it had on what came later, Virginia could never know.

THEY DANCED. They took their time over a leisurely dessert and specialty coffees. Then they went to the piano bar in another part of the hotel for a nightcap. Virginia felt the simmer of tension between them. Sexual tension and something more. But neither of them, it seemed, was willing to suggest the inevitable: to go up to bed together.

Finally the hour of reckoning arrived. At midnight Lucas took her hand after they'd danced and, without a word, led her toward the exit. They went up to their room, a sumptuous suite under the eaves, with a huge bed and bathroom and a small sitting area, complete with fruit basket, roses and bottle of champagne in an ice bucket. Virginia knew that the service was laid on by the hotel—at those prices, it should have been.

Lucas went to the big windows and drew open the curtains. The moon lit the edges of the snow-capped mountains that loomed beyond. The night was crystal clear. Virginia stood uncertainly in the center of the room.

Lucas turned and walked toward her and took her hands. She hoped they didn't feel as icy to him as they did to her.

"Do you want to sleep together tonight?" he asked bluntly. "I could sleep on the sofa."

"D-don't be silly," she said faintly. "We're married, aren't we?"

"Sweet Virginia," Lucas murmured, and bent his head to kiss her. She tensed, then made herself relax. It was horrible. She liked Lucas very much, more than any man she could remember ever caring for. She'd enjoyed kissing him before. She found him attractive, sexy and caring. Now she was his wife. Yet she'd never been able to have any kind of an intimate relationship with a man since Johnny had hurt her so terribly.

Would they never end, these feelings of repulsion?

He must have felt her withdraw, then resolutely try to relax. He straightened and ran his fingers lightly through her hair. "You're nervous."

"Yes. I guess I am."

"Know what?" She saw him grin in the dim light. Only one small lamp glowed on an end table. "I'm nervous, too."

She managed a sort of laugh. "You?"

"Yeah, me." He kissed her again, holding her face between his hands. "Guess what? I've never been married before."

"Me, neither." She felt his hands fumble with the zipper that closed her dress at the back and caught her breath. He was so gentle, yet firm. He meant what he'd said—he wanted a real wife. And she was determined to be one.

She undid the buttons of his shirt—his tie had been thrust into the pocket of his jacket earlier. He took a deep breath as she placed the palms of her hands against his chest, bare and warm and smooth.

"Oh, honey, I adore you. I want you so much," he whispered. Then, as he'd done so often before, he swept her up in his arms. But this time he carried her to the massive bed. Her heart beat wildly in her throat, and everywhere else. Lucas stripped off his shirt and tossed it onto a nearby chair, then gently peeled her dress from her. She shivered in her silk teddy and camisole.

"Beautiful," he said, his eyes glittering with desire. She felt her very soul shrink. Yet she knew she was committed to this; she knew that if she could get through it just once, it would get better. It had to. She couldn't go on forever fearing the physical side of life, the intimacy that must exist between two loving partners in marriage. Besides, with Lucas, it might be all right—at least she liked kissing him.

He pulled off her stockings, unhitching them from the old-fashioned garter belt she wore, then unsnapped that and removed it. It had been a gift, presented with giggles by Marcia a week before the wedding. That and the brief lacy nightie she hadn't dared to unpack from her bag.

Then, quickly, his desire as evident as her fear, he removed the rest of his clothing and stretched out on the bed beside her. He turned toward her, leaning on one elbow and traced the outlines of her breasts beneath the camisole, his eyes devouring her. Ravishing her. "I've dreamed of seeing you like this, Virginia."

His eyes caressed her from her toes to her hair, outspread on linen that was as white as the snow on the mountains. "You're gorgeous. I can't believe all this has happened, that you're my wife now. That we're married. That I've got a son."

He kissed her and edged his hand under her camisole to caress her breast. She shuddered, part desire and part plain, hideous fear. But he couldn't know that; he had to think it was only the trembling heat of her need for him. He *had* to believe that. He kissed her again, deeper this time and pulled her against him. She could feel his erection against her thigh. She wanted him. Oh, how she wanted him! She did.

"Lucas," she gasped, straining to sit up so she could remove her camisole. "Undress me. Hurry!"

Lucas complied, his breathing heavy, his erection pressing between her thighs, against the very center of her nakedness.

"Honey, slow down. I don't want to hurt you—"

"You won't!"

"I don't want to rush you—"

"Please!" she begged, and with no further urging, Lucas pushed into her, hard and hot and filling her completely. She gasped and froze in horror. It was no different—she couldn't breathe, she couldn't see, she was...she was *dying*.

Panicked, Virginia closed her mouth tight against Lucas's probing kisses. If she kissed him now, she would gag. She would scream. She had to keep her fear inside, deep in her throat, keep it all to herself.

It was only sex, for heaven's sake, not torture, she reminded herself. *Making love.* This was Lucas, the man she'd married, not some dreadful stranger who hurt her and hurt her and hurt her again....

"What's wrong, honey, what's wrong?" Lucas asked hoarsely, but his words sounded animalistic to her, squeezed out between breaths as he thrust deeper into her. And deeper. She shut her eyes and refused to answer him. She forced herself to wrap her arms around his neck so he couldn't see her face. She prayed it would be over soon.

Lucas's movements became stronger, more rhythmic, his breathing harsher. She arched to meet him, hoping he'd believe her frantic movements were inspired by passion, not terror.

Suddenly it didn't matter anymore. Lucas made a sound and she felt his seed spill inside her, hot and fluid. Then he groaned again, murmured something and collapsed on her, and she felt everything dissolve around her. She screamed and screamed again, clawing at him.

"What the—?" Lucas put one hand over her mouth to stop her screams and she fought him, scratching at his shoulders and neck, and tore his hand away from her mouth and screamed some more. Lucas rolled off her and pulled her into his arms, and the sound of her screaming, which she seemed to hear from outside her own body, was muffled, then stopped. She realized she was weeping uncontrollably, deep, dry, painful sobs, and Lucas was holding her close.

"Oh, shit, honey. I'm sorry. I'm so sorry. I...I just didn't think—"

The phone beside the bed rang. Lucas let it ring four times, then picked it up.

"Mr. Yellowfly?"

"Y-yes?" Lucas tried hard to control his breathing. He'd just had sex with his bride, mere minutes ago, and she'd damn near hollered the hotel down. He had a feeling it wasn't because of his superior lovemaking.

"This is Peter at the front desk, sir. I'm sorry to disturb you. We've had a call from a guest who reported hearing screams in the vicinity of your suite. Are you all right, sir?"

"I'm fine."

"Mrs. Yellowfly? Is she all right? Is she with you, sir?"

"She's fine. She's with me. She had, er, she had a bit of a surprise, that's all."

"Fine, sir. I'm glad to hear there's no problem."

Lucas hung up the phone wearily, wondering if Peter had overheard Virginia's frantic sobs. He hoped not.

There was a loud knock on the door. "Mr. Yellowfly?"

Lucas mumbled a couple of choice cowboy oaths and stumbled out of bed, grabbing the hotel-supplied terry robe from the chair nearby. He whipped open the door. Two men in hotel security uniforms stood there, worried looks on their faces.

"What can I do for you, gentlemen?"

"We met a guest in the elevator who said there was a commotion in your room, sir. We just wanted to check that everything was okay."

"Thank you for taking the trouble. Everything's just fine." He decided a flat lie would not be amiss. "My wife saw a bug."

"A bug? At the Banff Springs?" The older of the security men frowned. The other stood goggle-eyed behind him. "I'd better take care of that, sir—"

"It's taken care of. I squashed it," Lucas lied again. He was beyond caring. "I hit it with a shoe and threw it out the window."

"Out the window? Oh. Very good, sir. We're sorry to have bothered you." With a brief, curious glance over Lucas's shoulder, the senior security man bowed slightly and turned, the other one right behind him. Lucas was glad the bed was out of sight from the door.

He closed the door firmly, locked it and fastened the security latch. He wasn't opening it again; he didn't care who knocked.

Virginia was still sobbing faintly when he got into bed. He held her and stroked her back, hoping to soothe her. "I'm sorry, Lucas," she kept mumbling, between sobs. "I'm so sorry."

"Never mind, honey, just relax. Everything'll be all right."

He wanted to believe that. How he wanted to believe that. Then he thought back over the events of the past half hour or so. He'd thought she was as hot for him as he was for her. Obviously she'd been faking it. She was totally screwed up from that rape six years ago.

Maybe everything *wouldn't* be all right. At least not in the very near future.

He sighed. Poor Virginia. Poor him. What a hell of a way for a guy to spend his wedding night.

CHAPTER THIRTEEN

LUCAS COULDN'T SLEEP. He lay there for what seemed like hours, but when he looked at the faintly illuminated digital clock on the bedside table, it was just 2:00 a.m. Virginia had finally dozed off, exhausted. He'd held her until his arm cramped, then gently eased her away from him. He stretched out, arms above his head, and tried to think the whole thing through.

This had to do with Johnny. He was dead sure of it. *That bastard.* The rape was bad enough. But at least she had Robert. He knew she loved her son with all her heart. Despite the circumstances, he was damn sure she'd never regretted Robert's coming into her life, not for an instant.

But what if Johnny had left her afraid of men? Physically? What if that had been the real reason behind her admitted lack of interest in dating? He'd just assumed she'd had a few relationships since then, no matter what she'd said. They'd never talked about it. He'd always thought it best to let sleeping dogs lie. She was an adult; as far as he knew, she'd dealt with what had happened. It was past. It was none of his business.

Damn it. It *was* his business now. His wife

screamed when he made love to her. She was scared to death. She'd made up her mind she'd go through with their wedding night because she was a rational woman who knew very well that her husband wasn't the man who'd hurt her. But what had happened? It'd been goddamn Johnny Gagnon in bed with her. Not him. Not Lucas Yellowfly. Not the man who loved her.

He owed Gagnon. If he ever saw him in town…

For a moment Lucas's blood boiled, then he reminded himself that the law was there to take care of guys like Gagnon. Lucas had pledged himself to the law and to justice. Gagnon would be on parole. He'd have to be minding his p's and q's when he got out. He couldn't bother Virginia or Robert without risking trouble. Sure, he'd never been prosecuted for rape, but he'd spent the past five or six years in jail regardless, on other charges.

Why in hell Virginia hadn't had Johnny charged with rape was beyond him. Wait a minute—he should know better. He'd had clients himself who'd resisted pressing charges when they'd been sexually assaulted. When the time came to guide them through the legal process, they'd lost courage. The prospect of laying open their entire lives for the public to see had been overwhelming. And, as in Virginia's case, if a woman had had a previous relationship with the guy…well, juries were only human. Sometimes they reasoned that if she'd done it willingly before, what made this time any different? It became an issue of consent and the victim—

in this case, Virginia—could be dragged through hell.

Cruel and unjust, but true. Maybe that was why Virginia, even with her superior knowledge of the law, had done what a lot of women before her had done. She'd lost her nerve. Who could blame her?

Still, where did that leave them?

And, more specifically, where did it leave him? With a wife who was terrified of physical intimacy. It was his problem now, but it was Johnny Gagnon who was to blame. Lucas wanted to make love with his wife and he couldn't make love with his wife.

He turned and feasted his eyes on the woman sleeping beside him. *His bride.* He loved her. He'd never really loved anyone else, he knew that now, except maybe his mother and his sister and his dad, in the good times. And Tammy, of course. And one or two good buddies, like Adam, but that was different.

But nothing else was like this love he felt for Virginia. This held his entire future. His happiness. Children of their own, maybe. He reached out and lifted a curly tendril of her hair, spread in riotous abandon on the white linen of the pillow. It was soft and resilient, strong. Like Virginia. Beautiful. Like Virginia.

He ran his fingertip lightly over the bridge of her nose, down the curve of her cheek, not quite touching her, just tracing the outline of her features. Her lips were soft and relaxed in sleep. How he wanted to kiss her, to take her in his arms, to wake her slowly, to make love to her again. To have her respond, to smile, to look at him with a light in her eyes.

Not to scream in terror.

Lucas sighed and lay back and closed his eyes.

He had to make it happen. Somehow he had to make things work.

NEXT MORNING at breakfast, Lucas quietly asked Virginia to pack up her stuff. They were leaving.

"Leaving?" she asked, startled. It was a gorgeous day. The mountains beckoned. She thought maybe they could go for a long walk in the alpine meadows this afternoon. Or laze in the hot springs.

"I think we should," he said with a small smile. "Considering I told them you'd seen a bug in our room last night and that's why you screamed the place down."

"A b-bug?" She practically choked on her coffee. She felt her cheeks burn. She knew exactly what he was referring to, whether he mentioned it that morning or not.

"I was going to say a spider, but I didn't get that far," he replied with a glance at their waiter who hovered just outside hearing distance. "Everyone knows women hate spiders," he added in a low voice. "Right?"

Virginia couldn't help smiling. "And how did you dispose of the, er, bug?"

"I smacked it with a shoe and tossed it out the window," Lucas said, deadpan.

Virginia choked again, this time with laughter. "You didn't!"

"I did." Lucas put down his napkin and gestured for the bill. He quickly signed their room number and stood. "Let's go. Before the Rocky Mountain Insect Protection Society gets on our case."

Twenty minutes later, in the car, he told her they were headed back to Calgary. He'd booked them into the Palliser Hotel for the remainder of their honeymoon and purchased tickets to a play, made reservations at a fancy restaurant and lined up a hot-air-balloon ride for the next day.

"Not scared of heights, are you?" he asked with a sideways glance, driving a little faster than he should have, in her opinion.

"No. I'm looking forward to it." She was. She'd been horrified at her screaming fit the night before, probably no less horrified than he must have been. Lucas had said nothing. He seemed to understand intuitively that her fear was a legacy of the past, that it had nothing whatsoever to do with him. *Thank heaven.*

That was the truth. She could only pray things would be different the next time he wanted to make love to her. Whenever that next time might be. And she had to talk to him about it. She couldn't go through another night like last night.

Lucas was the perfect new husband. He was charming. He was sweet. He was funny. He knew just how to make her laugh, and they laughed a lot over the next couple of days. He always had an idea for something to do while they were in Calgary, whether it was a visit to the pioneer park or a trip to an exclusive jewelry shop to buy her some sterling-silver earrings, inset with the Alberta gemstone, korite, mined from ancient fossilized ammonite deposits in the St. Mary River Valley near Lethbridge.

She loved the hot-air-balloon ride and wished Robert could be with them to share it. Lucas promised he'd bring Robert and Tammy someday soon.

"Isn't it amazing?" she breathed, glancing up at the huge multicolored balloon suspended so high above them. Then, feeling brave, she peeked over the side to see the cattle and horses below—they looked like miniature farm animals—the fields laid out like a patchwork quilt.

"Yikes," she said softly, clutching Lucas's hand and stepping back. The wind blew his hair and he gazed over the side, his profile hard and chiseled and so handsome. His hair was very dark, as one would expect knowing his heritage. His eyes were shot with gold, a warm honey-brown that could look wickedly funny one minute and hot and passionate the next.

"Scared?" He grinned suddenly at her and put his arm firmly around her shoulders. She nestled into his solid warmth. He glanced up at the balloon high above them, too. The operator grinned and waved, adjusting the burner that shot heat upward into the balloon's silken skin to keep it flying.

"Not really," she whispered, sheltered and secure in Lucas's embrace. "It's just so...so amazing to think we can be in the sky like this, with just some hot air keeping us up, isn't it?"

Their eyes locked. Virginia felt her stomach tumble, and it wasn't just the lurch of the basket they stood in.

"It *is* amazing, Virginia," he said, and he kissed her. "It's like so many other things, isn't it? You've just got to trust it. Close your eyes and just trust it."

She nodded, feeling the wind whip moisture in her eyes. "I know what you mean," she said, blinking rapidly. "I do."

But for the three nights they stayed in Calgary, Lucas made no attempt to make love to her. They slept together in the big bed in their suite, and he held her and they talked until she fell asleep. She always fell asleep before he did, it seemed. And she fell asleep feeling safe for the first time in a long, long time.

IT ONLY TOOK A FEW HOURS to move into Lucas's big white house on Second Avenue. And it only took a few days to fall into a routine.

Lucas left for work early every morning and Virginia walked Tammy and Robert to school. Then she went into the office to complete the research she'd started for Lucas and work on the plan she'd begun for updating the law firm's computer and communications system. Sometimes she had lunch with Lucas; sometimes she had lunch with Nancy, who'd been agog at what she considered to be their whirlwind office romance, but who'd adjusted rapidly. Natasha Jarvis still walked the children home from school, only now they both came home to the same place.

Robert had his bunk beds in the room next to

Tammy's, and his disappointment at not being able to continue his I Spy game on the townsfolk of Glory was tempered by the discovery that the small square door in his wall led to a secret space under the eaves of the old house, a space probably used at one time for storing luggage and boxes of unused household items. It became Robert and Teddy's secret fort and was soon outfitted with foam mattresses and sleeping bags and stacks of *Archie* and *Caspar the Ghost* comics. Lucas installed a single low-wattage bare bulb in the hiding space, and Robert was in heaven.

After ten days at home, Lucas still hadn't tried to make love to her. Virginia was worried. But worried enough to...do what? She didn't know. She was past the point of seeking advice from women's magazines. It was up to her, really. Lucas was no doubt waiting for some signal. Maybe she should see a doctor about her problem. Maybe she needed therapy. But was the time right for that? She had just gotten married. Maybe she should give marriage and Lucas a chance.

Virginia often brought work home, which she'd go through after dinner when Lucas had to work late. He was just finishing an important trial preparation and, since they'd returned from their short honeymoon, had worked late several nights. Was it because he wanted to avoid her? More than once, Virginia had been in bed when he'd come home and she'd faked sleep. She was appalled at herself and at her deception. But she was more appalled at the thought of her husband making love with her.

Tonight—a Tuesday—Virginia sat up late copying some notes she'd made on a visit that day to the land-registry office in Lethbridge. She kept stopping, listening to the occasional creak and sigh of the old house, sure she could hear something else. It was windy, and many of the leaves had already blown off the Norway maples in the backyard. She reminded herself that all the curtains were drawn. No one could look in and see her working there by herself. And Lucas had phoned fifteen minutes earlier to tell her he'd be leaving soon.

She heard it again. A muffled, scraping sound.

Virginia got to her feet, feeling her heart jump into overdrive. The children were both fast asleep upstairs—weren't they? She walked quietly to the foot of the stairs.

Robert was perched on the top step, his limp toy husky tucked under his chin, a baby gesture. The dog had suffered all these years from a gradual dribble of its stuffing, which was now terminal. Robert also had his quilt tucked around him, as though he'd been sitting there a long time and was cold.

"Robert! What are you doing up, honey?" she asked softly, slowly going up the stairs toward her son. He looked so small and young sitting there, his dark hair rumpled, his eyes asking big important questions. He *was* small and young. She didn't need to remind herself that to her he was practically still a baby.

She sank down beside him and put her arm around him. He leaned against her and sighed. "Did you have a bad dream, honey?"

He shook his head.

"Couldn't you sleep?"

He shook his head again. "No," he muttered in a gruff voice, and sighed again.

"What were you thinking about?" She stroked his rumpled hair from his forehead, hardly daring to ask.

Robert was silent for a long time. Finally he stirred and looked up into her face. "Is Lucas my *real* dad, Mom? You can tell me. I won't care."

Virginia was startled. Hadn't they been through this already? "No, honey. He's not. Remember he told you that once when we were in the truck? That was the truth."

"When we went to the Grizzly place?"

"Yes." She took his hand and held it warmly between both of hers. "But Lucas is your dad now, isn't he? We're a family now, you and me and him. And—" she was suddenly inspired "—Tammy's your cousin now. I'll bet you like that."

"I guess so. But..." He hesitated.

"But what, honey?"

"I want a real dad, Mom. Just like Teddy's got. His dad takes him fishing and camping and they go to movies and dig up stuff down at the river. Arrowheads and neat stuff. I want to do that with *my* dad, too."

"Families are all different, Robert. You know that. Remember Amy Pilchard? The little girl who lived next door to us in Stettler?"

He nodded gravely.

"She was adopted. Her mommy and daddy

picked her to be their very own little girl. That's just as real as can be, even though they didn't have her in a hospital or anything.'' Virginia bit her lip, praying Robert was old enough to understand.

"But Teddy's got his own mom and dad. And so do lots of kids in Glory.''

"And now you do, too,'' she said gently. "Lucas isn't your real, *real* dad, but I'm your real mom and Lucas is going to adopt you so you'll really be his little boy. Like Amy and her mom and dad.''

"Forever and ever?''

Virginia nodded. "Forever and ever.'' Was there such a thing as forever? Was it fair to pretend to a child that there was?

"And Grandpa Lake's going to take you fishing pretty soon. He told me he's looking for a little fishing rod just the right size for you. Maybe Lucas will take you fishing, too, if you want. I don't know if he likes fishing or not. Not everyone does, you know.''

Robert sighed, a big sigh that came all the way from his toes and made her heart ache. "I know. I don't want to kill the fish or anything. I just want to see them wiggle around.''

Virginia stood, three steps lower, and picked him up. "Now it's time for my big boy to go to sleep. Don't forget it's school tomorrow and Mrs. Brown is taking everyone to the sheep farm.''

Robert smiled sleepily. "I know. And there's going to be baby sheep there, too. Maybe pigs. Tammy said.'' He put his arm around her neck and allowed her to carry him to his room and tuck him into bed.

He yawned and snuggled up to his toy husky and Virginia knew he'd be asleep within minutes. She bent down and kissed him. His baby scent had given way a year or two ago to the sourish little-boy smell, what she imagined dirt to smell like, and new jeans. It wasn't often Robert allowed her to kiss him anymore, but he did at bedtime and when they were alone.

She closed the door carefully behind her. How many nights had he lain awake wondering? How happy was he—really—with her marriage? Was she wrong not to tell him about Johnny? But what could she say?

She had no doubt he liked Lucas. Liked him a lot. But he knew Lucas wasn't his real father. And that seemed to matter a great deal to her son. Maybe the answer was to have more children. A baby. A brother or sister for Robert. To make sure they really were a family. Virginia had started birth-control pills just before her marriage. Getting pregnant had seemed like the last thing she'd ever want then. *Another nightmare.* But it didn't have to be that way, did it? She wasn't alone or lonely anymore.

Of course, to get pregnant, you had to make love with your husband occasionally.

When she got back down the stairs, she heard the characteristic sound of Lucas fumbling with his key at the front door. Her heart leaped. Already she knew that sound as well as she knew the sound of her own heartbeat.

Thank goodness!

Lucas opened the door, handsome, a little tired-looking, his eyes going straight to hers. He always seemed happy to see her. She smiled nervously and stepped toward him.

"Hey!" He reached for her and she wrapped her arms around his neck and burrowed her face in his shoulder. "Whoa...this is nice. Look, I brought us a couple slices of cheesecake from Molly's. She was just closing up."

Lucas stepped back from her and wrestled off his jacket. He handed her a brown paper bag. She peeked in. "Lemon?"

"Yeah." He hung his jacket in the hall closet. "I knew you liked lemon. Was I right?"

"You were." Virginia allowed herself to smile. She was happy to see Lucas tonight. Happier than ever before. Was it her talk with Robert? Had that brought home to her just how lucky they were, both of them?

Lucas stepped close to her again and pulled her into his arms. "Mmm." He kissed her, a kiss that started out brief and warm, as so many of his kisses were lately, and then turned into something else as she responded. She felt her blood hammer in her ears. She let the brown bag drop to the surface of the nearby hall table and slid both arms around Lucas and pressed herself against him.

"Oh, baby," he whispered. He kissed her once more, then, to her dismay, withdrew. He picked up his briefcase and tossed it onto the hall table, retrieved the brown bag and walked through to the kitchen. Virginia followed.

"Any coffee on? How about some decaf?" he asked her, running water into the sink.

Virginia hesitated a second or two. "Sure."

"I'll make it." Lucas whistled as he went through the familiar motions of measuring out the water and ground coffee. He told her a joke that Pete had told him, then mentioned that Nancy had a new boyfriend; both he and Pete thought so, anyway. Virginia wondered what sort of facts or nonfacts a couple of men would base that deduction on, but didn't ask. She wasn't interested in Pete's jokes or Nancy's new boyfriend.

She was interested in how her blood had tumbled in her veins, a slow, galactic rush, when her husband had come in the door. She was interested in the taste of his kisses, which she still felt on her mouth. Not coffee or cheesecake. She was interested in seeing him take his clothes off and climb into their bed with her....

"Lucas," she said, and went up to him, putting her hand on his arm. With the other hand she blindly reached for the coffeemaker and pushed the On button to Off.

"Hey, hon—" He looked surprised.

"Let's go upstairs," she said. "Let's go to bed."

"Oh, sweetheart," Lucas said, burying his face in her hair. "That's the best idea I've heard all day." He kissed her, a fierce lover's kiss, and Virginia raised herself on tiptoe to meet him. *Yes!* This was what she wanted.

Then, somehow, they were upstairs in their darkened bedroom. The wind creaked in the maple outside the window. Virginia realized they were whispering, less at the thought of waking the children—who were sound asleep at the other end of the hall behind closed doors—than at the enormity of what they were doing.

They were husband and wife; they were going to make love freely and with open hearts for the first time. Finally.

Then they were both under the light down duvet. Virginia giggled as Lucas reached for her in the dark. She wrapped her arms around his neck and her legs around his body. She felt him, ready and hard, pushing eagerly against her.

"Let's take this slowly, honey," Lucas said, and urged her down on the bed beside him. He began to kiss her face, her neck, her breasts, until she was frantic with desire. And then, when she didn't think she could stand it anymore, he moved over her, and she arched to meet him.

The feeling, as he pressed into her, was like a shock of icy water. Ice and broken glass and a lingering, horrible death. Panic nearly choked her and she fought it back, wave after wave, as Lucas began to move rhythmically over her, murmuring her name, caressing her hair, kissing her mouth as she tried not to gag. Did he realize? Did he *know?*

It was no good. As Lucas burst inside her, she stiffened, her body jumping with fear, her mind jittering with panic. She shoved her fist in her open mouth to stop her screams. Only the thought of the children down the hall, safe and trusting, gave her the strength to stay silent.

But Lucas knew. He groaned and folded his arms around her and stilled her hot, trembling body. He murmured gentle sounds, words she couldn't make out. He sighed. She heard his heart race beneath her cheek and then gradually slow.

She'd tried; she'd wanted him—*she had!* But nothing made any difference at all. She wasn't a woman anymore. She was a living, breathing mannequin, someone who went through the gestures of being a mother, a wife, of being alive. Of going to work every day.

But at her very heart, she was icy cold.

She was terrified. She had to get help.

CHAPTER FOURTEEN

WHEN LUCAS CAME DOWN for breakfast the next morning, the two children were tucking into the cheesecake.

"No Cheerios?" He tossed his jacket on the back of a chair and punched the coffeemaker button to On.

"We found this stuff in the fridge," Tammy said. "Too bad there were only two pieces. You could've had one."

"Yeah." Lucas grinned. "Too bad." And if things had gone the way he'd hoped they would last night, he and Virginia would have gobbled up every crumb in bed, after a satisfactory sexual experience. He would even have brought up coffee and cups on a tray. He'd have done *anything*.

He popped two pieces of bread into the toaster and opened the fridge, surveying the contents. That was one nice thing about family life—always lots of goodies in the refrigerator. He pulled out a carton of yogurt and spooned some into a bowl, then sprinkled raisin granola on top.

"Breakfast," he said, setting his bowl on the table with a flourish.

"Yuck!" the two children said in unison, then

both shouted, "Jinx!" which he'd realized in the past month was what kids did when two of them accidentally said the same thing at the same time. As far as he could tell, there was no payoff.

He poured a coffee for himself and sat down at the table.

"Hi, Mom!"

Lucas glanced up. Virginia had paused at the door to the kitchen, still in her fuzzy pink bathrobe. She looked haunted. He didn't feel too bad, considering the amount of sleep he'd had last night—considering the amount of sleep he'd had since they'd gotten married. "Hi, Robert. Hi, Tammy."

"Good morning, sunshine," Lucas said, as he did every morning when he got downstairs before she did.

She gave him a wan smile. If he could have done her suffering for her, he would have. "Good morning, Lucas." She moved to the counter and poured herself a mug of coffee, then brought it to the table and joined them, sitting opposite Lucas. Her glance at him was strained, watchful. Her hair was loose and wild on her shoulders. Her freckles stood out boldly against the paleness of her skin.

"Field trip today, Robert?" he said, finishing the last of his cereal and yogurt.

"Yep. We're going to the Websters' farm. The whole class," he said proudly, looking at Tammy. "On a bus." Tammy seemed very sophisticated for grade three, in her short denim skirt and matching jacket. He'd bought the outfit for her the last week of August, along with several hundred dollars' worth of other things.

Tammy got up and put her plate and fork in the sink and opened the refrigerator. "Want me to make you a surprise lunch, Robbie?" she asked.

"Would you, honey?" Virginia said. Usually she made her son's lunch in the morning, but Tammy insisted on preparing her own.

"Sure." Tammy competently set the makings for sandwiches on the counter. She pulled four slices of bread out of a bag and began buttering them on a cutting board.

"No rice cakes, Tammy," Robert said sternly.

"Why not?" Lucas asked, slipping his jacket on. He bent quickly to kiss Virginia on the back of the neck. She smiled at him, a more confident smile than before. God, how he loved her! If they could just get through this, if they could just put this nightmare behind them... Was therapy the way to go? Was it too early to mention that? It wasn't something he felt good about; he'd always thought therapy was overrated and, well, for your basic incompetents who couldn't face up to reality. Of course, he was probably wrong about that, he thought wryly. He was probably wrong about lots of other things, too.

"Rice cakes are for girls," Robert said, sticking out his tongue. "Girl food. Yuck!"

Virginia remonstrated with her son, telling him to mind his manners and not to stick his tongue out at people, especially Tammy, who was going to all the trouble of making him a special lunch for his field trip.

Lucas paused at the hall entrance. "I'll be in court all morning, Virginia. Molly's at one?"

"Sure," she said, and nodded. When she smiled again, he walked back into the kitchen to drop a last kiss on her mouth. He headed toward the front door, stopping to grab gloves and scarf from the hall closet.

The day was bright but cold. It was nearly the middle of November already, and the days were noticeably shorter. Only one light snowfall, last week, but plenty of frost. He knew they'd get a lot more snow before Christmas.

Still no sign of Johnny Gagnon.

Thank heaven. With luck, maybe he'd never come back to Glory. Lucas started the BMW and let it idle for a few minutes, the exhaust filling the air behind him. He adjusted the rearview mirror; Virginia had driven the car yesterday, while hers was at the garage having winter tires installed. He'd walked home from work last night.

If Johnny came back, Lucas would know. He'd made a few inquiries among his friends in the system, and he was pretty sure he'd find out before Virginia did. When Johnny Gagnon came back—*if* he came back—Virginia was going to need all the support he could give her. Maybe he should talk to her about laying charges now, all these years after the fact. Would that help her put the whole damn thing behind her? Help her get on with the future? With him?

Luckily he worked in a profession where you couldn't waste time obsessing about your personal life. Your clients, especially in court, needed your full attention.

That morning Lucas was defending a man who'd been charged with hit-and-run. He'd allegedly knocked down an elderly lady who'd been jaywalking and then he'd driven on. The victim had sustained bruises and a slight concussion. Lucas's client claimed he wasn't driving at the time; he'd spent the afternoon in the tavern at the Glory Hotel and slept off his drunkenness in the feed room of his son-in-law's barn.

Unfortunately plenty of people had seen him drinking, but nobody had seen him sleeping it off, which meant his alibi wasn't exactly airtight. On the other hand, several witnesses had seen his car hit the woman. No one could swear as to who'd actually been driving the vehicle—the only oar Lucas had in an extremely leaky boat.

Of course, it was abundantly clear that if his client *was* telling the truth, he'd driven to his son-in-law's place dead drunk. But that wasn't the charge.

Lucas wasn't convinced of his client's complete innocence, but he intended to get him off on the suspicion that maybe someone else had been driving the car. Which could well have been the case with the Baxter bunch from out Cayley way. Lucas was sure a couple of his client's brothers and cousins shared one or two license plates that they switched from one wreck to another, depending on which was most drivable at the time. Naturally he didn't plan to mention that little detail.

As it was, the judge finished hearing the case by

noon. Not guilty. Lucas heaved a sigh of relief and gave his client a blistering lecture as they left the courtroom, telling him just how lucky he'd been and how one of these days Lucas wasn't going to get him off. Especially if he kept driving drunk. Ned Baxter was so pleased about his acquittal he insisted on buying Lucas a beer. Lucas demurred. Somehow he didn't think it would go over well to be seen hoisting a beer in the Glory Hotel with his hard-drinking client. Especially after beating a hit-and-run rap that most of the town felt pretty sure was warranted.

No doubt he'd be a long time getting paid, too. Ah, well, that was small-town practice for you. He'd get it out of Ned and his cousins one way or another before the next time one of them needed Lucas's services. Maybe a load of firewood. He could use it now that he had two fireplaces in his new house. Or maybe Ned could do a favor for someone Lucas owed—that was how it worked in small towns sometimes.

He headed over to Molly's. He knew he was early, but he thought he'd get a table and grab a coffee and read the paper, which he hadn't had time to do that morning. He walked in and stood for a moment, taking a quick look around to see who was there.

Donna Beaton was sitting at a table by herself, finishing up a salad and a cup of soup. She waved and he joined her, first picking up this week's *Plain Dealer* from a stack of free copies by the cash register.

"You by yourself?" He slid into the booth opposite her.

"Yes. I've got a new girl in the shop and I'm just grabbing a quick lunch. How've you been? How's marriage?"

He'd dated Donna for five or six months two years before. She was a little older than he was, a divorcée with two children, and she ran a busy little gift shop in town. Donna was a treasure. Half the men in town had gone out with her at one time or another, but she was still friends with them all. She had a talent for friendship.

"Great. I've been in love with Virginia Lake most of my life, you know." He grinned, setting down his newspaper and unwrapping the scarf from around his neck.

"Oh? I didn't know that." Donna looked interested. "You didn't tell me."

"Well, maybe not. I never thought I'd see her again." He held up his hand to the waitress to show he wanted coffee and pointed at an empty booth by the window, to indicate he'd be moving there by the time the coffee arrived. "Yeah. Old story. Bad boy falls for society girl. Her parents pack her out of town to keep them apart." Lucas heaved a dramatic sigh. "Now she's back in town and bad boy—who's now a good boy—marries her."

"Happy ending?" Donna's brown eyes gleamed with humor.

"Pretty much." Lucas leaned toward her. "I'm having some problems though, Donna. Maybe you'd understand, being a woman."

"Problems?"

"She was hurt bad, back in the past. I can't seem to beat it. Can't seem to get around it."

"Sex?" Donna mouthed.

Lucas nodded.

"An old boyfriend, I presume," she continued in a low voice.

"Yeah." Lucas sighed again. He had no intention of abusing Virginia's privacy by divulging the details. He'd just thought maybe Donna could give him some insight. She was good at that.

"Didn't Virginia go out with that Gagnon boy? Cecilia and Phil's nephew? The one who's been in and out of jail since he got out of high school?"

"Yeah. Where'd you hear that?" Lucas frowned—although he realized he wasn't the only one in town who knew about Virginia's past.

"Someone told me at the post office, I think." Donna returned to her soup. "Maybe it was Noah…but, no, that's not like him."

"Noah? You seeing Noah Winslow these days?"

She nodded, coloring slightly. Donna had to be in her late-thirties, but she showed an uncommon aptitude for every deeply feminine quality, including blushing. It was amazing. Maybe that was part of her enormous appeal to men of all kinds, young and old.

"Good for you. I didn't think Noah had time for anything but cows and semen counts and worrying about whether it was going to rain next week."

"You're too hard on him," Donna murmured,

and blotted her mouth with her napkin. "He's a very nice man."

"Post office—ha!" Lucas snorted. "Myrna Schultz, I'd guess. Hell. You don't need to send a letter in this town. You just need to stop in at the post office and say hello to Myrna."

"Never mind. Give Virginia time, Lucas. You've just been married…what? Three weeks?"

"Three weeks on Friday."

"You've got your whole life ahead of you. Don't rush her. I'm sure you'll work it out. Some things take time." Donna made a discreet motion with her head, directing Lucas's attention elsewhere. Lucas took a quick glance at a booth behind her. Henry Hilton, Cal Blake's foreman, had been courting Letty Esperanza for a couple of years now. They were still at the stage of Letty doing all the talking and Henry doing all the listening. Maybe that would never change. The old cowpoke was smiling at his Filipina sweetheart, his sparse gray hair combed down firmly, aided, from the look of it, by a little Brylcreem. His worn ten-gallon hat was handy on the seat beside him, just in case he had to take off somewhere in a hurry, Lucas supposed.

He grinned. Donna had a point.

"Maybe she's just shy?" Donna continued. "This has all been awfully fast, hasn't it?"

"I guess so." Lucas glanced out the window. "There she is now. As far as I'm concerned, she'll get all the time she needs." His voice softened and his companion looked at him sharply, pausing with her spoon in midair. Then she smiled and continued with her meal.

"Well," Lucas said, rising and picking up his scarf and newspaper. "I'd better grab that booth. She's meeting me for lunch."

"What happened with old Ned Baxter this morning?"

"Got him off."

"You didn't!" Donna laughed and shook her head. "You ought to be ashamed of yourself, Lucas Yellowfly! That old boozer?"

"That's the law, Donna. A man's entitled to a defense. That's what I did—I defended him."

Still smiling and shaking her head, Donna set her bowl aside and picked up her coffee cup.

Lucas watched Virginia enter the crowded diner and look around. Her face lit up when she saw him and he felt like rushing forward and kissing her right there in front of the whole town. He didn't. He stood, though, and smiled as she exchanged a few words with Donna, then took her seat opposite him. They sat down at the same time and he leaned forward and clasped her hands. They were cold. Her cheeks were rosy and her eyes shone.

"So?" she said. "How'd it go?"

"Got the old fool off."

"Congratulations!" At least Virginia understood what it meant to win a case. "You worked hard on that. What's the special?"

"Barley soup and a veggie burger. Yeah, I did. Now we need to move on to that Sparks business

again. Did you find out anything in Lethbridge yesterday?''

They talked about the case Virginia was research-
ing for him, but the whole time Lucas kept seeing
the fear on her face when he'd made love to her last
night. When would they talk about that? Not now,
certainly. But soon. He couldn't stand it anymore.
He didn't know which way to turn. She'd wanted
him last night, he knew that for a fact. Yet, once
they'd actually got started, she'd been thrown into
another panic. At least she hadn't screamed. Maybe
that was progress. Either way, it was damned hard
on a man's ego.

He listened to her through the buzz of the lunch-
time diner, only half-hearing what she was saying,
aware of people looking at them, surreptitiously
studying him and his bride. He thought of the secret
knowledge he now had of the sprinkling of freckles
on the inside of her left thigh. He still wasn't really
used to the joy of knowing she'd actually married
him. Of the town knowing she was his wife and that
he loved her. That they were a family now—Virginia and Robert and him. And Tammy, of course,
until Theresa sent for her.

''Lucas?''

''Mm?''

''About last night.'' She blushed and he ached at
the pain he saw in her eyes.

He put his hands over hers again, squeezed them
gently. ''Hey, never mind, honey—''

''I'm sorry. I really am. If you think I should get
some kind of help...''

"Maybe. We'll see." He squeezed her hands again. "If you want to go that route, that's up to you."

"I want things to be different, you know that. I'll do anything."

"I know. And they will be different. Eventually. We'll just keep trying." Maybe they could try some different positions; maybe they could find something that worked for her.

She smiled as though she didn't really believe him and turned her attention to the menu.

He wasn't giving up. *Ever!* This wasn't like some legal case—win some, lose some. That he could handle.

This one he had to win at all costs. He'd accept nothing less.

THAT NIGHT they were scheduled to go to the Lakes' for dinner. At first Virginia had assumed Tammy and Robert were invited, too, until her mother had gently set her straight.

"I think it's so hard on children, don't you? Having to be on their best behavior and make conversation with adults? Why don't you get a baby-sitter, darling, and I'll order pizza for them. They can have pizza at home on Grandma!"

Virginia had agreed, knowing her mother was right. Still, she wished her parents would develop a more up-to-date view of children, maybe even plan an evening around them for once. It wasn't as though she and Lucas were keen on these formal dinners with her parents' friends, anyway. Why not a family night with pizza and a video?

She sighed as she reached for a light wool dress in her closet. She'd been out of the shower for five minutes and had heard Lucas enter their bathroom while she was dressing.

She knew her mother and father would never change. It was just as well that the children were staying home, for their *own* sakes. The whole evening would no doubt be a major bore. She stepped into the dress and was just buttoning up the front when Lucas came out of the bathroom. He looked magnificent—still gleaming with droplets of water, a towel cinched around his waist. He was a beautiful man. And he loved her. Or so he'd told her many times. Why couldn't she trust him? Why couldn't she believe him in her heart?

There was no question that he made her pulse race. Just his physical presence there in the bedroom, sifting through his shirts in the closet, was enough to do that.

"What do you think?" he murmured. "Pink silk or white cotton?"

"I'd guess cotton. Maybe Sea Island? It's that kind of crowd," she said dryly. She went to her dresser and picked out the pearls her parents had given her for her twenty-first birthday.

"Here," Lucas said. "Let me fasten that." He shrugged on a pale yellow cotton shirt—a compromise, she suspected—and stepped behind her to fasten her pearls. She was aware of him behind her, all of him. Male, physical, exciting—the kind of man any woman would be happy to have in her bed. He dropped a kiss on her neck that sent shivers down to her toes and stepped back to do up his shirt buttons.

"There. Give me five minutes and I'll be ready. I didn't know that meeting with Sparks would take so long. We had to go through his financing bit by bit. He's still trying to pull off his land acquisition, although it looks like he won't be able to buy that piece from Danny Weaselfat, after all. There's no title unfortunately. The guy who sold it in the first place never had proper ownership at all."

Virginia was relieved that Lucas was talking about the case he was working on. She'd noticed that, although he'd said he didn't care to discuss business at home, he often did, especially when they were alone. In their bedroom. Was he trying to distance himself? As she always tried to do?

If so, perhaps there was less chance for the two of them to work things out than she hoped. Still, they could hardly be pawing each other when they had a dinner date in twenty minutes.

The Lakes had invited three other couples. Lucas's partner, Pete Horsfall and his wife, Babs—now *where* had she ever received such a name? Virginia wondered. The woman was pure battleship through and through, and her only interest, besides her grandchildren, was her garden. On the other side of the table, polished and gleaming with Doris Lake's finest china and crystal, were the retired publisher of the Glory weekly, the *Plain Dealer,* George Frizzell, and his sister, Bernice, who went everywhere with him. Frizzell's wife had died decades ago and his spinster sister had moved into the family home and taken over managing his life. George hadn't objected. By the time Lucas and Virginia arrived, only ten minutes late, the publisher was pretty well tanked, which was his state much of the time, according to her mother.

"We'd rather not invite him, dear," her mother had confided once. "He's such an *embarrassment* the way he nods off and starts snoring—sometimes even at the table! But he's an old friend and we've known him for years and we could hardly abandon him now, could we?"

The other couple consisted of one of the town's young doctors, Kate Pleasance, and her friend, a rather morose Ukrainian forester, introduced to them as Orest Boychuk.

Lucas was the soul of wit and charming manners. He'd brought Mrs. Lake a dozen white roses, which he delivered with a slight bow and a kiss on his mother-in-law's cheek. Virginia was impressed; so was her mother, who giggled. Her father beamed. If he'd had any question about Lucas's desirability as a son-in-law, it had all become a moot point weeks ago.

Virginia was glad of Lucas's affability, as she felt tense and uncomfortable, which she often did at her parents' home. It was almost as though she were the rebellious teenager again, the maverick worried her parents would hear about her latest escapade. Only, there was no latest escapade, just a recent society wedding to one of Glory's most eligible men, a wedding that must have fulfilled even the demanding expectations of her aunt Lily.

Her husband never pretended to be anything he wasn't—it was one of the qualities she found so attractive about him.

Kate Pleasance had to hurry off midway through dinner when she got a summons from the hospital. She apologized, but Virginia's father laughed it off, recalling the many times he'd had to interrupt an evening to deliver a baby or do emergency surgery.

"Don't be concerned," Mrs. Lake said. "We'll hold your dessert and coffee in case you're able to come back and join us. And, Orest, you'll stay, of course!"

The gloomy Ukrainian had nodded and, after accompanying his date to the door, returned to discuss hardy flowering shrubs in his deep, slow voice with Babs Horsfall.

The meal was over in less than two hours, for which Virginia was grateful. She supposed a few of these duty dinners were required, especially considering Lucas's position in the community, but she was going to put her foot down at once a month. She'd far rather spend time with her son and Lucas's niece.

And Lucas. Alone.

"Bridge, anyone?" her mother trilled, hands clasped hopefully in front of her. "We've got enough for two tables, even without Kate." She was discreetly excusing old George Frizzell, who was snoring gently in his chair.

"Not for me, Mother," Virginia said quickly.

"Oh, Virginia! You're such a good bridge player, too. And we used to have so much fun playing when you were younger."

Lucas rescued her. "Sorry, Doris. But I don't know the game."

"You don't? I *am* surprised." Doris Lake sounded resentful. "I thought you would have learned, if not as a teenager, then certainly in college." Virginia's mother seemed determined to believe, or have everyone else believe, that Lucas's upbringing had been just as normal and conservative as Virginia's.

"No, ma'am," Lucas drawled with a brief, sly look at Virginia. "In college I worked a couple part-time jobs to put myself through. I never had time. As for when I was a kid, why, my pa spent most days drunk—" Virginia noticed Bernice Frizzell give her brother an elbow "—and my mother worked fourteen hours a day cleaning other folks' houses. No spare time for cards. My own experience ran more to red dog and five-card stud in the bunkhouse or Saturday night after a rodeo. Playing for cash or beer."

"Oh." Doris Lake seemed as disappointed that he'd pointed out his "unusual" upbringing as she'd been that her social plans for an evening of bridge were fast evaporating. "Well, you'll play, won't you, Orest? You and Bernice make up a twosome, and with Pete and Babs, that's four." She threw Virginia a wounded look. "The doctor and I will play cribbage."

Virginia and Lucas left shortly after. Virginia

could hardly help giggling on the way to the car. It was cruel, she knew, to enjoy her mother's disappointment so thoroughly, but she remembered all the times her mother had embarrassed her with those stiff, snobbish manners—when she'd brought home kids her parents didn't approve of, for example. Or all the times she'd been railroaded into playing afternoon bridge with her mother's friends, an unsure, gangly thirteen-year-old with nowhere to go on a weekend. Not that tit-for-tat was an appropriate response for a thirty-year-old woman. And her mother was at heart a kind person—look how she put up with old George Frizzell.

"What's so funny?" Lucas demanded, opening the car door for her.

"My parents. When you told everyone how your dad was a drunk and your mother cleaned houses. Mother doesn't want to admit those things, you know. Especially now that you're related to them."

"She'll just have to take me as I am, honey," he replied, putting his hand on her shoulder and spinning her around to face him. "Just as you do."

He bowed his head and surprised her with a kiss. It was a deeply satisfying kiss that went on and on, under the crisp stars in the wide black Alberta sky. She clung to him, inhaling his unique scent—his freshly laundered clothing, the rich suede of his topcoat, the exciting scent of his skin. He held her tight and she reveled in the feeling. No one made her feel as safe and protected as Lucas did. No one made her feel as special.

Maybe tonight would be different.

But it wasn't. Lucas made love to her in the most excruciatingly slow, gentle, considerate way—and she responded. Her body was on fire, her mind was exploding, but the instant he joined with her, the panic rose until she felt as though the air had become thick. She choked and gasped and only barely stopped herself from crying out.

She wept afterward. Bitter tears. How could she believe—as he did—that this would ever change? How could she believe that he'd stay with her—as he said he would—no matter what?

CHAPTER FIFTEEN

JOHNNY GAGNON stepped on the gas as he reached the outskirts of the city. Sixty-five, seventy miles an hour. Two hours to Calgary, max, from Edmonton. It was great to be behind the wheel of a car again. He'd missed driving almost as much as he'd missed sex in the past six years, even if this station wagon Ed had found for him was a major piece of junk. Sounded like it could use a valve job. He'd put down three hundred on it and owed another four. Ed could wait for his money; he owed Johnny a favor or two.

Tante Cecile, bless her, had sent him a thousand dollars when he got out of the pen. The system provided him with a few bucks—the proceeds of all that jail labor. Man, it burned him up! They made you work and paid you peanuts for it. Six bucks a day! There was a bus ticket to Toronto from Kingston Penitentiary, courtesy of the Queen. Thank *you*, Queen Elizabeth, for all the great times he'd had in the Crowbar Hotel over the last six years. *Not!*

He was out now. Toronto had been a nice transition to the outside world. He'd dropped in on an old buddy and they'd gotten good and drunk. Just like the old days. Then they'd gone out looking for women. His buddy was too damn picky. He'd never spent time in jail like Johnny had. Maybe he wouldn't be so picky if he had.

Johnny had no intention of going back inside. He glanced at the speedometer and eased up. No way he wanted a speeding ticket, either. Even the thought of being back in prison made him sweat and get the shakes. This last rap was the longest he'd ever had—nine years and out in six for good behavior—and it was no picnic. For what kind of crime? It wasn't as though he'd hurt anyone or taken all that much cash from that stupid highway grocery store. Two hundred and fifty bucks? There was no justice, damn it.

It was the gun, his lawyer had told him, and the kidnapping that had brought the big sentence. And the car theft didn't help any.

Kidnapping? Ha! It had been a lark. Ginny had enjoyed it as much as he had, even though the bitch had had the nerve to testify against him. And she'd locked him in the cabin and run off with his vehicle! Some joke! Getting picked up hitchhiking by the Mounties the next morning, after breaking out of the cabin, hungover and hungry, was not his idea of a good time.

Still, he didn't hold it against her. They'd probably made Ginny testify. He figured he knew her well enough to know she'd never do it on her own. She'd never hurt him on purpose. No, that jerk of a father of hers and the cops had made her do it.

Oh, well. That was the past. Johnny Gagnon wasn't one to hold a grudge. Not for long, anyway. New day, new life. He'd flown to Edmonton, instead of Calgary, because he had a buddy in Edmonton who could get him wheels, cheap. No more stealing. That was this morning.

Now, it was off to Glory. He was in no hurry. His aunt had written to him and told him she'd lined up a job helping out in the Co-op warehouse. Not really his style, but it would do for now. Earn him points with his parole officer. One of the terms of his parole was that he'd have to stay in one place and get a job. Glory. What a laugh! As if he'd ever go back there unless he had to. But he was keeping his nose clean. No way would he end up inside again.

The highway signs indicated that the exits to the city of Red Deer were coming up. Johnny deliberated quickly. He was still horny as hell. Red Deer wasn't much of a town, in his opinion, but he knew there were a few hookers working the streets close to the tracks. Making up his mind, he put on his signal light and bore right, exiting the freeway.

It was damn cold; too cold for most hookers. And his heater wasn't working right. Johnny cruised slowly up and down the streets in the part of town he knew the prostitutes frequented. Only the old and the desperate out tonight. That was okay. He didn't have much money to spend on one, anyway.

He slowed and talked to a young girl in a tight leather skirt and high boots. She looked cold and lost and about sixteen. He wondered why she wasn't at home, studying for a high-school chemistry test. At the last minute he drove off. No way was he screwing a kid.

Finally he made a deal through the open window of his station wagon, and the hooker climbed into the car with him.

"You got a place?" he asked.

"The Corbett, three blocks down," she answered dully. She was late twenties, obviously been at it for quite a while. A lifer. Johnny didn't spend too much time on the ethics involved—she had something to sell that he wanted to buy. And he was no pervert or creep who'd beat her up after. Just a good, clean john with some cash in his pocket.

They parked behind the hotel, a seedy, run-down place. He knew the type. There'd be a scaly sink in the room, cheap curtains hanging wearily at the window, a sagging bed with a faded chenille bedspread. Maybe a TV, if she actually lived there, didn't just use the room for work.

He didn't waste much time on preliminaries. He put his money on the dresser while she stripped. Then he undressed himself quickly. He wasn't interested in the salad or the dessert. What he wanted was the main course.

Later, he lay in bed for a few minutes, watching the hooker as she got up and washed at the sink. He didn't even bother to ask her name. Man, how many times had he been in this situation? Too many. Maybe he should settle down. Part of the life plan for staying out of jail. What about Ginny Lake, the doctor's daughter? They'd always gotten along good. Two of a kind. And she'd be a lawyer now. That was rich—he could use a wife with a law degree!

Johnny got up and pulled on his pants and shirt. The prostitute had said nothing. She'd already dressed and tucked the money in her purse and looked like she was ready to go back on the street. He took another twenty from his pocket.

"Here you go, honey. Take care." He grinned and slapped her lightly on the shoulder. She gave him a wan smile.

Twenty minutes later he was back on the freeway, a cheeseburger and shake from a fast-food joint on the passenger seat beside him. It was close to midnight now, which meant he'd probably have to stay in Calgary, unless he wanted to burst into his aunt's place at two in the morning. He hated having to stay in a motel—alone? what a waste—and he only had just over a hundred bucks left. What with one thing and another—the plane fare, the deposit on the car, meals, necessities—he'd gone through his money pretty quickly.

Johnny turned on the radio and found a rock station out of Calgary. Golden oldies. Between bites of the burger, he sang along with a Neil Diamond tune.

Yep, that was him. A golden oldie. And Ginny, too. Damn, he felt great since that stop in Red Deer. A new man. Yessir, he was going to drop in at the doc's and find out where Ginny was living these days. Maybe if she was in Calgary or even up in Edmonton, he'd give her a call. She'd be glad to hear from him, he had no doubt about that. Especially when he told her he intended to go straight from now on.

You never knew. She might even want to pick up where they'd left off all those years ago.

One thing about him, Johnny thought with satisfaction—he was an optimist. Life was too damn short to look on the bad side of things.

CHAPTER SIXTEEN

LUCAS GOT THE NEWS from an unexpected source.

He was working in the office late one evening toward the end of November when the phone rang. Nancy had gone home for the day, of course, so he picked it up himself.

"Lucas? It's Donna."

"Donna!" This was a surprise. "How are you doing?"

"Fine. I heard something today I thought you might want to know."

Lucas frowned. "Yeah? What's that?"

"I saw Cecilia at the shop. She tells me Johnny's back. He's living with her and Phil, and he's working at the Co-op."

"Damn!" Lucas said softly. He'd hoped this day wouldn't come. He'd hoped circumstances would take Johnny Gagnon elsewhere. Anywhere but Glory.

"You okay?" came Donna's soft inquiry.

"Yeah, I'm fine." He chewed his lip. "Just wondering how I'm going to tell Virginia, that's all."

"Well." There was a pause. "Look, I've got to run, Lucas. Like I said, I just thought you should know."

"Big date?" He laughed, an empty sound he hoped would sound fairly normal to Donna. He owed her. She was right; he *did* want to know.

"Noah and I are going out to do some shopping in Calgary. Early Christmas stuff. The kids are with Steve."

"Uh-huh." Steve was Donna's ex. "Thanks, Donna. I appreciate your call."

He hung up, but he couldn't concentrate on the material in front of him anymore. Who could give a damn about land acquisitions and mortgages and financial finagling when the man who'd raped his wife was back in town?

Thank heaven he was already well started on the process of legally adopting Robert. Not that Gagnon could do anything about it, anyway. According to Virginia, he had no clue that he'd fathered a child. No one did; she'd put "father unknown" on the birth certificate. Lucas had his own opinions about that—no way he'd want to father a child himself and not be told about it—but he could understand what had been going through Virginia's mind when the time came to fill out the details. She'd been terrified of Gagnon. She'd dreaded him coming back into her life, especially now that she had a child. She loved Robert. It would kill her if Gagnon somehow took a notion to fight for his paternal rights.

It wouldn't happen. Not if he, Lucas, had anything to do with it. If he had to, he'd lie. Get Virginia to lie. Make out that he was the kid's real father. It could've happened like that. They could have had an affair back then, in Calgary. Anyone would believe that story after the big fuss Doc and Doris Lake had made about him taking their daughter to her graduation dance. Then shipping her off to New Brunswick right after.

The big question facing him now was how—and when—to tell *her?* He couldn't take the chance of Virginia running into Gagnon unexpectedly somewhere in town. He couldn't take the chance of some busybody, someone like Myrna Schultz, getting the news to her first.

That evening they ordered in Chinese food and rented two videos the children wanted. Virginia made popcorn and they all sat through *Babe,* Robert's choice, after *The Babysitter's Club,* which had been Tammy's choice. Lucas thought he'd dislocate his jaw trying to keep from yawning. The children were in heaven, and if Virginia was bored, she didn't show it.

Lucas resolved that the next family night they staged, the adults would choose at least one of the movies. When they finally went up to bed after tucking in the children, Lucas decided this wasn't the time to bring up Johnny Gagnon's presence in Glory.

He fell asleep with Virginia in his arms, as he had so many nights. They didn't make love. They rarely tried anymore. Lucas wanted to continue trying, but Virginia seemed so overwhelmed by the suggestion and seemed to feel so terribly guilty about their unhappy efforts that Lucas had decided to give the entire subject a rest. Maybe once she got this business with Gagnon behind her, she could put the whole thing into perspective again. Or they'd seek counseling together, which he'd already decided had to be the next step, as she'd suggested.

It had to work eventually. In the meantime, nothing could have been more frustrating than to lie there beside the woman he loved and not be able to touch her beyond hugs and brief kisses. She was his wife; he wanted an intimate, physical relationship with her. Sex. He wanted to bury himself deep inside her. He wanted to make a child with her someday. He wanted her to cry out and beg him for more....

It was driving him crazy. Was it driving her crazy, too? Maybe. But in a far different way than it was affecting him. If anything, he'd seen her spirit seep away until she was just a shadow of the woman he remembered. As a teenager, she'd been full of fire and rebellion. Fiercely proud and protective. Deeply principled. Courageous, bold. She was a shell of that woman. That was what fear had done to her.

And he loved her just the same.

He'd loved her then and he loved her now. That would never change, not as long as he was who he was.

Saturday the Yellowfly family spent the day at a mall in Calgary, doing some shopping for winter clothes for the children. That evening they had plans to go to the Herrara home together. The Herraras had four children, and Tammy and Robert loved to visit them. Lucas found it a bit wearing, he had to admit. They had kids and animals and boots and boxes of cereal and small, broken toys from fast-food joints spilling, it seemed, from every corner of their bungalow.

Virginia walked into the bedroom as he was getting ready. He stood before the mirror, tying his tie and met her bemused look.

"What?" He didn't mean to snap—it had just come out that way.

"We're going to the Herraras," she said. "I don't think Paul will be wearing a jacket and tie, do you?"

"Damn!" Lucas didn't know what he'd been thinking. What was in his brain? He'd been in a fog ever since Donna had told him the news about Johnny. Mostly he'd been preoccupied with how he was going to tell Virginia.

"Lucas?" She approached him from behind and met his gaze in the mirror as he stripped off the tie and started to unbutton his shirt. "Is something wrong? You seem, well, very distracted lately."

He held her gaze and finished unbuttoning the shirt. He felt his jaw harden.

"Lucas?" she repeated.

"Johnny's back in town."

She paled and put one hand on his shoulder, and he turned to pull her into his arms. "Don't worry, honey. There's nothing he can do."

"But—"

"He's on parole. He's working as a swamper on a truck for the Co-op, apparently, and he's living with his aunt and uncle. There's nothing he can do to you, or to us. You're married to me now. I wish you'd realize that." Lucas felt his own frustration boil up. Damn it. Sometimes he wondered if she was overreacting to the whole thing with Gagnon. And who was suffering? Him, that was who. Maybe it was the aggravation, pure and simple, of having no sex life. As far as that went, he'd been better off when he was a bachelor, he sometimes thought with dismay.

She stepped back. "What are you saying, Lucas? That I shouldn't be concerned that the man who fathered my son is back in town? That the man who kidnapped and *raped* me—" her voice rose "—is someone I should just *forget about?*"

"I don't mean that, damn it." Lucas stalked over to the walk-in closet and selected a casual knit shirt. Angrily he pulled it over his head. "But I've got to wonder, Virginia. Is this business with Gagnon just an excuse not to sleep with me? It's been years since it happened. How long am I going to have to share my bed with him? The rest of my life? So he's back in town—so what? What's that got to do with *us?*"

Lucas immediately regretted his words. But it was too late. Virginia had gone white. Then he saw her clench her fists and march out of their bedroom, ramrod-straight. "I'll be waiting in the car with the kids," she called over her shoulder.

Great, Lucas thought, tucking his shirt into his pants and cinching his belt. Just great. He firmed his jaw and followed her out.

Their first fight. And over that lousy two-bit piece of machismo, Johnny Gagnon. What in the name of God had he done to deserve this? All he wanted was a wife and a family. Some peace and quiet. Sex, once in a while. Was that too much to expect? He was prepared to do his part—support her emotionally and financially, adopt her kid, love her with all his heart. Do whatever the people he cared about wanted him to do.

What the hell was wrong with that?

Later that evening he tried to make it up to Virginia. She was having none of it. Maybe what they said about redheads wasn't all fictitious. She was stubborn. She was icy and furious by turns. She'd been perfectly civil to him at the Herraras', but he didn't think they'd missed the fact that she had smiles for everyone except him.

"You married me because you thought you could help me and Robert," she said in the kitchen after the children had gone to bed. She went through the motions of making tea, every movement stiff and exaggerated. You'd think the conversation they'd started in their bedroom hours ago had never been interrupted.

"I married you because I was in love with you," he corrected. "That other—that just speeded up events. I'd planned to court you, take my time, wait until you were in love with me, too. It had nothing to do with Gagnon coming back."

"Now you're blaming me because we have no sex life," she bit out angrily, changing the subject.

"I told you right from the start that I wanted a real wife. A real marriage. That usually means a sex life, yes. Guilty as charged. But I'm not blaming you."

"You are!" She whirled, eyes flashing. "Now you're *lying* to me."

Lucas moved toward her, but she stepped back. "Look, honey," he said quietly, "I didn't realize you'd react to making love the way you did. I don't think *you* even knew. But we've been working on it. We've been trying, haven't we?" He put his hand on her shoulder and this time she let him. Her gaze dropped to the placket on his shirt. "I think things are getting better," he murmured. "I just wish they were better for you." He pulled her into his arms and bent, resting his head on her crown. "I just want things to be good for you, honey. That's all I care about."

"Oh, Lucas," she moaned. "What a mess this all is."

He had to agree, but wisely—he thought—said nothing, just tightened his hold on her and rocked her slowly. The two of them swayed gently in the kitchen and Lucas saw the neighbor's cat on the windowsill outside look in, then yowl and leap off into the darkness. He smiled.

"It's going to get better, honey. I promise. Do you want me to go over to the Co-op and have a word with Gagnon?"

"No. I think it's better if I just run into him somewhere in town. At least I know now. At least I can prepare myself. Maybe I *am* being ridiculous about it." Lucas rocked slowly and stroked the back of her head. "Maybe I've just made it such a big thing that I can't think straight anymore. Maybe Johnny doesn't even—" she sobbed and Lucas was sure she'd meant to laugh "—remember what happened!"

"Maybe not." Lucas hadn't thought of that possibility. After all, the man had been drunk as a skunk, according to Virginia. He'd known of sexual-assault cases in the past where the man had used drunkenness as a defense and gotten off. "Maybe it would be best if he *doesn't* remember—what do you think?"

"Maybe." Virginia was silent for a long time. He felt her arms go around him, and after a while, she held him as tightly as he held her. "Let's go to bed, Lucas. I'm so tired. I just want you to hold me," she whispered.

Lucas held her until she fell asleep. For many hours he stared at the ceiling in their bedroom, running through this eventuality, then that. The best thing, he decided, would be to have her meet Gagnon as soon as possible. If they were ever going to put this behind them, they had to get that out of the way. Short of inviting the bastard to dinner, Lucas was going to make every effort to ensure that when she did run into Gagnon, he'd be there with her.

Maybe it was time they did a little Christmas shopping at the Glory Co-op.

HE COULDN'T STAY with her twenty-four hours a day. And then, as it happened, Gagnon beat him to the punch, anyway.

On Tuesday the next week Nancy brought in the mail after lunch, as was her habit. Lucas flipped through the stack, pleasantly aware that Virginia worked just a dozen or so feet away from him, near the firm's law library stacks. She'd ordered new

computers, but they hadn't arrived yet. Before they
did, he and Pete were going to have some work done
to enlarge her office and rearrange the reception
area. The work, which would be carried out by Gus
McCready's firm, was due to be completed during
the Christmas break.

A letter from his sister. Lucas stopped and set the
other mail aside. Why was she writing him at the
office, instead of home? Maybe she had some news
she didn't want him to share with Tammy right
away.

"Letter from Theresa," he said, and waved it in
the air.

"Oh?" Virginia seemed distracted. He should
know better than to interrupt her while she worked.

"Maybe she wants Tammy back." Lucas slit the
envelope with his letter opener and began to read
the first of several single-spaced pages. "I hope not.
I'm going to miss that kid."

He barely noticed when Nancy popped her head
in the door and said, "Someone to see you, Mrs.
Yellowfly." Nancy got a kick out of calling Virginia
by her married name. Virginia went out and Lucas
read on.

Theresa, it seemed, was doing very well on the
program she'd started. She'd had several sweat-
lodge sessions, some counseling and—this was the
big news—had decided to get in touch with
Tammy's father after all these years and tell him
about his daughter. She didn't want Lucas to say
anything to Tammy yet.

Lucas was interested. He knew nothing about

Tammy's father or the circumstances of his niece's birth. Theresa wrote that Tammy had been conceived while she was on a nursing job in the Queen Charlotte Islands. She and her employer, a married man fifteen years older and a Kwakiutl Indian who owned a hardware store in Tahsis, had fallen in love and had had an affair. She'd felt horrible, as the man's wife was dying of cancer. So had he. When the wife finally died, Theresa had left the Queen Charlottes, never telling her employer that she was pregnant. She'd changed her mind now, nine years later, and was going to tell him he had a daughter. She'd had a change of heart and felt enough time had gone by that she could face the truth. She felt she owed it to her former lover and—

"Psst!"

It was Nancy, frowning and gesturing to him.

"Uh-huh?" He looked up from the letter, faintly annoyed that he'd been interrupted.

"I think you'd better come out here," she whispered with several exaggerated expressions of shock and distaste and a few wild hand gestures.

Virginia!

Lucas threw down the letter and practically vaulted over his desk. He took two strides to his office door, straightening his tie and jacket as he did. What the hell—

It was Gagnon.

He was standing in the reception area, a big smile on his handsome face. He hadn't changed much over the years; if anything, he was better-looking than before. Lucas had vaguely remembered a mustache. The man was clean shaven now.

"Well, if it isn't old Lucas Yellowfly!" Gagnon stepped forward, hand extended. After a moment's hesitation, Lucas moved toward him and shook it briefly.

"Gagnon. How are you?" he asked stiffly with a quick glance at Virginia. She'd gone pale. Her hands, gripping the back of one of the reception chairs, were white at the knuckles.

"Not bad, man. Not bad." Gagnon was still grinning.

"That's good to hear. What can we do for you, Johnny?" Lucas said more formally.

"Just wanted to take my old pal Virginia here out for lunch. Her and me go way back, y'know. Way, way back. All the way to high school."

"So I understand." Lucas looked at Virginia, eyebrow raised. Lunch with this character? It really was not his place to say she couldn't go.

He turned back to Gagnon. "I guess you know that Virginia is now my wife. We were married a while ago. Maybe all three of us should go for lunch?" He smiled, but he really wasn't joking. Nor did he want to spend an hour with Virginia and the man who'd raped her. He didn't know if he could be held responsible for his actions if he did.

"Your wife? Damn, when did that happen? Er…congratulations, I mean. When was the happy day, if I might ask?"

"A month or so ago. The beginning of November."

"Well, I'll be…" Gagnon shook his head. "Son of a gun. Didn't think the doc'd want a buck Indian for a son-in-law. Well, well."

"Times change," Lucas said through his teeth, barely restraining the urge to step forward and plant his fist in Gagnon's face. "For some of us."

Gagnon laughed heartily. "That's a good one! Matter of fact, I'm just out of jail myself. Intend to stay out, too," he added with a nod and a sideways glance at Nancy. The receptionist was rapt, behind her desk, not missing a word.

"Well, if I can't interest anyone here in lunch with a man who's seen the error of his ways, I guess I'll be going." He stepped back and replaced the Glory Co-op cap on his dark head. "Sorry to bother you, folks. Be seein' you around."

With that he stepped out the door and was gone.

Lucas breathed a sigh of relief. He moved toward Virginia. "How you doing, honey?" he asked in a low voice, hoping Nancy couldn't overhear.

"I'm fine, Lucas," Virginia said. "I feel just fine."

They stepped into Lucas's office and he closed the door and pulled her into his arms.

"Hey." She laughed softly. "Remember what you said about being strictly professional on the job?"

"That was before we were married." He looked intently into her face. She really did seem okay. As though this long-awaited meeting hadn't been as bad as she'd expected. "Now that we're married, I can kiss my wife anywhere I want, including the office, right?''

''Right.'' She gazed up at him. She took a deep breath, held it for a few seconds, then let it out. ''I do feel fine, Lucas. I don't know why I dreaded that so much. I'm glad it's over, though. He's just a creep. A plain, ordinary creep and I'm really not afraid of him.''

''Honest?''

''Honest. Now let me get back to work.''

Lucas watched her return to her desk and gather some papers and snap a rubber band around them. She looked up once and smiled.

He smiled back, but when he returned his attention to his mail, he couldn't keep his mind on it. Was that really all there was to meeting Johnny Gagnon again? Had all the trepidation been for nothing?

More important—where did that leave their love life?

THAT EVENING Lucas was disappointed to learn that Virginia had already made plans to help Marcia Herrara sew some outfits for the annual Christmas concert. She didn't get home until midnight and crept into bed so carefully that Lucas knew very well she wasn't interested in lovemaking.

The next night she complained of aches and pains and, after he'd gone to bed, told him she was taking a long, hot bath. She was in the bathroom for ages, until he finally put his book down and turned out the light. He feigned sleep when she, again, crept into bed, swaddled in her longest, thickest flannel nightgown.

Then, the following day, she announced to him that her period had started. Lucas couldn't recall ever receiving an announcement like that in such a pleased tone. As far as he knew, most women didn't really look forward to that time of month; in this case, he was pretty sure it was the temporary "hands off" that Virginia welcomed. Who could argue with Mother Nature?

When her period seemed to go on and on, he gave up. The writing was clearly on the wall and Lucas Yellowfly could read what it said: Johnny Gagnon wasn't the problem—*he* was.

His wife didn't want to make love with him. That was plain as day to him now.

It was the worst-case scenario he hadn't allowed himself to face before.

CHAPTER SEVENTEEN

WHY IN HELL hadn't anyone told him she'd married
that goddamn Indian?

Johnny was furious as he made his way to the
Glory Hotel for a plate of *poutine* and a beer. He'd
likely find some of his buddies in the tavern there.
He had an hour off and had to be back at the Co-
op by half past one, or that high-and-mighty Ted
Eberle would have his hide.

That was another thing—the day he'd ever
thought he'd be working for trash like Eberle!

Ah, well, his life wasn't his own. Yet. But things
were going to change after Christmas. A couple of
weeks, maybe a month or two, of toeing the line,
and he'd see if his parole officer would go for him
leaving town, taking up somewhere else. He
couldn't stand living under his aunt and uncle's roof
much longer. They wouldn't let him bring any
women in and they didn't approve of drinking and
they made him turn the TV down when they went
to bed. Not to mention they made him feel guilty as
hell because he wouldn't go to church with them
every Sunday. Once a Catholic, always a Catholic—
why else did he feel so guilty? Damn, you'd think

he was a little kid the way he got treated around here.

Now this!

Johnny couldn't deny he felt hurt. Not that him and Ginny Lake really had anything going. Hell, he'd even been married for a couple years in between the time the two of them had been an item and when he'd seen her last. Sure, they'd had some good times when they were teenagers, back when she was still in high school and he'd been working for Walt Friesen. That was a long time ago…but didn't old times count? Couldn't she just have lunch with him for old times' sake—never mind standing there like she'd seen some ghost and putting the rattles into that goggle-eyed secretary or whatever she was?

Damn it. That wasn't the Ginny Lake he remembered. The Ginny he remembered would've been up for some fun. Lunch, for sure. A little reminiscing. A few laughs. Maybe even a beer or two after work. Not send him packing like that. Or bring out that brand-new husband of hers in his fancy suit. Yellowfly!

He'd always known that uppity half-breed had the hots for his girl. This wasn't the first time. Yellowfly had taken her to her grad dance back when he had every intention of taking her himself, except he'd been unexpectedly detained as a guest of Her Majesty. That was in Fort Saskatchewan for stealing a car. His first serious rap.

He'd been mad as hell when he found out Yellowfly had dated her while he was in the clink. And then her daddy had packed her off down East shortly after, and he hadn't seen her since.

Except of course, for that little visit they'd had when he'd run into her while he was robbing the Bragg Creek grocery. She'd come with him easy enough. Kidnapping! That was what the cops called it and that was what he'd done time for. But it was no more kidnapping than…than he was the man in the moon!

Johnny frowned. He remembered how mad he'd been when he woke up the next day and found out she'd left and locked him in the cabin. He'd hollered and hammered at the door until he realized that she really was gone. Then he'd gotten dressed and busted his way out the bedroom window. That was when he discovered she'd hot-wired the Jeep and taken off with it. He'd been madder than a hornet. If he'd caught up to her then, he wasn't sure what he'd have done. But that was a long time ago. He'd forgiven her. He might have done the same thing if he was in her situation. Maybe she'd had a big date or something. Who the hell knew why she'd high-tailed it out of there so fast?

"Johnny!"

He looked around the relative gloom of the Glory Hotel tavern and caught the eye of his friend, Gil Baxter, sitting with another guy. Morris Jack. He walked over and joined them.

"Thought you had plans for lunch today," Gil teased with a sly glance at Morris.

"Yeah. Fell through. Hey—coupla draft and a menu!" he yelled at the waitress.

"Lady let you down?"

"Maybe. Why in hell didn't one of you fellas tell me she was married?" He still felt sore about that.

The waitress slapped down a torn and stained menu and two glasses of draft beer and sauntered off to deliver a hamburger to another customer.

"She married?" That was Morris, who wasn't the brightest at the best of times, and this was not one of his best times. Johnny counted five empty beer glasses in front of him.

"Yeah, married that lawyer fella, Lucas Yellowfly," Gil said, frowning at his companion. "While back? Last month? *You* remember, Moe."

Morris nodded. "Yeah, guess I do," he muttered.

Johnny knew damn well he didn't. But so what. He took a deep draft of his beer and wiped the foam from his upper lip. "Man, that tastes good. So, I guess you knew, right, Gil? You shoulda told me."

"I heard somewheres. A wedding ring don't stop a lady from having lunch with an old friend, though, does it?"

"No," Johnny admitted sourly. He looked around the bar. He'd better be careful. If he ordered another round of beer, he might get in trouble with Eberle this afternoon. "Ah, to hell with her," he said with a throwaway gesture. "There's other skirts in this hick town, eh, Morris?" He laughed.

Morris nodded agreeably.

"I suppose she married that Indian 'cause of the kid," Gil went on.

"Kid?" Johnny glanced sharply at his friend. "What kid? She never used to have no kid."

"Little fella, name of Robert. Five, six years old. He's in kindergarten over at the school. My cousin's kid is in the same class. Mrs. Brown's."

"That old bag! She still teaching?" Johnny gave the waitress his order for *poutine* and a bacon burger and took a sip from his second glass of beer.

"Yep. Some things don't change around here, buddy. You know that."

"So, whose kid is it? She musta got married for a while, I guess." Man, the news you missed when you were inside for a few years.

"Not as far as I know. 'Course I don't travel in the town's top social circles, y'understand." He winked at Morris, who gave him a gummy smile. "Could be she's divorced. She just came back this summer. August. Started working for old Horsfall and Yellowfly, and first thing you know, her and Yellowfly get hitched. Big la-di-da wedding. The doctor's daughter, you know," Gil drawled. "You shoulda got outa the slammer a little sooner, buddy. Coulda been you."

"Yeah, sure." Johnny dug into his plate of *poutine,* a greasy, high-calorie mélange of french fries, cheese curds and steaming hot gravy. It was the western version of old-fashioned Quebec fare that had become popular in the last decade or so.

So she had a kid, did she? Well, so much for that. Married, a kid, working for a couple lawyers. She was well out of his life. She must've had a bun in the oven about the last time he saw her. Or got one pretty quick after, if the kid was in school already. She never mentioned being involved with any guy when he'd seen her. But then, he'd been pretty drunk most of the day or two they'd spent together. It wasn't as though he remembered *everything* that'd happened that weekend, or everything she'd said.

He frowned and bit into his burger. There'd always been something that bothered him about that time up at Bragg Creek. When he'd gotten dressed, he'd found a pair of panties on the floor, ripped, over by one of the bed legs. He wasn't sure how they got there. Maybe his buddy that owned the cabin had brought a babe up one weekend and they'd been so hot they'd forgotten her underwear on the floor. He'd never had a chance to ask.

Johnny stood and wiped his mouth with his sleeve. ''Gotta get back. See you guys later, eh?''

They both nodded. Johnny left the tavern and began to make his way to the Co-op. He dug his hands deep in the pockets of his jeans and hunched down into his denim jacket collar. Damn, it was cold! He slipped once on the icy sidewalk and swore.

Any way you looked at it, he'd been done dirty. Gil hadn't told him, which made him seem like a complete dope in front of everybody in that law office, that bug-eyed secretary and all. And Ginny had practically acted like she'd never seen him before. After the time they'd had? Ha! She'd been a virgin when they started going out—she wasn't by the time she graduated. No way she'd forgotten that particular little detail. And now she had a kid. And a bigshot husband, even if he was half Indian. And a good job. Probably making decent money, too.

Looked like everything had gone right for Ginny Lake.

And everything had gone wrong for him.

Hell, it wasn't fair. It wasn't fair at all.

A FEW DAYS after Johnny had come to the office to see her, Lucas got a call from his sister. Typically for Theresa—or so Lucas said—she'd decided on the spur of the moment to spend Christmas with them. As a matter of fact, she was in Calgary now, and if he could drive up and get her at the airport, she'd greatly appreciate it. Lucas told her to rent a car, instead, which she did.

That evening Virginia met Lucas's sister. Tammy was thrilled at the unexpected visit from her mother, and the two of them spent the whole first evening together in Tammy's room, catching up on news.

Theresa was a small, dark-haired, dark-skinned woman with huge brown eyes. She looked a little like Lucas, but he told Virginia she resembled their father's family more. She was quiet and very neat in her habits, very plainly dressed. Almost no makeup. Virginia would never have dreamed that she had a drug-and-alcohol problem. According to Theresa, she no longer did.

She said so with such an air of conviction that Virginia believed her. She was annoyed to see Lucas glance over his sister's head and smile. He obviously wasn't quite as ready to believe as she was, but then, she reminded herself, he'd probably heard those promises before.

Virginia couldn't help but admire Theresa for the

stand she'd taken on Tammy's father, too. Apparently the man had been elated to reestablish contact. He'd never forgotten Theresa and was thrilled to learn he had a daughter. Virginia hoped that even more would come of it. For Tammy to find a father after all this time would be a truly happy ending.

Poor Robert and Tammy. So far, they'd both grown up without fathers. Would she ever be able to assume a live-and-let-live attitude such as Theresa's? Of course, Theresa Yellowfly hadn't been raped, and her child's father was an upstanding citizen, a widower, a businessman—not a convicted criminal out on parole.

Besides, now Robert had Lucas as a father. *As long as they could work things out…*

Could they? Some days Virginia felt grim. The Christmas season, the most hopeful time of the year, was fast approaching, yet she'd never felt lower. Not even when she'd been pregnant, alone and with few prospects.

She didn't know what to do. She was damned if she made love with her husband and damned if she didn't.

The truth was, she didn't really want to make love with Lucas anymore. She couldn't help thinking she'd been nothing but a fraud since she'd married him. Seeing Johnny in the office had brought it home to her. First of all, she'd seen her former lover as he really was: a small-town loser.

Then, later the next afternoon, when she and Robert had met Johnny briefly on the street, she'd been almost paralyzed with fear until she realized he hadn't given Robert a second glance. He'd seemed more interested in apologizing for showing up at the office the day before. As if her reaction would have been different if he'd phoned first!

He clearly didn't have a clue about Robert, which made her worries on that score over the past six years seem ridiculous. Moving from place to place, the bus trip to Regina to have her baby, the subterfuge with her parents. It all added up to the actions of an idiot now.

Then there was the business of the rape. As Lucas said, it was a long time ago. What Lucas didn't say—was too gentlemanly to say—was, Why didn't she yell rape then if it was such a big deal? Have him charged?

And her answer to herself had to be, *Yes, Virginia, why didn't you?* She hated the truth. She knew Johnny'd been drunk when he raped her. She knew he might have very little recollection of the time they'd spent together, let alone the rape.

Virginia had always felt that her first real boyfriend, her teenage lover, was basically a good-hearted person. Even his crimes were more on the level of misguided impulse and foolishness than they were true evil. She wondered if he'd even regard what had happened as rape. Maybe he'd thought she was just being coy when she tried to fight him off. He'd have very little concept of being repulsed by a woman, especially a woman with whom he'd once had a relationship. In Johnny's world, he no doubt saw himself as a major stud. The kind of guy women were nuts about.

She'd justified her inaction back then by reminding herself that he was going to jail, anyway, for the armed robbery and kidnapping and car theft. Why bother adding the rape? It would just involve her in a horrible, messy court case and bring her parents into it and— Virginia had just felt she couldn't face that. Doris Lake would never have survived the notoriety.

She hoped she'd made the right decision. She'd never know, would she? Unless another woman was raped by Gagnon, and then she'd never forgive herself for keeping quiet.

In the meantime…*that man was Robert's father!*

And she was married to a kind, gentle, handsome man who loved her, yet she hated the thought of taking off her clothes and going to bed with him at night. Having sex with him. She was a fraud as a woman. Lucas had said he wanted a real marriage. How long was he going to put up with this? She had to do something.

They'd made love once since she'd seen Johnny and it hadn't gone very well. She'd managed to control her panic—she hadn't cried out—but she hadn't fooled Lucas, either. He'd given up, frustrated, halfway through. Which made *her* feel terrible, too. After all, he must be thoroughly frustrated, both emotionally and physically.

But did she want to be the kind of woman who faked pleasure when she made love with her husband?

Definitely not.

Which left her…where? She cared deeply for Lucas. She'd never met a man she liked more. He made her feel happy about herself and Robert most of the time. He was terrific with his niece. He was good with the kids, always found time to spend with them. Helped them with their homework, took them places on the weekends.

He was good and considerate with her. She couldn't have found a better husband if she'd been actively looking, which she hadn't. She'd lucked into this marriage and now she wanted it to last.

But Lucas was an attractive, healthy, virile man. He was bound to turn elsewhere sooner or later. She didn't think she could bear that. Yet they couldn't continue this sham of a marriage forever. Something had to give.

Thinking about it affected her health. She woke up a week before Christmas violently ill. After a session in the bathroom, she stumbled out and told Lucas that although she felt a little better now, she thought she'd stay home for the day. Theresa, she knew, would be visiting an old school friend in Pincher Creek, then picking up Tammy from school and taking her to her grandmother's apartment in Calgary for the night. Lucas's sister had been staying with them, off and on, since her arrival in Alberta the week before.

"You do that, honey," Lucas said, always thoughtful, although she hated the way he looked at her sometimes lately. With pain in his eyes. With a secret, yearning expression. She hated the way he changed the subject now whenever she veered toward discussing the source of their problems—her feelings about sex.

It was almost as though he blamed himself as much as she blamed herself. Virginia felt doubly unhappy to think she'd caused that, too.

"I'll see how I feel at noon," she said, crawling back into their bed. The bed was warm and comfortable. She edged over to Lucas's side and buried her face in his pillow. What frustration! To be so turned on by your own husband, yet unable to find satisfaction with him.

"You stay in bed. Take it easy," Lucas said when he got out of the shower. "I'll get the kids off to school. Tammy can make the lunches. I'll zip back at noon and see how you're doing."

"You don't need to check on me," she said weakly.

"I want to," he said, and came over and sat on the edge of the bed. He leaned down and kissed her forehead. "I don't like to think of you alone all day. It should be an easy day at the office. I'll have lunch at home, just like I used to before I got married."

"Okay," she said, and smiled. She was glad he'd be coming home at noon. Maybe, if she felt better, she'd get up and make them something good for lunch. She wasn't much of a cook, but she could certainly manage an omelet. Mrs. Vandenbroek's sister kept them supplied with farm-fresh eggs, and Tammy had grown a little herb garden in the kitchen for a school project. She could raid it for fresh parsley and chives.

She must have fallen asleep, for when she woke

up, she felt a lot better. The house was very quiet, and the sun was bright on the snow outside. Christmas was so close and she still had so much to do. The house was partly decorated but they didn't have a tree yet and she had a lot of baking planned. Luckily, on the weekend, her mother and Mrs. Vandenbroek had both stopped by for a visit, bearing homemade Christmas cakes for the family. She really wanted this first Christmas to be special.

Maybe she'd just been overtired from lack of sleep. So many nights she'd lain awake lately, fretting about their situation. She'd pretty well decided to try the therapy route and had made an appointment with Kate Pleasance for after the New Year. She hadn't mentioned her decision to Lucas yet.

They planned to stay home Christmas morning, then go to Virginia's parents for a big turkey dinner. Boxing Day they'd spend at home with Lucas's mother and aunt and sister, who would stay on for a few days. The house was big enough for all kinds of company, and Virginia was looking forward to getting to know her husband's family better.

Virginia swung her feet over the side of the bed and stood up gingerly. She felt fine. Good, in fact. She glanced at the clock on the dresser. Just half-past eleven. She'd have a quick shower, get dressed, make a nice omelet for the two of them. Have a glass of wine, even. Maybe they could discuss her decision to seek therapy over lunch.

Or maybe not. Virginia dreaded that particular discussion. She knew Lucas didn't have a whole lot of faith in the counseling process. Look how skeptical he was of Theresa's progress. He said he had an open mind, but like most men, she suspected, he preferred to think he could fix his problems himself. Until now, he'd insisted things would work themselves out. It wasn't happening. Even he had to admit that.

Virginia took a quick shower with the new lavender soap her mother had given her, along with some other toiletries, some of which she'd passed on to Tammy, who was at the age where she enjoyed fancy soaps and creams and bath stuff. She toweled her hair vigorously, deciding to leave it down to air-dry.

Then she stood in front of the closet with just a towel around her, looking for something to wear. She decided not to dress, as she didn't think she'd go to work today, after all. She'd get some Christmas baking done. She slipped on a pink floral caftan that Lucas had particularly admired. Virginia was starting to feel a little more than normal excitement that her husband was coming home for lunch.

She was starting to feel like a honeymooner. She liked the sensation of the silk on her bare skin. She'd have everything ready when he got home—just in case they went upstairs.

One of these days—or nights—something *had* to give.

Virginia hurried down the staircase, humming. She felt better than she had for a long time. Maybe it was the extra sleep. Maybe it was Christmas coming. Maybe it was being in a family after such a long time spent alone with Robert.

Maybe it was the prospect of her sexy, handsome husband coming through that door....

Virginia heard a car. Lucas couldn't be here this early, could he? It wasn't even twelve yet.

She went to the window to peek out. An old, beat-up station wagon was parked right in front. And getting out on the driver's side was Johnny Gagnon.

CHAPTER EIGHTEEN

LUCAS LEFT WORK early. He couldn't deny he'd been thinking about Virginia all morning. When he wasn't worrying about her being sick, maybe sick enough to need a doctor, he was imagining her naked in their bed.

He couldn't win. And he wasn't getting much work done. He'd sat in on a meeting with Pete and one of his clients, supposedly to take notes and ask questions, and when he looked at his pad of legal paper later, there were only two items jotted down. He'd have to apologize to Pete this afternoon.

Nancy had a cold, too. She sniffled and blew her nose and coughed and croaked so often on the phone that Lucas sent her home. He ducked into Pete's office before he left to tell him. Pete nodded affably—no sense everyone being sick with Christmas coming up.

And it wasn't as though the week before Christmas was all that busy, anyway. It was after Christmas that the break-and-enters, drunk-and-disorderlies and driving-under-the-influence charges started rolling in. January tended to be one of the firm's busiest months.

Lucas shrugged on his jacket for the short walk

home. He looked forward to getting his lungs full of cold, clean air. It was a beautiful, clear day. The snow that had fallen the night before had settled on all the low spots and the fences and rooftops, making everything sparkling white and glistening. The sun on the snow almost hurt his eyes.

Lucas hoped Virginia was feeling better. If she wasn't, he just might take the afternoon off, too, and stay home with her. Spoon chamomile tea into her. Go over some briefs in front of the fireplace. No matter what happened between them—or didn't happen, to be more accurate—he loved her. He'd never met another woman like Virginia and he didn't expect to. No matter how difficult things seemed at times, he always kept his mind fastened on the possibilities. He truly believed that if they had the will, the two of them, they could find the way. He definitely had the will. And he believed, in his heart, that Virginia did, too.

He rounded the last corner onto Second Avenue. Their house was a block and a half down. Lucas sauntered along, enjoying the sights of a prairie town in winter. The dogs trotting down the newly plowed street, stopping regularly to sniff car tires and leave their calling cards in the snowbanks. The never-say-die clothesline devotees, who had their sheets and tea towels and their mens' long johns pegged out, a long line waving stiffly in the breeze, frozen solid. Lucas remembered his own mother bringing in clothes like that in winter, to drape over a wooden rack to finish drying inside. She swore

that clothes air-dried—or freeze-dried, in this case—
smelled better.

When he got a little closer to home, he narrowed
his eyes against the glare. Whose car was that
parked outside the house? Virginia had company?
Lucas wasn't familiar with the old station wagon.
Alberta plates. It had to be from around here. The
doctor's? Not Kate Pleasance's, that was for sure,
not an old beater like that.

Then, as he got closer, he saw the driver's door
open and Johnny Gagnon get out. He stood, one foot
on the roadway, the other on the running board.

"Hey, Yellowfly—where's your missus?" he
called.

Lucas's blood heated to near boiling. What the
hell was *he* doing here?

"Are you referring to my wife?" he asked coldly.

"Ginny. Yeah, I guess she's your wife now, but
I have to say I always think of her as my girl,"
Johnny drawled insolently. Lucas wished he could
see Gagnon's eyes behind those dark aviator-type
sunglasses he wore.

Lucas said nothing. He came closer to the car and
stopped. He would deal with this before he went in
the house. He'd get rid of this nuisance.

"You *could* say I knew her pretty well back
then," Johnny went on. It was almost as though he
was taunting Lucas. "Guess she remembers me, too.
I called your office this morning and the girl said
Ginny's home sick today. She's scared to open the
door, though. Maybe she's afraid of what she'll do,
eh? Face-to-face with a *real* man—"

"What's your business, Gagnon?" Lucas interrupted. "Maybe you'd better move on. Seems you aren't wanted here. By my wife or by me." Lucas barely restrained himself. So the bastard had been banging on the door already, scaring Virginia half to death, no doubt. She said she wasn't afraid of him any longer, but he didn't entirely believe that.

"Maybe not now," Gagnon drawled. "But there was a time she couldn't keep her hands off of me, if you know what I mean...." He winked.

"Get out!" Lucas stepped forward, hands clenched. He had to be careful. He'd vowed many, many years ago that he wouldn't let his temper get the best of him in this kind of situation. Guys like Johnny Gagnon were the physical type. Using their fists was all they understood. Lucas had sworn off physical violence the day he'd woken up, hungover after a rodeo bar fight, to realize that one of his buddies had lost the use of an eye in the fracas. No one knew who'd hit whom, but Lucas had sworn off fighting then and there. Since that day he'd never laid a hand on anyone in anger. A piece of garbage like Gagnon wasn't going to bait him enough to start—

"She looks like she's a pretty cold fish now. Maybe you'll have better luck with her than I did the last few times we were together. Ya know what I mean? Maybe she's the kinda woman that likes a little buck with her—"

Lucas hit him. He didn't know when he'd crossed those last few feet that separated him and Gagnon. He didn't know when he'd taken off his leather gloves. He didn't know when he'd tossed his jacket in the snowbank.

"You son of a bitch!" Gagnon leaped at him with a howl of rage. His sunglasses had gone flying with Lucas's punch and Lucas saw now that his eyes were red and bloodshot. He looked like he'd been drinking. Lucas took Gagnon's fist on his jaw like a load of bricks. He grunted and stepped back, then he went for Gagnon again. He hit him in the face with one fist, in the belly with the other.

Gagnon groaned and came up, fists flying. Lucas felt something hit him in the eye, something that was like another load of bricks, then he saw stars as Gagnon connected with the bridge of his nose.

He leaped for the other man and they went down in a thrashing mess of arms and legs and blood and snow. Lucas felt Gagnon grab his necktie and he swore—another goddamn reason not to wear a tie! He pummeled Gagnon's head into the snowbank and yelled, and amazingly, Gagnon let go of his tie.

"Lucas! Stop it! For God's sake—you're going to kill him!" Virginia had the front door open and was shrieking at the two men.

Lucas's head cleared. He sat up on Gagnon and then, just to make his point, grabbed a handful of snow and washed his face for him. Gagnon howled, spitting snow and sputtering oaths.

Lucas stood up. "He's too goddamn worthless to kill," he panted, stepping aside from the still-prone Gagnon. He prodded Gagnon with the toe of his boot. "Get up, you useless bastard. And get out of here.'' The man lying in the roadway rolled to his side and sprang to his feet.

He staggered toward the open door of his station wagon and shook his fist at Lucas. "You son of a bitch! You're gonna pay for this. I'll get you, I swear I will.''

He banged the door, started the car and slammed it into gear, his wheels spinning on the slick surface of the snowy road. Lucas tossed him a rude gesture, which was returned through the open window.

"Hey, you forgot your sunglasses!" Lucas shouted, picking them up and holding them in the air.

"Up yours!" Gagnon roared out his window.

Lucas snapped them in two and threw them back in the snowbank. Another childish move, but he just couldn't help himself.

Gagnon took the corner in a cloud of blue smoke. Good riddance. Sounded like the rust bucket could use a little engine work, too. "And don't come back!" he yelled after Gagnon, aware the other man couldn't hear him. It was satisfying to yell, all the same.

Lucas glanced around the neighborhood. The street was quiet. He hoped no one had witnessed the fight, but he knew the kind of thing that went on behind closed curtains. New neighbor, town lawyer, new wife—some impression he'd make on Second Avenue.

Now that it was over, Lucas was seized with an almost unstoppable desire to laugh. He bent over and grabbed up his jacket and gloves, realizing only then that his nose was still bleeding. His shirt was red with blood.

"*Lucas.* You crazy fool." Virginia was down the steps in her thin dress and her bare feet. She whimpered and touched his face with her fingertips. "Get in the house so I can take care of this for you. I don't *believe* you two—like a couple of kids in the school yard."

Lucas made it up the steps. All of a sudden he felt about a hundred years old. He was a lawyer; he was no rodeo rider anymore. No wrangler's helper. He wasn't in shape for this kind of thing. And Gagnon knew how to throw a punch. He'd no doubt picked up a few pointers in the pen.

Lucas staggered as he entered the house and grabbed for the door frame. Virginia gave a squeal of dismay and pushed him in, closing the door behind him. He heard the click as she locked it. Lucas grinned. "Hey, it's not that bad, honey. Just a little blood."

"Just a little blood! Look at your eye— Here, let me help you into the bathroom." Virginia held his arm and guided him into the main-floor bathroom. He let her lead him in, feeling, amazingly, like he'd put back a mickey of cheap rum in one or two big gulps. His knees were shaky. He gripped the sides of the sink and leaned forward and watched as blood from his nose dripped lazily onto the porcelain.

"Lucas, you're crazy! What were you doing, fighting with…with that creep? He's dangerous. He's a criminal, for crying out loud! You could have been seriously hurt."

Lucas frowned. That wasn't quite the way he'd seen it. "Hey, who rubbed whose face in the snow? I guess I got in a couple of good licks myself—"

"*Oh!*" Virginia made a frustrated sound and began to unbutton his shirt. "Let me get this shirt off. It's covered in— Yuck!" She unbuttoned it, reaching around him as he leaned over the sink, and made him straighten while she peeled it off. She tossed it into the corner.

"Turn around. Let's see how bad you are."

Lucas obediently turned around and closed his eyes. The left side of his face felt full of pins and needles and he could feel his brow and cheek swelling. He'd have a doozy of a black eye tomorrow. His nose had pretty well quit bleeding, though. He felt Virginia's careful fingers probing his face. Then there was the sound of the faucet running and the cool, welcome feel of a damp facecloth as she gently wiped the blood and sweat away. It hurt but felt good at the same time.

He smiled crookedly and opened his eyes. "What's for lunch? I've worked up a hell of an appetite."

"Oh, you!" she said, but Lucas caught her stifling a smile all the same.

She turned the tub faucets on full blast. "Why don't you take off the rest of your clothes and get in the tub? I'll find an ice pack for that eye. Stay here, I'll be right back."

She was gone before Lucas could make up his mind whether or not to ask her if she'd take off the rest of his clothes for him. Then he figured he could manage with a little difficulty. Any more teasing, and she was likely to take a swat at him herself.

Awkwardly he stripped off his pants and socks and stood there for a moment in his underwear. Then he thought, *What the hell,* and stripped that off, too. It wasn't as though she'd never seen him with nothing on. He sat down heavily on the closed toilet seat and rested against the tank, eyes shut. Damn, he felt weak—

"Oh!" Virginia was back. She had a plastic two-pound sack of frozen peas in her hand and her cheeks were a little flushed. Probably more from the domestic crisis, Lucas thought with a flash of sarcasm, than his state of undress.

"Here." She carefully positioned the bag of frozen peas over his eye, letting it extend onto his bruised and sore nose. He'd closed his eyes again, but he felt her knees against his and had the distinct impression that she was leaning over him. He suspected that if he opened his one good eye he could look right down that loose dress thing she was wearing. He refrained.

He heard the sink tap run, and then she was gently blotting at his face again, murmuring little encouragements and tiny "Oh!"'s and "Does that hurt?" Then, amazingly, he felt her soft lips on his face, here and there and here again. He opened his good eye. She was directly in front of him, her face flushed, her eyes bright and hazy at the same time, and yes, he could look right down the front of her dress as she bent over him, clear down to her belly and beyond, and she wasn't wearing a stitch under that pink flowered thing. Not a stitch.

Suddenly he felt her take his face in her hands, gently, and position it so that she could place her mouth on this. "Oh, Lucas," she moaned, and he felt his entire body respond, from his painful black eye down to his bare feet. And everything in between... "Kiss me." She climbed onto his lap and pressed her lips against his.

He couldn't believe what was happening. She was kissing him like a frenzied woman, touching him everywhere and moaning softly, like a woman in pain. *Or a woman feeling intense sexual desire.*

In the name of heaven, was this really happening? After all this time? Lucas's response was immediate. He reached up and slid his hands under her dress.

"Oh, honey...kiss me again," he breathed, and she did, and then she frantically hiked up her dress and settled herself on his lap and he felt her wriggle around, seeking him, until he thought he'd go crazy.

"The bath," he gasped with the last rational thought that remained in his head. "Better turn the water off."

With a moan of exasperation, she leaned over as far as she could without leaving his lap and turned off the faucets. Then she was wriggling again, her breath hot and fast in his face, her lips seizing his again. Lucas felt her fit herself over him and moan and then he was inside her. He gripped her hips as she began to whimper and gasp and move frantically over him.

"Oh, baby!" He held her tightly as she arched

over him and cried out again and again, cries of deep, incredible delight that came straight from her soul. Lucas felt his own responses, delayed at the miracle of what was happening to him, to her, catch up, and with a few deep surges, he emptied himself in her, and she gasped again and cried out and then sagged against him, sobbing. *With release, with joy, with pleasure.* He felt her hot breath on his chest, her hair tangled and wild on his face.

Damn. What had just happened? Was this the end of their problems in bed? He had to believe… He *did* believe…

"Oh, Lucas," she said, lifting her head and staring into his eyes. He saw the wonder, the questions, in her beautiful teary eyes and couldn't keep from grinning. "I can't believe it. I just can't believe it. I…I just wanted to…to do it. I wanted you. I couldn't wait. I…I've never felt like that before!" She looked embarrassed.

He bent forward and tasted her lips, full and soft and moist. "Believe it, honey." He kissed her deeply and felt himself stiffen inside her again. *This was crazy!* Her breath came in sudden little pants and he unbuttoned the top of her dress so that he could see her breasts, small and round and perfect, in front of him as she arched again and again, moving frantically on his lap, seeking the sensation that had been denied her for so long. Lucas took the tip of one rosy breast into his mouth and she cried out, rocking on his lap as he held her bottom tightly against him. As she climaxed again, so, too, did he.

"Oh, honey," he managed, when he caught his

breath. "I never thought of something like this. Maybe I should get a black eye more often, eh?"

She laughed weakly. Lucas lifted the dress off her altogether. After a moment or so—the two of them grinning at each other like teenagers—he stood, with her legs still wrapped around him and his hands firmly on her bottom supporting her, and stepped into the tub.

Luckily it was an old-fashioned cast-iron model, long and with a sloped back. They lay together in the warm water and she gently sponged him from head to toe and then he sponged her, stopping now and again to kiss her here and there. Her knee, her toes—one by one—her shoulder. It was wonderful. They talked quietly. It was as though they'd just discovered each other—which, in a sense, they had.

They talked and kissed and touched each other all over. Then, finally, they got out and dried each other off. Virginia picked up her caftan and slipped it on and Lucas wrapped a towel around his middle. "Lunch?" he said with a grin.

"Give me five minutes," she said, and left the bathroom. Lucas wiped the fogged-up mirror with another towel and took a good look at himself in the mirror. "Wow." He turned his face from left to right, examining the damage. The bridge of his nose was bruised and there was a scratch on one cheek. His black eye was going to be a whopper, frozen peas or no frozen peas. Damn that Gagnon—he'd had a nasty right.

Then he paused. No, *thank* you, Johnny Gagnon. How it had happened or what the reasons might be, something else had come out of that fight with Gagnon—and it was something he would always be grateful for. Virginia wasn't afraid anymore. She'd put the horrible experience of being raped by Gagnon behind her. Their lives were going to be lived in the present now, not the past.

Maybe they'd still fill this big old house with kids and toys and dogs. Maybe they'd still build a family together.

Lucas whistled as he went down to the kitchen. His life was now perfect. The table was set for two. A chilled bottle of white wine sat in an ice bucket on the table. There were two glasses and Virginia was just putting a delicious-looking omelet on the table.

He opened the wine and poured some into each glass, then handed one to his wife. "Cheers, Virginia," he said.

"Yes." She raised her glass, smiling into his eyes. Hers were soft and happy, no longer haunted. Lucas felt truly blessed. "Cheers."

There was no question of either of them going to the office that afternoon. After demolishing the omelet, they left the dishes on the table and went upstairs with their glasses and the remaining half bottle of wine. Lucas wanted to introduce their marital bed to their newfound marital pleasures.

Which they did. The afternoon hours sped away, until suddenly, feeling as guilty as teenagers caught in the act, they heard the door open downstairs.

The children were home from school already!

No, it must be Natasha and Robert—he'd forgotten for a moment that Theresa had taken Tammy to Calgary.

Virginia dashed into the en suite bathroom and Lucas quickly pulled on a pair of jeans and a T-shirt. He heard Virginia say something from the bathroom, but it was just a mumble; he couldn't quite hear her words. He strode out, closing the bedroom door behind him.

"Robert?" he called from the top of the stairs.

"It's me! Natasha." The girl was standing in the foyer, wearing her hat and gloves and coat. She had a key, Lucas remembered, to use when she brought the children home from school. She was alone. "Is Robert here?"

"Robert?" Lucas glanced at his watch. It was already half-past three. He and Virginia had completely forgotten about the time. "Isn't he with you?"

"I thought that guy must have brought him home by now."

"Guy?"

"At the school. He met us on the sidewalk and said Mrs. Yellowfly wanted him to pick up Robert. I knew she was sick. Robert said he'd met him, that he was a friend of his mom's. I thought it was okay. I saw the car here when I walked home for lunch today, so I thought it must be all right." Natasha paused, looking worried. "It's okay, isn't it? I went to the library, but then I started thinking maybe I should've checked with Mrs. Yellowfly and so I just stopped by to make sure everything's all right."

"Friend of Virginia's?" Lucas said slowly, horror dawning. "Was he driving a station wagon?"

"Yeah." Natasha took a step farther into the house. "Mr. Yellowfly—you okay?"

Lucas gripped the banister until the muscles in his arms and hands hurt. How was he going to tell Virginia?

Johnny Gagnon had gone to Sam Steele Elementary and taken her son.

CHAPTER NINETEEN

VIRGINIA OPENED the door to their bedroom and tucked her shirt into her jeans. Her face was flushed, she was barefoot and busy finger-combing her hair as she came out, in the midst of telling him something.

"...forgotten about Tammy not being there today but— *Lucas, what's wrong?*"

"Did you send anybody to the school to pick up Robert?" He had to be sure.

"No." Her eyes locked on his.

"Johnny must have gone to the school—"

"Where's Robert?" Virginia rushed to the railing and looked down. Natasha looked up helplessly. Virginia screamed, *"Omigod! Where's Robert? Where's my baby?"*

She rushed down the stairs before Lucas could stop her and grabbed Natasha's hand in both of hers. "Where's my baby, Nattie? Where's *my baby?*"

Natasha turned beet-red and Lucas knew she was about to burst into tears.

Lucas raced downstairs. "Virginia!" He gripped her shoulder and she tried to fight him off. "Get hold of yourself."

She whirled around to face him, tears streaming

down her cheeks. "How can I do that? That...that *bastard* has my son!" Lucas caught a glimpse of Natasha's wide-eyed shock from the corner of his eye. "We've got to *go,* Lucas. We've got to find him—"

"Hold on. Let's stop and think this through."

"While he's driving away with Robert? Maybe out of the province? No way!" Virginia shoved her feet into her boots and grabbed for her car keys. Lucas seized her wrist.

"What are you doing? Where are you going?"

"To the school. Then...then I'll drive around and try to find them."

"That's crazy. Sit down here for a minute." He led her to a chair and gently pushed her into it. She covered her face with both hands and started to sob. It was a terrible, dry sound that tore Lucas's heart out.

"Should I g-go? Mr. Yellowfly?" Natasha looked completely bewildered. "Should I call the police or something? I'm so sorry. I...I thought it was all right..."

"Never mind, Nattie. No, my wife didn't send a friend to pick up Robert." Lucas dragged both hands through his hair. He must look like hell— black eye, bare feet, T-shirt, hair on end. "It's just that we figure we know who Robert's with. He's not a friend. He's... I can't explain it now. Maybe you better go on home. Don't worry. I'll call the police if we think it's necessary."

He ushered the teenager toward the door. She was beside herself, but Lucas didn't have time to comfort her now. His wife needed him. "Look, it's something that could have happened to anybody, Natasha. Don't blame yourself. Robert will be back soon, I'm sure. It's just a shock, that's all. Thanks for coming by to tell us. That was a big help."

He shut the door behind her and strode back to Virginia, who'd stopped sobbing and was now staring wild-eyed over his shoulder. At nothing. Or—who knew?—maybe at all her worst nightmares coming true....

"What do you mean, he'll be back soon? You don't know! You don't know *anything!* You don't know what that bastard's got in mind!"

"Listen, honey. Think! What kind of car did he have? Did you happen to see the license plate? Damn it, I didn't pay any attention," Lucas muttered, almost to himself. He could have kicked himself for not noticing a detail like that now that it was so crucial. But who went around memorizing license plates on other people's cars? "The car was a Chevy. Or a Pontiac. Station wagon. And it was brown—"

"No, it was green. Dark green." Virginia sounded very certain. She was watching him now, as though she expected that he'd come up with some answers. That they'd actually get somewhere—fast.

"Okay, dark-colored. Green or brown. Rusty. Probably ten or fifteen years old. Damn it—I'm no car guy. I'm not sure." He straightened. "We'd better call the cops and then I'll go over to the school with you and try to find out what happened. Natasha says she saw him on the sidewalk. That means he probably wasn't even inside the building. How would he have known what Robert looked like?"

"I met him once on the street downtown. I had Robert with me." Virginia moaned, grabbing his arm. Her pupils were dilated. "I've got to find my son. I want my baby *now*, Lucas. It's winter. It's cold. Who knows where that creep is taking him?"

Virginia was on her feet again. She followed him to the phone. He punched in the number of the local police station, his mind reeling. He gave the details as he knew them and listened to the affable tsk-tsking of the constable on duty. He decided he had to make it clear to the on-duty officer that this was serious. "We're pretty sure who the kidnapper is, Wilkie—he's done it before. He's got a record—check it. It's Johnny Gagnon. Yes, *that* Johnny Gagnon. No, there's no ransom note, damn it—he took the kid from school half an hour ago. That's kidnapping in my books! Okay? Fine."

He hung up and turned to Virginia. "They're sending someone over to take a statement. He'll be here in a few minutes. Hey, where you going?"

"To the school. I want to find out what happened before all the teachers leave for the day, see if anybody else saw anything—"

"What about the cop?"

"You can send him there to find me. I've got to *do* something! I can't just stand here." Virginia shrugged on her winter coat and turned to him, wiping at her tears with the back of her hand. "Lucas?"

He took a step toward her and pulled her into his arms. "What, baby?"

"I'm scared."

Lucas held her tight. "Me, too, honey. Me, too."

GETTING THE KID into his car had been a piece of cake. He wished he could be there when Yellowfly found out. He wanted to see that son of a bitch's face. Ginny deserved a good scare, too, after what she'd put him through back at her law office that day. Pretending she'd never seen him before!

He'd planned to drop in to the school office at five minutes to three and say Mrs. Yellowfly had sent him for Robert and ask which room was Mrs. Brown's. But he hadn't even had to get the kid. The bell had rung just as he was sauntering down to room 114, thinking how little things had changed— even the hallway was the same putrid green—since he'd gone there as a boy. So he'd gone back and stood by the door as the kids started to come out.

He'd spotted Robert right away, walking by himself. Lucky he remembered him from that time he'd seen him on the street with Ginny. The kid bought the story about being sent by his mom to pick him up, no questions asked.

There were a few teachers around, including Mrs. Brown. She didn't seem to recall him, which was just as well. How many kids had she seen through kindergarten? How many brats like him? Thousands, probably. He was almost down the sidewalk with the kid when that nosy baby-sitter ran into them, Natalie or Natasha somebody.

He didn't have to talk much. Robert said he was

going with him, that he was an old friend of his mom's and that he'd see her later.

Yeah, they'd see her later, all right. Much later.

Then—just to be on the safe side—as they headed out of town with Robert happily licking a Grizzly double chocolate ice cream in the front seat, he'd stopped at the hospital parking lot to do a little license-plate switcheroo. Just in case. Didn't want the cops chasing him if they had his license number on their computer, which he was pretty sure they did.

Ha! Johnny Gagnon was no dummy.

He picked a Jaguar to switch plates with and enjoyed the little joke. Some poor old doc—he'd probably be working late, sewing up some poor sucker's innards, and wouldn't even notice his plates had been switched.

He'd only stopped by Ginny's house to say goodbye, damn it, tell her he was leaving town. He'd just been trying to act decent, show her there were no hard feelings. Then she'd peeked through the curtains but wouldn't open the door. It made him mad. Jeez, you'd think he was some kind of criminal!

Eberle had put in a bad word about him with the management at the Co-op and Johnny'd been fired. His parole officer wasn't happy, but he'd given Johnny permission—written permission, even—to leave town for a few days, maybe find a job and a place to stay somewheres else. If he had no luck, he'd agreed to come back to Glory. But that was a lie. No way was he coming back to this dump. He'd find work in Pincher Creek or Stavely or High River. Anywhere but here.

Johnny climbed back into the car after switching the plates and gingerly touched his cheekbone. It hurt, but hadn't bruised up the way he'd thought it would. His gut was sore, where Yellowfly had sucker-punched him. After the little dustup on Second Avenue, he'd gone home, showered, changed, packed his bags to leave town and then, on the way out, had another idea. It was almost three o'clock. He'd pick up Ginny's kid from school and take him for a ride in the country. And then, when the Yellowflys were ready to have heart attacks, he'd return the kid, no harm done.

He glanced sideways. Seemed like a nice enough little guy. Quiet, but asked a few questions, too. Crazy about ice cream, but what kid wasn't?

"You warm enough, kid?" Johnny fiddled with the heater controls. Still wasn't working right. He had a bone to pick with Ed next time he saw him for selling him this bucket of bolts.

"No, I'm fine, mister," the kid said, looking up through those big glasses and smiling. Kinda cute, really. "Say, where'd you meet my mom, anyway?"

"We went to school together."

"Really?"

Johnny couldn't resist. "You betcha. We went all through school together, right here in Glory. She was my girlfriend in high school, did you know that?"

"Really? That's neat. Did you have Mrs. Brown?"

"As a matter of fact, I did."

"Cool!" Robert vigorously licked his cone. "Did you like her?"

"Nah." Johnny grinned at the boy. They were headed out of town—where to, he had no idea. He hadn't thought that far.

Robert giggled. "Why not?"

"Too strict. How about you—you like her?"

The boy sighed. "I adore her," he said.

"*Adore* her?" Johnny laughed. "That's a pretty big word for a kid your age."

"Yep." Robert kicked his feet. He had to be cold; Johnny was chilly in his ski jacket. "Tammy taught me that one. She teaches me a lot of big words. Do you know Tammy?"

"Not really," Johnny admitted cautiously.

"Well, she's kinda like my big sister. She's related to Lucas. He's my dad, you know. Since my mom married him. That makes Tammy and me cousins, sorta."

"Yeah," Johnny said through his teeth, "I know your dad, all right. Hey, kid. Where you want to go?"

"Aren't we supposed to go home? My mom will be wondering where I am."

"Nah. She told me to take you out for a little spin. Show you a good time," Johnny lied. "Give her a break for a couple hours. She ain't feeling too good. So, what d'you want to do? Go to Calgary?"

"Calgary?" The boy's eyes were huge. "All the way *there?*"

"Sure, why not?" Johnny smiled. He was getting to like the little guy. Didn't look much like Ginny, with all that dark hair, but he kind of reminded him of someone or something. Couldn't think what, though. "Or how about Lethbridge or High River? Your wish is my command," he teased in a TV voice.

"Okay, let's go then!" Robert giggled again. "I'm supposed to clear the table tonight, too, but Tammy can do it twice for a change. Hey, this is fun, mister!"

Johnny flicked on the radio and got a country-and-western station from Medicine Hat. He wondered if Ginny and Yellowfly would've called the cops right off or not. He hoped not. But if they had, the fuzz would be looking for plates that were on a car parked in the doctor's lot at the hospital.

They drove in silence for a while, listening to the chat on the radio. At one point the deejay rattled off a bunch of birthday greetings to listeners in southern Alberta and Saskatchewan, and the boy piped up.

"That's where I was born, you know," he said, "Saska...Sasach...well, Regina. My mom went there on a bus and had me."

"She did?" Johnny frowned. "So when's your birthday?"

"When's yours?" Robert asked slyly, and Johnny decided to play along.

"November tenth," he said.

"Mine's February twenty-seventh."

"How old are you—six?"

"Five. Tammy's nearly nine. Her birthday's in January. How old are you?"

"Hey, don't you know you're not supposed to ask old people that? It ain't polite."

Robert laughed.

They were approaching High River. It was nearly six o'clock and dark already.

"You hungry, kid?"

"For what?"

The kid was no dummy. Johnny felt a warm glimmer of appreciation for his quick answers. "What if I said for a nice big salad with carrots and beets and stuff? Or bean sprouts?"

"No thanks!"

"How about for McDonald's? Or Subway?"

"McDonald's!"

"Okay. We'll see what's going on in High River."

Johnny wheeled off the highway and onto the exit for the town of High River. The town, built along the Highwood River, was alight with Christmas decorations. Robert's eyes shone as Johnny cruised slowly up and down Main Street, then along the tracks, then back onto the access highway where the fast-food strip was.

They decided to go inside, instead of using the drive-through, although Johnny was a little worried that news of him taking the kid might have spread through the district already. But he was damn cold and the kid had to be cold, too. They ordered a couple of Big Mac meals and chocolate shakes. Then they sat at one of the brightly lit plastic tables and dug into their meals. Robert was a good eater, Johnny noted, with another flicker of satisfaction.

He worked his way right through the burger and halfway through the fries before he slowed down.

"Hey, can I ask you a question, mister?" he said, wiping his fingers carefully on one of the napkins that came with their order.

"Sure, kid," Johnny said, about to take a big mouthful of burger. "Ask away."

"Are you my real dad?"

Johnny practically choked on his pickle. "Your real *dad*. What the hell you talking about, kid?"

"My real dad. I asked my mom and she won't tell me. Lucas isn't my real dad, you know. He's my dad 'cause him and my mom are married and he adopted me and all that, but..." Robert sighed and looked into the distance where there was a kiddie area with balls and little kiddie rides. When he looked back, his eyes were suspiciously bright. "I just wish I knew, that's all. I thought you might be the one."

Calmly he picked up a french fry and dipped it in the paper ketchup cup, then stuffed it in his mouth.

Johnny didn't know what to say. He'd been sucker-punched again, and this time by a kid. His *dad?* Slowly he chewed a bite of burger, frowning.

He was a nice kid. And obviously Ginny had been fooling around with someone she wasn't all that proud of, or she'd have told him who his dad was. Born the end of February... He frowned again and set his burger down on the table. He felt a coughing fit coming on.

"Can I go goof around at the playland for a while, mister?"

"Uh, sure, kid." Johnny managed to choke back the cough. "Go ahead."

She must've gotten pregnant about the time he'd seen her, the time he'd taken her up to Bob's cabin on the Powderface Trail.

Holy cow. Holy shit. Holy hell.

Maybe he *was*...

Johnny counted backward on his fingers. The kid was born the last week in February. It was the middle of May he'd robbed that grocery. The sixteenth, how could he forget?

That made it a week or two either way but...it could have happened.

Johnny felt his heart pounding like a hammer mill. *Holy shit.* His *dad?*

Had they screwed, him and Ginny? He couldn't remember. He'd got into the rye pretty heavy, he remembered. And he remembered some soup she'd made and the leftover pepperoni he'd found in a package on the sofa and eaten for breakfast next morning...*and the torn panties under the bed.*

Johnny crossed himself—instinct—then cursed himself for being such a damn fool.

Man, if it was true—how in hell would *he* ever know? It wasn't as though she'd look him up in the slammer and tell him she wanted child support, was it?

And did he even *want* to know the truth? The notion scared the shit out of him. He wasn't daddy material, no way. It was partly what they'd split over, him and his ex-wife. She'd wanted him to keep his nose clean and start a family. He didn't know what scared him most, the prospect of working nine to five or being responsible for some kid coming into the world. Some poor little kid who'd get knocked around and disappointed like most kids were.

He stared at the dark-haired boy in the play area. Robert was throwing himself from a small platform and laughing as he nearly buried himself in plastic balls. Johnny saw two other kids playing there, both girls.

His son. Maybe. He pushed the rest of his meal away. He wasn't hungry anymore, and that didn't happen too often.

He leaned forward and watched Robert. Now what? He had a lot of thinking to do. This changed everything.

"Hey, Robert!" he yelled, and the kid stood at the fence that separated the dining area from the play area.

"Yeah?"

"Let's forget Calgary, huh?"

The boy hesitated, just for a second, then shrugged. "Doesn't matter to me, mister."

"What about a movie?"

"Sure!"

"Five minutes, okay?"

"Okay!" Robert ran back into the plastic balls. "Yahoo!" He threw himself face-forward into the balls, then, grinning like an idiot, glanced at the two girls to see if they approved.

His father's kid, Johnny thought, his chest swelling. Hot damn. He needed to think.

And to pee.

He got up and headed for the men's, crossing his fingers that the High River cinema was running something suitable for kids.

Suitable for kids? When had he ever had a thought like that before?

Luckily some Disney flick was on, and midweek on a cold evening there weren't too many people in the theater. Johnny bought Robert a big box of popcorn and a giant Coke. He bought some cherry licorice twists and a box of Cracker Jacks for himself. He sat there, listening to the kid giggle at the funny spots—Johnny laughed a few times himself—and watching him stuff popcorn into his face, and wondered what to do next.

He had to go back. Pronto. This was no longer a gag. Ginny'd be sick with worry. He hated to admit it, but he didn't want her to think he was the kind of guy who'd just kidnap a kid for the hell of it. Even if he was. She didn't *know* he'd just done it for a lark and that he'd never hurt him or anything, and now that he thought he might be the kid's dad, it mattered what she thought of him.

The movie wasn't over for another hour. Then nearly forty minutes on the road back to Glory. Maybe more, since he'd seen a few snowflakes coming down on the way to the theater. He'd better call her.

"I'll be right back, kid," he whispered, feeling in

his jeans pocket for some change. "Gotta make a phone call, tell your ma you're all right. Okay?"

"Sure." The boy barely glanced away from the screen.

"And, hey—" Johnny leaned back toward the boy when he got to the end of the aisle "—don't go off with anybody, eh? There's a lotta nuts in the world, y'know. Looking for kids 'n' stuff."

"Yeah, yeah, I know."

Johnny walked back to the lobby to find a pay phone. Damn, he hoped that the doc hadn't gone home for the evening. He'd have to change the license plates back. Wasn't *that* a hell of a note.

Well, he thought, picking up the receiver and starting to feed his quarters into the phone slot, *guess there's a first time for everything.*

CHAPTER TWENTY

THE PHONE IN THE KITCHEN sounded like a fire alarm to Virginia's strained nerves. She grabbed it on the second ring.

"Ginny, it's—"

"Johnny! Where are you? *Where's Robert?*" She clutched the receiver so tightly she heard her knuckles crack. The relief! The incredible roiling of her stomach in relief...

"The kid's fine. Look, we gotta talk—"

"Where is he? I mean, right this minute—where is he? Let me talk to him!" She whirled and met Lucas's astonished gaze. He mouthed, "Where?" and she shrugged.

"You can't talk to him. I'm at a pay phone. He's in the theater watching a movie."

"A *movie!* My God, Johnny, don't you realize this is serious? You took my son from school. You *kidnapped* him!"

"Listen here, this is what we've gotta talk about. I'm bringing him back. Okay? Right away. Soon as the movie's over."

"What movie?" Why did she ask that? She had to know, crazy as it was.

There was a pause of a second or two, then
Johnny said, *"Scream, Part Two."*

"You're crazy! That's no movie for a five-year-
old kid! You—"

"Man, can't you take a joke, Ginny? Of course I
wouldn't take a kid to a movie like that." He
sounded irritable all of a sudden, and she panicked.
She didn't want to irritate him; he had Robert. *Dear
God, how could she forget that?* "It's some Disney
flick, I don't remember what the hell it's called."

"Where are you?" She prayed that even now, the
telephone company, on orders from the police, were
tracing this call.

"High River."

"High River! What in the world are you doing
up there?" Which was a crazy question, as she already knew they were at a theater. Watching a
movie!

"Never mind that. Listen, I'll be back before ten,
I promise."

There was a long delay, as though he was trying
to think of something more to say.

"What else, Johnny?" She didn't have a good
feeling about this.

"He asked me if I was his dad."

"He what?" She tried to laugh it off. "I don't
know why he'd say something ridiculous like that."

"That's what I thought. The kid told me his birthday. It don't take no Einstein to figure you musta
been expecting when I saw you last. Either that
or..." His voice was genuinely perplexed. "We
didn't *do* nothing, did we? Up there at the cabin?"

Virginia saw red.

"You don't know what *happened?*" Her voice rose. "You kidnapped me and you got stinking drunk and..." Virginia was shouting, her voice cracking. Fresh tears poured down her cheeks.

Lucas stepped forward and reached for the phone. "Here, let me take that."

"No!" She pulled away. "And then you *raped* me, you bastard! I hate you. I hate the thought of you. I hate what you've done to me and my family."

"Settle down, Ginny." Johnny sounded shocked. "For cripe's sake, settle down."

She still couldn't believe that he really had no recollection of what had happened, yet at the same time she felt huge relief that she'd never told anyone but Lucas. *He didn't know; the stupid bastard was too drunk to remember anything.* He might have gotten off with some judge or jury either at trial or appeal, and she'd have been dragged through all that, she and her family, and everyone would know that her son was the result of rape by a drunken fool with a criminal record.

Her first love. The wild and crazy boy she'd once loved with all her heart. He'd ruined all her plans; he'd broken her heart.

It was too much; it was unbearable. She wanted her son in her arms. She wanted the whole day to wipe itself from their memory—hers and Lucas's and Robert's. And poor Natasha's. And her own parents', whose immediate sympathy and offers of help had moved her deeply. Her father—she still couldn't believe it—had wanted to phone all his colleagues and get them out looking for the boy. Literally out there with dogs and flashlights. Maybe she'd been wrong about their feelings for her son. Maybe they'd just been unable to express what they'd felt all these years.

No. She didn't want the day's memory wiped out. That would mean all the good things would be wiped out, too. That she'd discovered how much she loved Lucas. That her parents really did care about their only grandchild, her son. *That Robert had been born at all.*

"Please deposit another dollar in coins immediately or this call will be disconnected," came the toneless voice of a mechanical operator.

Virginia heard the clink of a few coins.

"Jeez, that's all I got."

She had to know. "Did you tell him...did you tell him you might be?"

"No. I figured that was your business—I'm no dad type. That's up to you, Ginny, what you do. Look, I gotta—"

The call was disconnected. Weakly she handed the receiver to Lucas, who hung it up and pulled her into his arms.

"I'm sorry, honey," he said, cradling her against his chest. "I'm so sorry."

She sobbed. Her heart was breaking. Johnny was bringing back her son, he said—and, damn her, she still believed him—but her life was broken into a million pieces.

No matter what kind of person Johnny Gagnon was, no matter how he'd broken her heart and ruined all her dreams, he was still her son's father. She could not deny her son a father.

Like it or not, she had to live with that fact.

"You want a cup of tea, honey?" Lucas sounded worried.

She wiped her face with the back of her hands and nodded. She didn't want tea, but he needed something to do. Something that made him feel he was helping her. Thank heaven for Lucas Yellowfly! Thank heaven he'd stood by her through all this.

"Lucas?" she whispered, and he looked down at her. She reached up and touched his bruised cheek softly. "Thank you. For everything. I love you so much. I'm so glad you took a chance on me."

"Oh, Virginia!" Lucas hugged her and kissed the top of her head. "Some chance! Robert's coming home. Everything will work out now, you'll see, honey."

"Promise?" She laughed shakily and stepped back, out of the circle of his arms.

"I can't promise. You know that. But I'll do my best. I'll do my best to make sure things work out for us. For Robert. Hell, even for Johnny, if that's the way you and Robert want it."

"I love you, Lucas," she said steadily, meeting his gaze, loving the flame that shot through the dark depths of his eyes. Loving the feeling that still resonated through her body since their afternoon together, the feeling of being well and truly loved.

"I love you, too, babe. I always have."

She knew he meant it. He went to the counter and plugged in the kettle. She had promised her parents she'd call the instant she heard anything. She dialed their number with trembling fingers.

"Mom? I heard from Johnny. Yes, he's got Robert, and Robert's okay. They're watching a movie somewhere—can you believe it?" She hiccupped, then sniffed and tried to smile through her tears. She held the receiver in both hands. "Yeah, crazy Johnny Gagnon. Mom, there's something I have to tell you and Dad. I should have told you years ago, but I just couldn't—Johnny is Robert's father. Yes. Yes, he is. Okay. Thank you, Mom. Thank you. Yes. Give Dad a hug for me. I'll tell you about it some other time." She wiped her eyes with her sleeve and said goodbye.

Lucas looked shocked.

"I had to tell them, Lucas," she said as she went back to the table. "I've held this in for way too long. Now Johnny suspects, anyway. Robert put the idea in his head. Whether I like it or not, I'm going to have to face up to it."

Without a word Lucas thrust a mug of tea at her. She sat down and warmed her trembling fingers on the hot ceramic. Lucas sat opposite her at the kitchen table, eying her with concern.

"So Robert asked him if he was his dad, the same way he asked me that time?"

"Yes." Virginia shook her head; she wanted to laugh and cry at the same time. "I've got to face up to it, don't I? My son won't let me do anything else."

"Do you think we should talk to the cops, honey?

Find out if they were monitoring the call—and if they could go to High River and pick Robert up?''

Virginia considered. How would that experience affect her son? Cops bursting into a darkened movie theater, grabbing him, arresting the man he'd just asked about being his real dad. The man he'd eventually find out *was* his real dad.

"I don't think so, Lucas. You know—" she shook her head and her voice cracked "—crazy as this is, I actually believe Johnny. I actually believe he'll have Robert back by ten. Am I crazy, Lucas? Am I?"

"You're not crazy, honey. It's natural. Your good feelings are there all the time, beneath the surface. Beneath the bad feelings. He's not only Robert's father, he's somebody you once cared about a lot."

Virginia sipped at her tea. Lucas had laced it with honey. It was sweet and good, and she felt energy running through her system again. "This has always been my worst nightmare, Lucas," she whispered. "That Johnny might come and take my son away."

"He's bringing him back now. Didn't he say that?"

"Yes."

"And you think he'll do what he says? You truly believe him?"

Virginia stared at her husband. "You can call me a fool from the middle both ways, Lucas, but I do. I believe him. I still don't believe, in my heart, that he's an evil man." She searched Lucas's gaze for support and saw plenty. "You know what I mean? Considering all he's done to me and all the grief he's caused me...I still have Robert," she whispered. "I still have my son."

Lucas reached across the table and covered her hand with his. "Never forget that. Never forget that Robert is what my ma used to call the silver lining. She said every cloud has one. Me going to law school was what made scrubbing other peoples' floors worthwhile, she always said. Robert's your silver lining in this business with Gagnon."

Suddenly Virginia put down her cup and gripped her head with both hands. "*Lucas!* I'm living in some kind of la-la land. Johnny's got my *son!* He's in High River. What if he changes his mind and doesn't bring him back? Or what if he's drinking and they get in an accident on the way?"

"Virginia—"

She stood up, pushing her mug away. "I'm going there. I'm getting Robert myself."

"In High River?" Lucas stood, too.

"I've got to! I can't just sit and wait here until ten. What if he doesn't show up? What then? It's only a half hour drive."

She grabbed her coat and thrust her bare feet into her winter boots. Lucas grabbed her shoulder.

"It's forty minutes. And you're in no condition to drive."

"Yes, I am." She dug in her coat pocket and pulled out her car keys. "Maybe you want to stay here, in case they come back and I miss them—"

"I'm coming with you. We'll take the BMW—Damn!"

"What's wrong?"

"I forgot—I left my car at the office. At noon."
Lucas smiled. "We'll have to take your old beast.
Or the pickup."

"My car."

Virginia felt better when she was on the road. It
had started to snow and the falling snow in the high
beams of the Mazda nearly blinded her. The tears
that kept gushing unexpectedly didn't help. All she
could think of was Robert, how tiny and pink and
helpless he'd been when he was born. The grim hospital room where she'd had her son. How much she
loved him. And then she'd think of how angry she
was with Johnny. It helped, after all these years, to
get it all out.

"That stupid bastard! He didn't even *remember*
it, Lucas!" She turned to look at him in the dim
light from the dash and the car swerved slightly.
"Can you believe that?"

"Watch what you're doing, damn it!"

"He didn't even *remember* what he did to me. He
raped me. He forced me. It still makes me sick to
my stomach when I think about it. It's not right. It's
not fair. He should have to *pay* for what he did, the
way I had to pay—"

"Pull over!"

"What?"

"I said pull over and stop the car. I'm driving."

Obediently Virginia slowed and pulled the car
onto the shoulder of the highway. The snow was
sticking to the windshield and her boots when she
got out to trade places with Lucas. She was relieved
that he'd offered to drive.

Lucas let her vent all her feelings. He drove slowly and carefully—more slowly than she would have liked—through the snowstorm. By the time they reached High River, she wasn't sure she was doing the right thing, after all. What would Robert think? He'd wonder why they'd driven there to get him, why her eyes were so red. She had to get hold of herself. She pulled down the visor and put on the map light and tried to repair some of the damage. She ran a brush through her hair, which was about all she could do, then rummaged through the glove box and found some tissues to scrub her eyes.

"The theater's just down the street here." Lucas turned the corner carefully and slowed as they approached the brightly lit building. Christmas lights sparkled everywhere on the fresh snow. "Looks like the movie's just let out."

Knots of people emerged from the door of the theater. Lucas stopped right in front in a No Parking zone. Virginia rolled down her window. Lucas opened his door and got out.

"Do you see them?" she called softly. *Oh, Robert! Johnny.*

Suddenly she saw them. They hadn't spotted her. Robert was holding Johnny's hand and skipping along at his side, looking up and talking a mile a minute. He clutched a bedraggled half-empty bag of popcorn in his other hand. Johnny was smiling and replying to the boy.

Virginia's heart stopped. This was her son and his father. She *had* to make room in her life for Johnny

Gagnon, no matter what she felt. There was no other way.

"Mom!" Robert had seen them. He ran toward the car and Virginia got out. She didn't know whether to hug him or not. She wanted to pick him up and stuff him in the car and drive away into the night. As far and fast as she could, to get away from this man. But she knew she couldn't do that.

Johnny hung back, but he showed no sign of taking off.

"We went to McDonald's and I got a giant Coke at the movies. I couldn't finish it. And he bought me ice cream from that Grizzly place. And we saw this really funny movie and— Hey, mister!" the boy shouted. "Here's my mom and dad!"

His dad. Lucas.

"Are you okay, Robert?" She couldn't help it. It was the mother in her.

"Okay? Yeah! I'm having a lot of fun. It's already way past my bedtime. Boy, wait till I tell Tammy and Teddy about this. They're gonna be mad...." He grinned.

Johnny came forward, hunched a little, hands deep in his jeans pockets. He looked sheepish. She had a few things she'd like to tell him, but she wasn't going to do it here in public and in front of her son. No matter what kind of scumbag she thought Johnny Gagnon was, he happened to be her son's father and one day her son might want to have a relationship with him.

"See? My mom's here, mister!"

"I see that, kid."

Virginia bristled. She didn't like him talking to her son—their son—that way.

"I guess I'll go home with them now. Is that okay with you?" Robert looked anxiously into Johnny's face.

He grinned and reached out and ruffled Robert's hair. "That's just fine. See you around, eh, kid? Maybe we'll go ice-fishing pretty soon. Catch a big one. If you can't wait for spring, that is."

"Oh boy!" Robert opened the back door of the car and climbed in. He rolled down the window a few inches. "See ya, eh?" he echoed Johnny, and giggled. "Thanks for taking good care of me, mister." Then he rolled it back up.

"You've got a lot of nerve," she said in a low voice to Johnny. Lucas stepped up beside her. He hadn't said anything so far.

"I know, I know." Johnny took his hands out of his pockets and held them up briefly. "What can I say? I was mad. I wanted to scare you a little, the both of you. Yellowfly for punching my lights out, and you for pretending you didn't know me a while back. I had my reasons. I'm not the kind of guy who says sorry that easy, eh?"

"You raped me, you bastard!" Virginia's thoughts about not making a scene had evaporated. She had to say it; she had to say it to his face.

"That's what you said on the phone." Johnny's voice was low. Shocked. Almost apologetic. "Does that mean..." He couldn't seem to finish what he wanted to ask her.

"Yes," she said. "That means what you think it

does. Robert's your son. And mine. And don't you ever try and take him away from me or I'll…I'll have you strung up from the nearest tree so fast your head will spin. And I'll do it myself, too!''

"Hey—'' Lucas put his hand on her arm and she could hear the smile in his voice ''—no violence.''

"Yeah, take it easy, eh?'' Johnny stepped back and put up his hands again. ''You know me, I'm no father figure. You don't have to worry. Maybe take the kid fishing, maybe take him out for a burger now and then—that's all.'' He moved toward his station wagon, which was parked a few car lengths behind Virginia's—in a fire lane. Lucas moved around her car to get in the driver's side.

"Dr. Hornby?'' A uniformed policeman came forward. Virginia hadn't noticed the police car. She wouldn't have noticed the movie theater burning down, she'd been so focused on what she had to say to Johnny.

"What's goin' on?'' Johnny sounded alarmed.

"Well, we noticed you were parked in the fire lane here, sir, and then we ran a license check and found out you were a Dr. Mark Hornby from Glory. Is there anything wrong, sir? A medical emergency we don't know about?'' The officer looked Johnny up and down, clearly not impressed by the ''doctor's'' scruffy off-duty attire.

Virginia got back into the car and grinned. Lucas started the engine and turned toward her, eyebrow raised. Robert was quiet in the back seat. A quick glance showed her he was nearly asleep.

"What was that all about, honey?" Lucas asked softly, looking into the rearview mirror.

Virginia glanced out the window. Johnny Bandito! He'd never change. He was talking to the police officer, who had been joined by his partner. Probably talking real fast.

"Looks like he switched license plates with some poor doctor. Doctor's plates have a special logo, so they can park anywhere, you know—I guess that's what the cops noticed." She laughed. "Sounds just like Johnny! Probably thought they'd be out looking for the doctor, instead of him."

"No kidding."

"No kidding, Lucas. That's Johnny Gagnon."

Lucas smiled at her in the dimness and reached over to take her hand. "Home, darling?"

"Home."

They drove for a while, then Virginia remembered Robert's words. *My mom and dad.*

She squeezed Lucas's hand. "Did you hear what Robert said?"

"I did." Lucas smiled at her and returned the pressure on her hand.

"I'm so happy about that," she whispered, barely trusting her voice. Lucas was the kind of father a kid dreamed about. Kind, thoughtful, caring—a man to depend on.

Lucas didn't say anything. When he finally spoke, his voice was gruff with emotion. "I'll try to be the best dad any kid could ever have, honey."

"You will be," she said softly, her heart overflowing with love for her husband. "I know you will be."

When they got home, Lucas carried the sleepy Robert up to his room, helped Virginia put him to bed and stood in the half-open door for a while, watching him. Virginia could only guess what was going through his mind.

Her own mind was reeling from the events of the day. "I'm going to take a quick shower," she whispered to him. "Then bed. I'm exhausted. I must look a mess."

"You look beautiful to me," he whispered back, and she kissed him quickly before tiptoeing down the hall to their bedroom.

The hot water washed away her tension. *Her son was home; her family was complete.* She washed her hair and brushed her teeth. Somehow, talking directly to Johnny tonight, even under the stress of the situation, was another landmark. She'd gotten rid of something. Something that had eaten away at her and festered for years. *He didn't know he'd raped her; now he knew.* Now, at least in his own heart, he'd have to deal with that knowledge.

She pulled on her robe and belted it. She felt clean, really clean, for the first time in years.

Lucas had closed the door to Robert's room and gone downstairs to sit in front of the fire, which he'd lit. She sat down beside him and he put his arm around her.

"Happy?"

"Happier than I've ever been in my life, Lucas."

He tightened his arm around her. "Me, too."

She sighed. "One of these days I'm going to tell Robert that Johnny's his father. Not now, but when things settle down a little. We'll have to see if he gets out of the license-plate-switching business." She laughed and shook her head. "What a loser. Do you think he'll ever change, Lucas?"

"Probably not. Mind you, you know him a lot better than I do."

"I have a feeling you're going to get to know him a lot better, too," she said softly. "As the years go by."

Lucas touched his bruised eye gingerly. "I hope not."

Robert appeared at the top of the stairs. "I'm just getting some water, Mom." He stopped and narrowed his eyes when he saw Lucas. "Hey, Dad! Where'd you get that shiner?"

Lucas looked startled for a second or two. He touched his eye again. "I, er, had a little accident."

"Cool!" Robert continued down the hall toward the bathroom. "Boy, wait'll I tell Teddy my dad's got a shiner!"

Virginia moved closer to her husband. He put his arms around her. "He called you 'Dad,' again," she said, smiling. "He must mean it."

"I noticed," Lucas said proudly.

"You may not be his real father, but you're definitely his real dad."

"Yeah." Lucas looked even prouder. "Now I got me a real son and a real wife. Let's get busy and work on making a real brother or sister for Robert.

Another grandkid for Doris and the doc and my ma.
A cousin for Tammy. What do you say?''

Virginia laughed softly. ''I say, I'm ready whenever you are. But I'm not sure I'd call it work.''

Lucas laughed and kissed her.

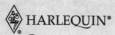
HARLEQUIN®
SUPERROMANCE

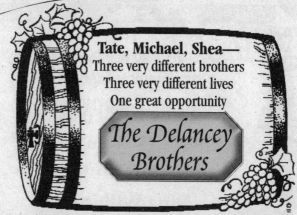

Tate, Michael, Shea—
Three very different brothers
Three very different lives
One great opportunity

The Delancey Brothers

June 1999—**Second to None (#842)**
by Muriel Jensen

What's a tough cop like Michael Delancey doing in a place like this? Mike was a hostage negotiator in Texas; now he's working at the Oregon winery he and his brothers have inherited.

Michael was ready for a change—but nothing could have prepared him for Veronica Callahan! Because Veronica and her day-care center represent the two things he swore he'd never have anything to do with again—women and children....

And watch for the third story in The Delancey Brothers series, Shea's story, *The Third Wise Man* in December 1999!

Available at your favorite retail outlet.

HARLEQUIN®
Makes any time special ™

Look us up on-line at: http://www.romance.net

HSTDB2

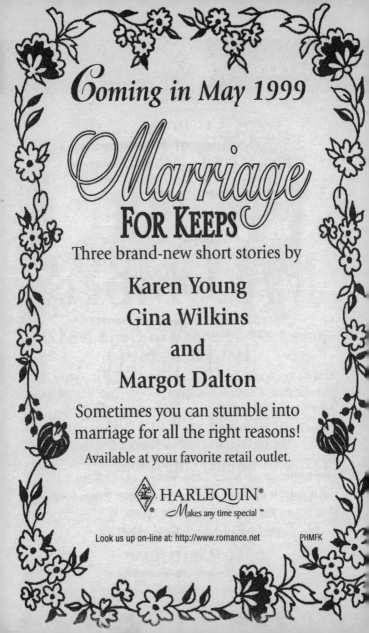

#840 IF HE COULD SEE ME NOW • Rebecca Winters
By the Year 2000: Satisfaction!
Rachel Maynard was rejected by her best friend's handsome brother,
Nikos Athas, and now—years later—she's determined to win his love.
Except that when she meets his older brother, Stasio, she realizes she's not
in love with Nikos at all. Because *real* satisfaction can only come from
being loved by a man of strength, passion and honor—a man like Stasio.

#841 WINTER SOLDIER • Marisa Carroll
In Uniform
When Lieutenant Leah Gentry goes overseas as part of a team that
will provide medical care for those in need, she figures she'll spend
long days doing fulfilling work. What she *doesn't* expect is to fall for
Dr. Adam Sauder. *Or* to return home pregnant with his child.

#842 SECOND TO NONE • Muriel Jensen
The Delancey Brothers
What's a tough cop doing in a place like this? Mike Delancey was one of
the best hostage negotiators in Texas. But he left it all behind to work in the
winery he and his brothers inherited. He was ready for a change but nothing
could have prepared him for Veronica Callahan—a woman with a *very*
interesting past.

#843 TRIAL COURTSHIP • Laura Abbot
Life is a trial for nine-year-old Nick Porter. His grandparents make him
eat broccoli and nag him about his clothes. Aunt Andrea's a great guardian,
but she's always on him about school and manners and stuff. At least there's
Tony. For a grown-up, he's *way* cool. Nick's seen how Tony and Andrea
look at each other. Maybe if he's lucky, Tony and Andrea will get together
and Nick'll get what he *really* wants—a family!

#844 FAMILY PRACTICE • Bobby Hutchinson
Emergency
Dr. Michael Forsythe's marriage is in trouble. He and his wife, Polly, have
not been able to cope with a devastating loss or offer each other the comfort
and reassurance they both need. It takes another crisis—and the unsettling
presence of a four-year-old child—to rekindle the deep love they still share.

#845 ALL-AMERICAN BABY • Peg Sutherland
Hope Springs
To heiress Melina Somerset—pregnant and on the run—the town of
Hope Springs looks like an ideal place to start over. Unfortunately, her
safety depends on a man she met months ago when she was living under an
assumed name. But this Ash Thorndyke is nothing like the man she used to
know. She'd loved that man enough to carry his child. *This* one she's not
sure she can trust.